*Pride Publishing books by M.C. Roth*

**Single Books**
The Drumbeat of His Heart
A Song for His Heart
Karma's Kiss
Greedy Boy

I0658902

# GREEDY BOY

## M.C. ROTH

Greedy Boy
ISBN # 978-1-80250-955-7
©Copyright M.C. Roth 2022
Cover Art by Erin Dameron-Hill ©Copyright June 2022
Interior text design by Claire Siemaszkiewicz
Pride Publishing

# GREEDY BOY

# Dedication

For Q.

# Chapter One

The building probably had more light switches than any other in the city, but with night pushing against its windows, it was nearly pitch black except for the tiny bleak emergency lights spotted along the stark walls. Within the compartmentalized offices, a few computer screens buzzed, with their colorful screensavers bouncing along with dizzying monotony.

Simon *could* switch the lights on as he crept through the building, but then someone might look up from the street below and wonder what was going on.

The office building emptied at six o'clock sharp every day. One by one the light switches were flicked off, so the entire building went dark as people filed out at the end of their shift. The neighboring condos were bound to contain a few curious souls who would call the cops at the first sign of something out of the ordinary.

Which was something he didn't wanted to risk when he wasn't supposed to be in the office in the first place.

There were only a few company rules that he'd discovered since he'd started working in the grand building a few years before. The strictest of them all was that he was never allowed to work late. His boss had called it a perk. He probably hadn't thought to warn Simon that the deserted halls looked like the inside of a haunted house after dark.

*Not that I haven't broken enough rules today.*

The biggest rule *should* have been that he wasn't allowed to kiss his boss. It should have been printed in giant gold letters at the top of his orientation papers, which he'd signed for human resources on day one. There had been the salary information, the confidentiality agreement and the listed restrictions to keep employees from stealing clients and going rogue.

There had been nothing about kissing.

Maybe he should have tried harder to pay attention to the sexual harassment video they'd made him watch that had been thirty years out of date? The boredom had been so complete that he had almost passed out in the tiny plastic folding chair.

The kiss hadn't been his fault!

* * * *

*Six hours earlier*

Simon let out a tired sigh as he organized a few things on his desk and filed a frustrating contract under 'G' as he got ready to wrap up the rest of his paperwork. Six o'clock was looming close, only an hour away according to the digital clock at the corner of his computer screen. Sixty minutes before he would head out of the door and into the swarming hive that was public transportation.

He reached for his bag, the fabric slipping against his fingertips, when he heard a sound coming from his boss's office—his very quiet and very professional boss, who hadn't even shouted when he'd stubbed his toe on his desk two days before.

He peeked in the office door, knowing that he didn't have to knock. Rich, dark wood filled the space that was decorated with expensive art and a bookshelf with a few first edition novels.

Rubric Mayvel, one of the richest and most desired men in the country, was facing his office window that overlooked the bustling city below. His shoulders were heaving, the rumpled fabric of his shirt stretched tight. The shattered remains of a shot glass lay among the carpet fibers, the bitterness of expensive bourbon in the air.

Drops of alcohol flowed down the window, and the tiny shards of glass stranded in the carpet glinted in the afternoon light. Mr. Mayvel didn't seem to notice the state of the window or the glass, his gaze drawn to the rushing traffic of the city below.

Simon didn't think twice before he rushed in, grabbing the small broom and dustpan that always hung conveniently by the door. Sweeping up a little bit of glass was nothing worse than having Mr. Mayvel's morning coffee ready for him when he strolled into the office five minutes early, his suit pressed and perfectly fitted on his tall, sleek body.

Simon copied, signed, faxed, emailed and did every other imaginable thing to the paperwork that went through his boss's office, so a little bit of glass on the floor wasn't beneath him. He was there to help, after all.

It was the same reason that Simon shielded his boss from solicitors, usually feeling terrible about hanging up on someone who was just trying to make a living. He even acted as a tiny guard outside Mr. Mayvel's office, mostly keeping secretaries or other interlopers away and distracting them by asking for details on the latest gossip.

Simon had a face that people liked to tell their secrets to, and he knew exactly who was screwing who in the office because of it—all seventy floors included. Not that he would ever tell anyone about what he learned or look at any of his colleagues differently. So what if Niamo had her boyfriend tie her up? That actually sounded kind of hot.

Kneeling on the office floor, he scraped the glass into the trash bin, leaving the stained window for the cleaners, knowing he would just make the smearing worse. He poured a glass of ice water, setting it on the desk before he prepared to retreat.

Mr. Mayvel hadn't looked away from the window when Simon had entered the room or when he'd bent over to pick a few stray shards out of the carpet, but that was nothing new.

Simon did his duties with as little inconvenience to Mr. Mayvel as possible, not to mention that Simon had the approximate sex appeal of flat ginger ale, while Mr. Mayvel put models to shame.

But when he started to back out of the room, he looked up to see Mr. Mayvel staring at him, as if he had lost his way while gazing out of the windowpane. His shoulders were slumped, and his suit was crumpled in a way that Simon had never seen before. His hair was limp from him running his hands through it over and over, and there were dark smudges under his eyes that Simon hadn't noticed earlier in the day.

"Are you okay?" Simon asked as he folded his hands behind his back to keep from fiddling. Mr. Mayvel always commented if Simon clicked his pen too many times or tapped his fingers on his desk while he was thinking.

The sky flamed golden in the afternoon light, shimmering against Mr. Mayvel's honey-colored hair and turning it almost bronze. The sight pulled at Simon, begging him to step closer.

Mr. Mayvel caught his gaze, dragging his tongue over his lower lip that looked swollen, as if he'd been chewing on it in distress. Simon wanted to speak up and ask Mr. Mayvel what he could do to help, but he was mesmerized by the sight. He would do anything the man needed, if only to take the broken look off his face.

Simon didn't realize that his *anything* included moving closer and cupping his boss's cheek in his palm. Mr. Mayvel leaned into the touch, his long lashes dancing over his cheeks as he closed his eyes. He was so beautiful but so lost.

Lifting up to the tips of his toes, Simon brought their lips together. He'd never imagined kissing Mr. Mayvel before, because he had kept the man squarely in the 'off-limits' corner of his mind.

Mr. Mayvel's lips were soft, yet firm, the lower one a bit swollen and warmer against his own. At the first touch, heat seared between them, building so quickly that Simon's reservations quickly spiraled beyond his control. Mr. Mayvel let out the smallest gasp, and

Simon pushed into his mouth with a groan, tasting bourbon along with the faintest hint of cigarettes.

He wasn't sure how long they kissed as he took complete control, even with his shorter stature. Mr. Mayvel showed no signs of resisting or fighting for dominance, melting against Simon like smooth chocolate. It was the sweetest kiss Simon could remember from the last year, if not longer, and it was with his boss.

Simon finally pulled back with dawning horror, ripping his hands away from where he had accidentally buried them in Mr. Mayvel's hair. Mr. Mayvel's lips were kiss-swollen and red, glistening as the sun peeked through the window. His eyes were half-lidded, with a blush across his cheeks that hid the darkness of the smudges under his eyes.

"I-I'm…"

It was the only thing that Simon managed to say before he turned and fled, pushing his way out of the office. His lips tingled, and he touched them as he rounded the corner, remembering the way Mr. Mayvel's mouth had felt against his.

How was he going to find a new job? His stomach sank as his heart pounded.

When he reached the elevator, he ran through the doors, pressing his back against the wall as he waited for the gates to close. His breaths came in short gasps, his vision starting to blot as he approached hyperventilation. His stomach twisted into so many knots he wasn't sure if he would ever be able to eat again.

"You okay, Simon?" Troy asked with a raised brow as he took a sip from his coffee mug. Simon hadn't noticed his coworker standing in the elevator when he had thrown himself inside.

A flush bloomed on his face. "S-sorry! I just f-forgot I had an appointment t-today and had to leave a f-few minutes early, so I'm running," Simon stammered, flushing hotter as the lie stuck on his tongue. He couldn't exactly tell Troy the truth, but the lie lay deep in the pit of his stomach, making him even heavier.

"Hmm-m," Troy said, tapping his finger to his lip before he pressed the back of his hand to Simon's forehead. "You might be getting sick, Simon. I've never heard of you forgetting anything, least of all an appointment. You are a bit flushed. Make sure you get straight to bed after." He pulled away, hitting the button for the parking garage and the main floor.

Troy had his own car there — a monstrosity of a Jeep that belonged to one or both of his boyfriends — but he knew that Simon took the bus home.

"Thanks, Troy." Simon melted against the back of the elevator as he tried to slow his breathing.

* * * *

*The present*

An hour after running from the office in a panic, he had realized that he'd managed to forget the keys to his apartment. He had tried to wait around for his roommate, Chris, but gave up after two hours. Chris' schedule was never consistent, and most days he had no idea when the guy was getting home.

Which was why he was creeping back into his office building hours after he should have been. He had to brave the haunted halls, though. If Chris was staying at his girlfriend's place for the night, then there was no telling when he would make it home. And bugging Chris on his cell was out of the question. He didn't want to bother him if he was at work or spending time with his girl.

It felt strange not stopping by the receptionist's desk to ask her how her day was going or to give her some fresh-baked cookies that he'd made the night before. He always traded the cookies for a single Life Savers mint that she kept in a special jar just for him. She always smiled, telling him that he shouldn't have gone through the trouble. It just made him want to bring more cookies.

The best part about bringing food was when it made someone smile. The worst part was when he burned it terribly enough that even Chris struggled to get it down. His oven was a finicky beast that had a raging temper during the most difficult of recipes.

The elevator was terrifyingly loud in a way that he'd never noticed before, but taking the dimly lit stairs was not an option that he wanted to face. With each floor he passed, the elevator thumped, the noise growing louder as the cable vibrated above. His ears popped as it continued to climb all the way to the top floor.

He leaned back against the mirrored glass, gripping the wall and taking deep breaths as sudden claustrophobia swooped in. The elevator was lit, thank God, but the light was flickering with each whirling sound, and the noise was riling his already-unsteady gut. He was almost ready to cry tears of joy when the soft ding announced his arrival at the right floor.

He stumbled out through the doors, taking a deep breath and sweeping his hands down his cheap dress shirt. The purple pastels complemented his build, but the real selling point was that it had been in the clearance section. It didn't fit as nicely as Mr. Mayvel's outfits did, but it suited him just fine. It even had a light-blue pocket square that had matched his eyes in the store mirror.

If he got caught, then at least he still looked presentable.

The elevator opened into a wide space that made up most of the top floor of the building. The walls were lined with different types of art, both paintings and modern sculptures that Simon still had no idea how they managed to get to the top floor. Along the far side was Mr. Mayvel's extensive office with Simon's workspace just outside the door so he could act as both a receptionist and a guard dog. To the right there was a boardroom that was equipped with any refreshment that a billionaire could ask for, and to the left was an ostentatious seating area that rubbed Simon the wrong way. It did have a nice view of the sunrise, though.

He shook his head as he crossed the distance to his desk. He couldn't believe that his key card had even worked on the doors, let alone the elevator. After a kiss like that, Mr. Mayvel should have fired him immediately and taken his card out of the system before his lips had dried.

Simon ran a hand through his hair as he looked down at the scattered papers on his desk. He hadn't quite finished his filing, and a few contracts were still splayed over the wooden surface. He could still file them. Then maybe he would do Mr. Mayvel a favor and pack up his stuff, so they didn't have to see each other in the morning.

As much as he needed his job to cover his skyrocketing rent, he wouldn't dream of making Mr.

Mayvel uncomfortable. *For once, why couldn't I keep it in my pants?*

He flipped one of the papers around, skimming over the name briefly before he slid it into the green folder in the top drawer of his desk.

A shout coming from Mr. Mayvel's office had him nearly jumping out of his skin. One paper on his desk fluttered to the ground as he jerked. Moments later, a second voice joined in—one that sounded an awful lot like his boss.

His heart fluttered as panic hit him with full force, slicking his palms and underarms. He whirled toward the office, noticing for the first time that the privacy blinds were shut, but a tiny bit of light was seeping through the cracks. He'd been so focused on his own desk that he'd never looked there.

Mr. Mayvel *never* asked him to stay late for meetings. In fact, he'd almost forbidden it. Maybe the reason he had been so upset earlier was that he'd needed Simon's help but had been too nice to ask him? Mr. Mayvel was the best boss he'd ever had by far, and he hardly ever asked Simon for anything above his normal duties.

Simon scrambled to the boardroom, leaving his desk in more chaos than when he'd arrived and stubbornly avoiding his bag. For the voices to be so loud, the meeting wasn't going as expected, and if Simon had one specialty, it was smoothing over tricky situations.

Why hadn't Mr. Mayvel asked him to stay? *He was probably going to before I decided to suck his face.*

It was time for redemption mode 2.0.

He flicked the coffee machine on before grabbing chilled glasses and a bottle of wine from the stocked wine cooler just inside the boardroom. Mr. Mayvel's clients were some of the most elite in the world, so it was usually fifty-fifty if they wanted booze or coffee.

He didn't have time to run for muffins — not by the sound of a masculine yell that reverberated in the space. He did have half a container of cookies left, though. They were ones that he'd been saving to give to Mr. Mayvel anyway. They had gone a little flat in the oven when the temperature had suddenly dipped for no apparent reason, but they would have to do.

He rushed back into Mr. Mayvel's office, not stopping to knock because he *never* had to. The entire building had an open-door policy, and Mr. Mayvel followed that rule to a *T*. It meant that Simon had learned more from overhearing phone calls than any other source.

He paused just inside the door, clutching the wine, glasses and cookies with his thin fingers. He could always be a waiter if he got canned. There weren't many people who could balance so many things with such small hands.

Five sets of eyes snapped to him at once, most of them looking much angrier than he expected for a business meeting. People got pissed over money all the time, but by the color of red on the tallest man's face, he was bordering on heart attack range.

Simon swallowed, forcing a smile onto his face as his confidence started to drain. The person closest to him was one of the most attractive women he'd ever seen, in a strictly observational sense, of course. He had no interest in women or any of their…parts.

Her thin legs were wrapped in leather, and a black tank hugged her form, leaving nothing to the imagination. His cock shrank as he came face to face with so much femininity. It was rare that he saw someone without a suit in the office, and he definitely hadn't seen someone in leather.

Most of the others weren't nearly as startling, two of them in simple jeans and T-shirts that also had no business in the building. The tallest man caught his attention, though, drawing his gaze and making his mouth run dry.

If sin and lust got busy and had a baby, then this was their child. He had dark hair that fell just past his ears in waves that longed to have someone's fingers in it. The suit that stretched over his back was perfectly fitted and definitely more expensive than Mr. Mayvel's. Hell, the man's shoes were probably worth more than Simon's apartment.

The redness rapidly drained from his face as he turned to Simon, leaving a startlingly pale complexion behind. Simon caught sight of a chiseled jaw with a hint of scruff and ice-blue eyes that drew him like a vortex. His lips were full but pressed into a thin line that made him even more attractive.

The man had his hand gripped in the front of Mr. Mayvel's suit, pinning him up against the glass where his shot glass had shattered hours before. With the force that it would take to pin someone like Mr. Mayvel, the man must've been built like a tank beneath his suit.

"Who is *this?*" the suited man asked, in *Russian*. The others shifted around the room, and the woman glared at Simon like he was a tasty treat that was not going to last long in the cupboard.

The Russian words flowed over his tongue as if they were meant to be there, with no detectable accent to speak of. Simon wanted to sigh. After all his hours of practice, he still managed to slaughter his attempted Russian accent.

Simon blinked once before planting a fresh smile on his lips. Mr. Mayvel was always dealing with foreign companies, which was one of the reasons that Simon had applied for the job as his assistant in the first place. He loved diversity in every form, which was probably why he loved languages as intensely as he did.

"Some kind of plaything?" asked the woman, switching to French so quickly that it took Simon a moment to catch up. Russian and French usually didn't coincide, but he wasn't one to judge.

"Hello, sorry I'm late," said Simon, going for English in a hope that it would be okay. He didn't want to insult anyone by picking French over Russian, and he definitely didn't want the lady's pointy boot in his eye. "I am Mr. Mayvel's assistant. Can I get anyone a cup of coffee or a glass of wine? I also have some cookies if anyone is interested. Sorry... They are homemade, but they do not contain any nut products."

Simon kept the smile on his face, starting to struggle to keep it genuine when no one responded. "We have several other premium liquors, if you would prefer. I can also grab a few extra chairs, as we seem to be two short."

He could sacrifice his desk chair, even though he'd just managed to get it adjusted for perfect lumbar support. He doubted he could smoothly move them to the boardroom at this point—not with Mr. Mayvel pinned against the glass.

"What do you think, boss?" asked the woman, this time in perfect Russian. She slid her hand down her thigh, skimming the leather that clung to every square inch.

*Don't look. Don't look. How does she not have camel toe? Crap.*

"Simon." Mr. Mayvel spoke up for the first time. His tanned face had gone pale, the dark shadows under his eyes looking even worse than Simon remembered. The hand at his chest tightened, the thin material bunching in the huge fist.

Things must've gone really wrong without him. He'd never had a meeting get physical before, even ones where a million dollars had gone missing.

There were a few scattered papers on the floor, but Simon didn't recognize them at a quick glance. He still had no idea who these people were.

"I can grab my laptop to take minutes if you could just give me one second, please. I'll bring it back with the coffee." Simon slipped past the woman, keeping a wide berth, before he set the wine on the polished table at the side of the office. The table was too small to fit all of them, but it would have to do.

"That's okay, Simon. We were just finishing up here," said the suited man as he released Mr. Mayvel, smoothing the front of his suit with the back of his hand. His English was as impeccable as his Russian.

Simon held back his sigh of relief as Mr. Mayvel went limp against the glass, his palms pressing against the surface. His knees were bent, and he was slowly sliding down the glass, despite the hard set of his jaw.

Simon cursed his past self again. Mr. Mayvel looked so tired that he could barely stand, and Simon had probably contributed to his stress by forcing a kiss on him. He had to turn this meeting around before it concluded.

"That's no problem at all, Mr...." Simon trailed off and offered his hand, closing the distance to the suited man. He was so much taller up close, and his shoulders were so broad that Simon felt suddenly tiny next to him. He refused to be intimidated, though. He'd promised himself never to judge a person by their looks alone.

Mr. Mayvel's eyes widened in his periphery.

"Leo Zoya," said the suited man as he straightened his own ensemble before accepting Simon's offered hand. His hand was warm, with a callused palm that Simon hadn't been expecting. He'd expected soft skin and manicured nails, but from that simple touch alone, he knew that Leo *worked* for a living.

Most businessmen had grips softer than their palms, their nails buffed and trimmed to even perfection. Mr. Zoya had a stray hangnail on his thumb, reddened, most likely from the man worrying at it. His nails were unpolished but not ragged.

Simon tried to keep his smile steady when he realized that he didn't recognize the name. There had been a few reports on his desk that he hadn't touched before he'd fled, and one of them probably had Mr. Zoya's name on it and his account portfolio.

Salvaging the situation was getting harder by the second.

His panic fled when Leo gripped his hand, tugging him until he stumbled forward and nearly collided with Leo's chest. Every inch closer he got made the man look bigger, his frame broad and strong beneath his tailored suit jacket. A hint of his forearm peeked from the jacket, showing off how thick and sculpted it was.

The warmth of his palm was…distracting.

Simon took a deep breath, getting a whiff of expensive cologne that made his knees wobble. He was professional, but he was also a hot-blooded man who hadn't been fucked in way too long. Leo was already straying from his 'off-limits' list to pure spank-bank material. His chiseled jaw and sparkling blue eyes weren't helping to keep the images out of his head, either. His nose was slightly crooked, as if it had been broken more than once, but his lips looked so soft and downright kissable.

Simon cleared his throat, refusing to drop his gaze. "Again, my apologies that I was late. There was a scheduling error, but I take full responsibility. Are you certain I can't get you anything while you are here? Perhaps a tour of the facilities?"

Simon was grasping at straws as he tried to keep his breathing calm. Mr. Zoya still hadn't let go of his hand, and his grip felt too good to go on for much longer. Dress pants were great...until he got hard. Then everyone would know exactly what size condoms he bought.

"I would like that, thank you," said Mr. Zoya, moving a step closer until their chests were almost touching. Simon saw the woman smirk from the corner of his eye, and he struggled not to take a step back. He had dealt with...intimidation techniques before, but this was a unique tactic. Too bad it wouldn't work on him.

"Right this way then, sir. Let me pour you a drink and we will start. May I ask if your colleagues would like to accompany us?" He doubted anyone had seen the art display while wearing leather pants or jeans before.

He watched as the blond man in a faded T-shirt perked up, his eyes going bright and a smile splitting his face.

"No. They will make sure that Mr. Mayvel finds his way to his vehicle unharmed. You can never be too careful in a big city at this time of night." The blond deflated as Mr. Zoya nodded once, releasing Simon and stepping back.

"Make him understand what happens when he defies me, but nothing permanent. We still need him to fix his error, after all," said Mr. Zoya in Russian, staring at Mr. Mayvel, who blanched.

*Something isn't right.*

Simon looked between his boss and Mr. Zoya, asking the question without words. He could have the police here at a moment's notice, but he didn't want to read the situation wrong. They could have been talking about lowering the commission percentage, but Simon wasn't sure.

Mr. Mayvel nodded as he pushed away from the window, his knees still looking unsteady. "Simon, please give Mr. Zoya a full tour. I would appreciate the escort. One can never be too careful." He smiled, but it looked forced, and the paleness of his cheeks didn't diminish.

Simon looked back over his shoulder as he walked from the office, trying to ignore the hand that was on the small of his back. The heat of it sank directly through his shirt, sending a shiver up his spine. Mr. Zoya was incredibly…distracting, making it even more difficult to make sure Mr. Mayvel was okay.

"Let me grab you some wine, Mr. Zoya," he said, trying to look for an excuse to get back into the office. Something just wasn't right, and he really didn't want to leave Mr. Mayvel alone when his gut was telling him to stay.

"I'm fine, thank you, and please call me Leo." He shook his head as a small smile quirked at the corner of his lips. "What did you want to show me?"

*My cock.* Simon smothered his brain's reaction, struggling to remain professional when Leo moved his hand an inch lower on Simon's back. Any farther and he would be getting into dangerous territory.

"Are you an art fan?" asked Simon, taking another deep breath and smoothing the front of his shirt self-consciously. There was a stubborn wrinkle across his chest that was probably from sitting against his apartment door for a few hours.

Most people in business seemed to have an appreciation for some kind of art. Mr. Mayvel preferred paintings and landscaped canvasses, the most expensive pieces lining the space outside his office. Simon liked them so much more than the modern art monstrosities that resembled an open concept imagining of his intestines.

"Hmmm, not really. It takes something very special to catch my eye." Leo's crystal gaze stayed locked with Simon's, his dark brows rising as he slowly licked his lips. "How long have you worked with Rubric?"

They'd come to a stop a few steps outside the office, but Leo urged him on, his hand slipping even lower. Simon felt himself flushing and he clenched his hands into fists to keep from pushing Leo's hand even lower.

"Five years," said Simon, his voice surprisingly steady. His career accomplishments were nothing compared to Mr. Mayvel's, who had started the company out of his parents' garage when he'd been seventeen.

They strolled past a muddled watercolor canvas depicting a famous pond somewhere. Apparently, it was worth six figures, even if Simon didn't understand the appeal. His niece had better watercolor skills.

Leo never once looked at the canvas, his gaze fixed on Simon.

"And you help him with all of his business ventures? Or just his late-night escapades?" asked Leo, his voice dipping as he stilled his hand on Simon's back, his pinky resting just above his waistband.

Simon sucked his lower lip into his mouth, chewing on it to try to will the deepening flush from his face. Leo's voice was like liquid sex with a side of aphrodisiacs, and it had sounded even better with the roll of Russian behind his consonants.

"I'm not screwing him, if that's what you're asking," said Simon, slapping his hand over his mouth as his eyes went wide. Leo stopped, his dark brows hitting his hairline as he leaned back, a deep laugh pushing from his throat.

Simon swallowed with a loud click, following every movement as Leo's lips parted over his teeth, showing off straight pearly whites. He hadn't known that laughing could be erotic, but Leo had nailed that as well.

"I'm so sorry, Mr. Zoya. I—"

"Leo, remember?" His grin pulled wide. One of his incisors was slightly crooked, and there was a small chip out of the corner. It could have happened at the same time his nose had been broken.

*He works for his wealth, and he came from the bottom.*

Simon felt himself relaxing. He loved a good story, and Leo looked like a man with a great story. He wasn't going to get anywhere by trying to be polite.

"I'm sorry, Leo," said Simon, letting himself relax and press into the hand at his waist. It dipped lower, skimming under the edge of his waistband. "I handle all Mayvel's business affairs. There is nothing that goes through his office that hasn't been approved by me."

Leo took a step forward, forcing Simon to take a step back so they didn't collide. Simon looked over his shoulder, sidestepping a priceless canvas so that his back hit the wall instead. Leo moved in, placing one hand on the wall, and leaning down over Simon, his hair falling around them like a curtain.

"Are you sure?" asked Leo, stopping when their lips were only inches apart. Simon could smell the quality of his cologne, and the mint on his breath mixed with a bite of alcohol. His blue eyes looked to be made of crystal — like the kind that floated on the surface of a frozen lake on a sunny day.

"Yes," said Simon, grunting as his back pressed against the wall. He had nowhere to go. His cock twitched in his dress pants, and he knew by the smirk on Leo's lips that he had seen it as well.

"Then we can continue our meeting over dinner," said Leo, leaning back and holding out his arm.

There should have been more hesitation than three seconds before Simon's cock won the battle between yes and no.

"Just let me grab my keys."

# Chapter Two

"Did you need me to make reservations?" Simon asked as he searched through his desk drawer. He always kept his keys in the same spot, but everything had blurred together as soon as his cock had gone hard. He was certain that Leo's eyes were on his ass, and he couldn't help but give it a little wiggle.

"No need. You're going to come home with me. I'll make you dinner, then you'll suck my cock as a thank you. If you're good, I'll fuck you and let you come — unless you had other plans," Leo drawled, as if the weather were a more interesting topic than fucking.

*Holy shit in a handbasket.* He didn't even need a pick-up line, and Simon was already sold. He'd always liked them big and strong. Getting them to look his way was usually the trick, but Leo was already looking.

"No plans," said Simon, nearly stumbling over his words to get them out of his mouth faster. His face flushed, and he stared down at the scuff on the toe of his shoe. *Desperate much?*

"This won't get your boss a contract," said Leo, crossing his arms and leaning back with a frown on his lips. His icy blue eyes looked straight into Simon's soul.

"I'm not a whore," said Simon, meeting Leo's gaze dead-on, ignoring the heat that surged in his chest. "You seem like an interesting person, and I'd like to get to know you."

It wasn't the whole truth, but it was darn close. He was more interested in getting to know Leo's cock and the way his callused hands would feel on his smooth skin. Maybe Leo's lips could erase the phantom of Mr. Mayvel's and ease his guilt.

"And?" asked Leo, closing Simon in until his ass pressed into the edge of his desk. Leo slotted between his legs like he belonged there, and Simon had to crank his head back to keep their gazes locked.

"I'm really fucking horny," said Simon, barely above a whisper. Mr. Mayvel had left him hard and aching, and he needed release more than he needed dinner.

Leo let out a chuckle, grasping Simon by the elbow before he stepped back and tugged him toward the elevator. His palm blazed through the thin layer of Simon's dress shirt and his skin prickled, his hair standing on end. *This is going to be so good.*

"Let me help you with that."

* * * *

Simon was ready to bury himself under a rock. Not only had he sworn in front of a client, but he'd had to get hard and admit that he wanted him, too. Things like that just didn't happen to him. Attractive men didn't look his way, but he'd flirted with two in the same day.

*I have to go buy a lottery ticket.* If he did get fired, at least he would win his usual free play.

Leo was different, though. It didn't feel like he was going to end up as a notch on the back page of Simon's journal. No one could fake a look of desire like that—not unless he was secretly an actor or an extremely steady drunk.

He'd dealt with horny old businessmen before, and he thwarted them if they tried to grab his ass or invite him over for 'drinks'. Anyone he had worked with had always stayed on the 'off-limits' list, and yet, he was ready to jump into bed with Leo, a client with unknown value and net worth.

*If I'm already getting fired, then I might as well get fucked.* His cock had started throbbing in his pants the moment that Leo had pinned him against the desk, his voice going dark and dangerous as he not-so-subtly called Simon a whore.

That voice promised a fuck that was hard enough to make Simon forget his own name, which was exactly what he needed. His palms slicked again, and he wiped them on his pants, adjusting the fabric so it draped over his crotch instead of peaking.

He was breathing hard and clenching his hands by the time they reached the dark ground floor. Leo turned toward the parking garage, and Simon had to rush to keep up with his longer stride. Leo knew his way around in the dark, moving smoothly between the desks and alleys as if he'd done it many times before. Not once did he look back, as if he knew that Simon would follow him without prompting.

Entering the garage was like entering a whole new world. The air was thick and reeked of stale gasoline and oil, unlike the artificial freshness of the office. The yellow lines were crisp, some reserved with bright letters and others open for visitors. The echo of their footsteps was louder than Simon's breaths in the oppressive concrete spiral.

Mr. Mayvel's Aston Martin was in its usual spot right next to the entrance, which was a place that was permanently reserved for him and his plethora of personal vehicles. Simon nodded to himself, glad that his boss would be able to find his way home. It wasn't that he had to go far to his penthouse, but it was still a relief. His escort would keep any after-hour rapists away from his car, too.

Next to it—and sticking out like a sore thumb against the black Aston—was a bright silver SUV. Simon tilted his head, more than surprised when Leo strode toward it. He had expected something a little bit…more.

He reevaluated the man with a fresh view that seemed to evolve with every moment in his presence. Leo obviously worked hard and had a shit-ton of money to be one of Mr. Mayvel's clients, but he apparently didn't like to flaunt it. People that came from nothing usually wanted to display their worth to show the world how far they'd come. There were only a select few who came from wealth then decided to turn over a new leaf.

The interior simmered with the bland perfume that always lingered with newer vehicles, and the engine was surprisingly quiet as Leo pushed the illuminated start button. He reached down under the steering wheel, pulling the column up and locking it higher, before reaching down and adjusting the seat back as well.

"I hate getting in this thing after Clas," said Leo, a small smile on his lips as he straightened his suit jacket that had rumpled as he tried to get comfortable.

Simon pulled the belt across his chest, before snapping it into place. "It's not your car? Sorry… I just assumed." He bit the corner of his lip, chewing gently when Leo raised one brow.

"It's mine, but I never drive it. It's too much of a hassle when you can just have someone drive for you." He tucked his hair behind his ears with long fingers before he eased out of the parking spot.

"The others? Will they find their way home okay?" Simon worried his lip harder as he thought about stranding Leo's underdressed colleagues. "I can call them a cab or a rideshare, if you prefer. It would be no charge, of course." Simon reached for his phone, ready to dial. He had the contacts to get a top-notch ride for clients, and enough of an expense account that he didn't have to worry about it.

"They'll find their own way home. They have some business to wrap up first." Leo turned away, focusing on the road as he turned into traffic. His profile stood out against the city lights, not helping Simon's pants situation in the least. The thrill of anticipation was sweet.

His thoughts turned to what Leo had told his colleagues in flawless Russian. They seemed like a bit of a rough crowd, but that might have been from the sight of jeans in Mr. Mayvel's flawless office. Leo had seemed honest enough so far, at least, when it came to his plans for the night. His anger toward Mr. Mayvel seemed to have disappeared, his gaze casting out into the bustling night life.

Sometimes they lost contracts, and clients were obviously upset. As long as Mr. Mayvel came through with a game plan, Simon knew that everything would work itself out. He didn't get this far in the business to get bogged down by one unhappy rich guy.

Simon was still thinking and worrying his bottom lip to the point of bruising when they pulled up beside a massive condo unit. Leo parked right out front in a spot that seemed to be reserved for him.

Simon looked up as they stepped out of the SUV, craning his neck back to try to get a peek of smothered stars over the top of the building. It was impossible. They definitely weren't in his neck of the woods, but the area looked more like where Mr. Mayvel would live.

An actual doorman let them through the entrance, holding it open for them and nodding at Leo as he greeted them. Beyond the door looked more like a hotel entrance than any condo building he'd been into. It screamed exclusive, with polished floors, air so chilly that he wished that he had a coat as well as the distant scent of lingering chlorine.

He tried to keep his breathing calm when they stepped into the elevator, only to be greeted by another concierge who spoke to Leo as if they were old friends. *Who pays these people to stand here and say hello at this time of night?*

"Straight to the penthouse today, sir?" he asked, the polished buttons on the front of his uniform shimmering in the elevator's light. With the tap of a card and a code input, they were ascending.

Simon's gut twisted. He was about to get fucked by a guy who owned a penthouse in this building? He swallowed, his tongue sticking to the roof of his mouth.

Multi-millionaire wouldn't even cover it. His earlier assessment of Leo wasn't holding up.

When the elevator door opened, Simon had to remind himself to breathe. The space was beautiful and yet sterile, with mostly black and white tones and a few shades in between. It had more square footage than Simon's childhood home and not nearly as many walls. Marble floors shone beneath the pot lights, a silver grain carving its way through the pearly surface. Every countertop was granite, and the cupboards were ebony. Leather furniture dotted the living room on the other side of the kitchen.

"You are welcome to shower before dinner." Leo strolled to the kitchen, which was the closest space to the elevator after the short hallway. He unbuttoned his jacket and set it over the back of a chair at the expansive island. His pale-blue shirt stretched over his shoulders, the custom material having a hard time keeping up with the man's strength. He released the top two buttons on his shirt, the smooth expanse of his pale chest peeking through.

Simon's cock twitched, going from soft to semi in record time. Leo looked delectable, and that small peek of skin had Simon ready to drop to his knees. Every movement was graceful and strong, even though he was built like a sleek tanker.

A glint of something at Leo's waist caught his eye. It was silver and shiny, but Leo was already turning and walking to a door beyond the living room.

"I'd like to help, if that's okay. I'm an okay cook, and it doesn't seem fair that you have to make it all just for me." Simon slipped his shoes off, carefully placing them on the mat. Leo hadn't bothered to remove his, but Simon didn't want to track dirt over the marble. A shiny surface like that had to be brutal to clean.

Leo glanced back over his shoulder, his brows nearly hitting his hairline as he gave Simon a once-over. Simon failed to keep another flush from his cheeks as he shuffled into the kitchen, waiting for Leo to return from what was, presumably, the bedroom. He *was* an okay cook, at least, according to his roommate.

When Leo came back to the kitchen, he pulled a bundle of vegetables from the fridge, piling them on an empty space in front of Simon.

*Scallions, garlic, mushrooms, cherry tomatoes and fresh chives. All things I can handle, but seriously? Who keeps fresh chives?* Simon cradled the vegetables in his hands, taking two trips to get all the mushrooms over to the sink.

"Can you chop those?" asked Leo, who was already turning for the stove. After a few clicks the flames caught and he swirled oil around the pan as it started to heat.

Simon minced the garlic into perfect tiny chunks, tossing it into the pan and grinning at the sizzling burst of sound and scent. Leo eyed the garlic, a smile flickering over his lips, before he lifted the pan and tossed the contents to coat them with hot oil.

Leo's hand flexed on the frying pan handle as he blended the ingredients, the movement making his whole arm tense so it strained at the fabric of his shirt. An office may have been the place that Simon had met Leo, but Leo obviously belonged in the kitchen.

Simon forced his gaze back to the task at hand before he lost a finger as he sliced the first few mushrooms. At least it would have been for a good cause.

Even though the kitchen was intimidating and sleek, it was still just a kitchen, with fancy plates and the one set of tongs that made it impossible to close one drawer because the tongs were stuck open. Some of the tension eased as he spotted a potato masher with a slightly bent handle. No matter how much money Leo had, he was still just a man.

Simon searched through the ebony cupboards for a plate, finally finding one so high that he had to climb up on the counter a bit to reach.

Lining cherry tomatoes up on the cutting board, he pressed a plate down on top of them to keep them in place. He slid a sharp knife through them, halving fifteen at once, instead of chopping them individually.

"What are you doing?" asked Leo, moving in behind Simon and making his breath catch. Simon's hand trembled as he set up the remaining ten tomatoes, placing the plate on top just a tad too hard. One of them squished, its seeds oozing over the board. The heat of Leo's chest was pressing against his back and...*oh God*, he was getting hard...again.

"Just a trick to save time," said Simon, his voice an uncomfortable squeak.

Instead of pulling away, Leo moved closer, sliding his hand down Simon's wrist, before he set his finger on the back of the knife.

"I've never seen that trick before," said Leo, his lips so close to Simon's ear that he could feel the tickle of his breath. "What else do you have up your sleeve, Simon?"

"I-It's nothing," he stammered, his grip faltering as he nearly sliced his finger on the sharp blade. He could feel something hard against his ass and he hoped it was what he thought. He couldn't remember if Leo had worn a belt or not.

He let the knife drop to the counter, gripping the edge of the granite and biting his lip. Tomato juice clung to his fingertips, smearing the surface. He forced himself to stay still, despite the desire to grind back. *Why am I still wearing pants?* He should have taken them off with his shoes.

"Here, let me help." Leo took up the knife and the plate, slicing the tomatoes in half with one smooth cut. "I'm going to have to remember that." He chuckled, the noise sliding down Simon's spine as he scooped up the halves and turned away.

Simon panted against the countertop. He couldn't take much more of this before he snapped.

By the time dinner was complete, Simon was able to turn around without embarrassing himself. He cursed when Leo looked completely unaffected. *Is it my imagination?* Maybe this whole thing *was* a dream, and he was about to wake up at home in his tiny twin bed, or worse, outside his apartment door.

He slipped into a chair at the island, waiting until Leo took the first bite before he brought the pasta to his lips. Flavor burst over his tongue, a warmth of rich cream and tomatoes sinking down his throat. He groaned, shoving another forkful into his mouth as his stomach grumbled for more.

"Would you like dessert?" asked Leo from the head of the island after Simon's fork had started to scrape the bottom of the dish. Leo set his fork to the side, licking the sauce from his lips.

Simon finished grinding the bottom of his bowl, longing for another bite, even though his belly was near bursting. It was probably the best pasta that he had ever had, and Leo had whipped it up within a few minutes with zero effort.

"If it's as good as the main course, then yes please," said Simon, running a hand over his belly. It wasn't polite to turn down a meal, especially when Leo was going so far out of his way to make him feel comfortable. He'd already shed his socks at Leo's urging, but he wished he had taken the opportunity to ditch his belt. He was way too full.

"It might even be better," said Leo, leaning down until his elbows rested on the dark surface of the island. He pushed his bowl aside, crooking his finger to summon Simon. Simon stood as if he was a marionette on strings, ready to follow its master's directions.

"I made a promise, and I intend to keep it." Leo swiveled as Simon approached, gripping Simon's hips and guiding him between his parted thighs.

Simon's gaze flashed down to Leo's lips and the remnants of sauce that still glistened there. Lower still, a tent rose in Leo's slacks, banishing all thoughts of food.

Leo's words from the office rolled over him again.

*"You're going to come home with me. I'll make you dinner, then you'll suck my cock as a thank you. If you're good, I'll fuck you and let you come."*

*Oh God.* Leo wanted him to suck his cock as dessert. His cock swelled as he stared at the trapped beast in Leo's pants. He looked huge through the fabric, and Simon knew he was going to be in for a challenge. He *loved* a challenge.

He braced his hands on Leo's thighs, sliding them up the inside of his legs until he was only a hair's-breadth away from his prize. He teased the skin, flicking the thin fabric that tented over Leo's groin before he let his hands fall away.

Leo twitched, his grip tightening and his brow furrowing when Simon withdrew.

"Get on your knees," said Leo, his eyes so dark that they were nearly black, with only a hint of crystal around the edges.

*Holy sweet fuck.* Leo needed to order him around more, because those four words were built on a foundation of sin.

Simon slid to his knees, biting his lip as he came face to face with Leo's arousal. Even through the expensive cologne, the man smelled good enough that Simon's mouth immediately started to water. He could only imagine how he would taste.

"When was the last time you were tested?" asked Simon, looking up through his lashes. "I mean, I would really like to taste you, but I can grab a condom if you're more comfortable." Nothing ruined a blow job faster than the taste of latex, and where most people despised the taste of cum, Simon loved it. It was that little bit salty, little bit sweet with a touch of thickness—like a chocolate pretzel ice cream sundae.

"I'm negative across the board," said Leo as he threaded a hand through Simon's hair, tugging him closer. "Pull me out and put your mouth on me. I want to see how much you can take."

*Why did I eat so much?* He wouldn't be able to deep throat Leo properly with his belly so full, but he hoped he could still make him enjoy it. His hands trembled as he flicked the black button open, tugging the short zipper down slowly to reveal a pair of Superman boxers. He let out a snort, glancing up to Leo, who had gone a touch pink.

"I — uh forgot about those."

It was the first glimpse of the person underneath the iron skin that seemed to cover Leo like armor. There was so much more to Leo than just a gorgeous suit and an expensive condo. Something twinged in Simon's chest, but he shook his head. It was just his cock getting to him, nothing more.

"I like them," said Simon, letting out a small chuckle before he reached for the band on the boxers, tugging them down. Leo's cock bounced free like it deserved its own goddam parade. He was long *and* thick, which had Simon a little worried. But he was absolutely gorgeous. He paused before he leaned in, biting his lip hard to suppress a groan.

"I've never sucked someone that wasn't cut," said Simon, licking his lips and experimentally running his finger over the flushed head that was peeking through the foreskin. The glans looked darker than his own cut cock as he gathered a drop of pearly liquid and brought it to his lips. It tasted thick and heady and fucking perfect.

"It's the same, but I'm more sensitive around the head. Just be careful with your teeth." Leo's breath hitched when Simon slid his finger over his slit again, spreading pre-cum over the glans and sliding along the edge of his foreskin. Leo's cock flexed, the foreskin pulling back as he hardened and exposing more of the head.

Following the same path as his finger, Simon took a deep breath and leaned in, licking the gathering liquid and swirling his tongue over the tip. Leo's hips twitched, begging for more, even as the man stayed silent, letting Simon take his time.

He ran his tongue along the edge of Leo's foreskin, dipping into each wrinkle and ridge, before closing his mouth over the head and sucking with everything he had. Leo barely fit in his mouth, and there was so much more of him to go. He circled the base with his hand, shuddering as he got his first grip.

The taste was a tad stronger than expected, with a hint of soap. The skin was smooth and glossy, sliding freely and shivering against his tongue. Leo seemed more sensitive than some of the guy's he'd been with, but the mechanics seemed about the same.

Throwing caution to the wind and begging his full stomach to stay calm, he lowered himself onto Leo's cock, using every trick he knew. He swirled his tongue, reveling at the weight in his mouth and the heaviness of Leo's balls in his hand. He was trimmed, with only a bit of hair on his groin, but his treasure trail remained.

"Fuck, you're good with your mouth," said Leo as he fisted Simon's hair, bringing him closer and rocking his hips.

Simon groaned as Leo took over, hitting the back of his throat soft enough that he didn't gag and giving him time to breathe and relax between thrusts. Simon wanted to show him what he could really do and drop all the way down on his cock until he could feel it in his throat, but he didn't want to tempt fate on a full stomach.

Leo's breaths came faster as Simon traced the vein on the underside of his cock, swallowing the bitterness that flooded his mouth as Leo's balls drew up.

"You ready for me?" Leo asked, his voice strained and deep.

Peering up through his lashes, Simon felt his own cock twitch, begging for release or even a bit of attention. He hummed, more than ready to taste Leo on his tongue and swallow him down. Their eyes locked, and heat sank into Simon's core.

Leo thrust one last time, rocking into Simon's mouth before pulling back, shooting his cum over Simon's tongue. Simon managed to keep the grimace off his face when it went from perfect to too much of a good thing.

Leo's expression made the bitterness worth it. As Leo tilted his head back, his lips went soft and a breathy moan pushed through his lips. He slid his eyes closed, his dark lashes fluttering on his cheeks.

*Fuck.* Simon was going to come.

"Good boy." Leo tugged him to his feet, bringing their lips together and spearing into Simon's mouth to share his taste. It was the first time that they had kissed, and it was one of the most intense kisses of Simon's life. It sizzled along his spine and raised goosebumps all over his skin as Leo sucked his tongue, fucking into his mouth like he had with his cock. It was completely dominating, leaving Simon little chance to think, let alone breathe. His head swam, his cock so hard that it was painful and straining against his slacks like a forgotten toy.

"Please," said Simon, as he panted against Leo's lips. He hoped that Leo could get hard again and follow through on his promise. There was nothing more that Simon wanted right now than to be fucked into utter bliss. He wanted his hole to ache, glistening with slick and flushing red and swollen from stretching so wide around Leo's cock.

"Please fuck me," he begged, surging up to Leo's lips again and dragging him down to meet him, begging to be dominated.

"Let me take you to bed."

# Chapter Three

The bedroom was massive, with a king-sized mattress on a sturdy ebony frame, adorned with silk sheets that glistened under the lights. There was a fluffy white rug at the base, and a single black nightstand with a carved brass lamp that was already on and ready for them. The walk-in closet was ajar and substantial enough to make any fashionista spontaneously orgasm. There was another closed door, which he assumed guarded the entrance to a bathroom.

Simon hardly saw any of it. He was too focused on Leo's hands as he pulled Simon's shirt over his head before going to his belt and dropping his pants and plain black boxers in one go. The room was chilled, as if the air-conditioning was set too high, and it brought his nipples to painful peaks, despite the heat of their entwined mouths.

Leo had lost his pants along the way, and only one sock clung to his ankle. His shirt was still on, the seams nearly bursting as he flexed to divest Simon of the last of his modesty. His thighs were thick with a sparse dusting of light hair that darkened farther down his calves.

When Leo started on his shirt buttons, Simon was suddenly certain that he was dreaming. The pale expanse of Leo's chest gave way to solid pecs and pert nipples that looked harder than his own. There was a slight dip at the base of his sternum that ended where his six-pack began.

As Leo's shirt dropped to the floor, Simon caught sight of his lateral muscles, and his mouth watered. Leo was fucking built and could probably dead lift a small car. Simon had almost expected tattoos, but his skin was flawless and pale, except for a thin pink scar near the top of his right shoulder.

Simon skimmed his fingers along the scar. It looked like it would have hurt more than he could bear. He could not deal with pain well, unless it was his ass that was getting the beating.

"A knife," said Leo, following Simon's touch with his own, before grasping Simon's hand and bringing it to his lips. "I was the last person that they ever cut," he said in flawless Russian.

*Fuck.* The way the words rolled out of Leo's mouth made Simon want to burn. He loved languages, but he'd never been with anyone who'd spoken to him like that when he was already hard. Leo could probably recite a recipe in Russian, and it would make Simon ache.

He wanted to kiss the scar, but Leo was too tall for his lips to reach, so he settled on the divot of his collar. At least the person who had cut Leo had changed their ways, leaving their violence behind so they didn't hurt anyone else.

"May I fuck you?" asked Leo as he slowly pushed Simon back toward the bed. Simon's knees hit the edge and he collapsed, the breath rushing from his lungs as he fell against the bed.

The silk sheets slithered against his skin, chilling and heating him at the same time. They were so soft, and yet, almost uncomfortable as they slid against him, as if they had a life of their own. And the bed itself sank beneath him, as the thickest pillowtop he'd ever felt squished against his back.

Leo followed a moment later, driving all rational thoughts from his mind. He opened his legs wide, welcoming Leo between them and wrapping his legs around his hips before using his heels to pull him closer. He ground up against Leo's cock, groaning when he found that he was already hard and dripping again.

"So eager." Leo let out a chuckle as he nipped at Simon's lips, dropping lower to kiss along his neck and suck a bruise into the spot beneath his ear. It would be impossible to cover, and everyone at work would know that Simon had been fucked. The thought made him shudder.

"I need to hear you say it, Simon. Do you want me to fuck you? I can stop now if it's too much." He nipped at one of Simon's nipples, pinching the other before soothing it with his tongue.

"Yes. Yes. Please, yes," Simon chanted as he dragged Leo back to his lips, losing himself in his mouth. He was so hard that pre-cum was dripping from his cock, sliding between them and bringing him closer to the edge. He wasn't sure if he'd even be able to make it until Leo was inside him.

Leo dipped his hands down Simon's sides to his ass, pulling him wide and exposing him to the air. His hole clenched automatically with a mix of arousal and trepidation. He was going to come too soon. He just knew it.

"Just p-put it in," he stammered through another groan as heat built to dangerous levels in his groin. "I'm not going to last. You don't have to prep me." It was bound to burn like a motherfucker, and it was probably going to feel like he was splitting in half, but it was exactly what Simon needed to keep away from the edge.

He liked it rough and didn't mind when it hurt, but he hated coming early. If he did, he was too sensitive to let his partner finish inside him as their rough thrusts pushed him beyond pleasure to a dangerous space that was something...else.

"I don't want to hurt you," said Leo, pulling back with concern etched on his face. "I'm big, baby, real big. I'll split your ass in two." He reached for a condom and lube, only leaving Simon's body for a second before he was settling his weight back and lining up their cocks. Simon hissed at the contact, curling his toes and biting his lip.

"That, please do that. I want to feel you for a week." He knew it was a terrible idea, even as he craved it. It was going to be a week of extra pillows on his chair and bran muffins. The pain would keep him from coming right away, though...probably.

"Fuck, baby. Your mouth is so fucking filthy." The foil condom wrapper crinkled as Leo tore it open and smoothed it down his cock with one hand, using his other to slather lube over Simon's hole. He swirled his fingers around his entrance, never dipping inside.

"You look so tight, baby. Have you ever taken a cock as big as mine?" Leo asked as he lined himself up, rubbing the head of his cock over Simon's hole.

*Oh fuck.* Leo felt huge and he hadn't done anything except rub against him. Simon frantically thought back to the partners that he'd had since coming out with an onslaught of rainbow flags.

"No, not even close." He shook his head, trembling when his rim strained against the impeding intrusion. His past partners had mostly been average, with a few that exceeded expectations. Technique had always seemed to matter more than size anyway.

Leo paused, shooting his brows to his hairline as he hovered over Simon, holding himself up with one hand on the bed. "Are you sure you don't want any prep?" The hand on his cock was already moving down to Simon's entrance.

"Oh, God." Simon bit his lip hard. He knew he would come as soon as Leo touched him. His hand went to his cock, desperate to stave it off, but knowing that he wouldn't make it in time. One touch and he was done for.

A blaring ringtone splashed a bucket of freezing water over his body, putting him on instant alert. There was only one person who had that ringtone, and at this time of day, it was bound to be an emergency.

Leo leaned back, going rigid as his face wrinkled in confusion. He looked toward Simon's discarded pants and the cell phone blaring within. Maybe the glare was because it was Britney Spears' *Criminal* blaring through the speaker as the most epic cock block of the year.

Simon scrambled from the bed, his cock forgotten as he dove for his pants and grasped the phone within. His sweaty hands slipped over the phone's surface, and it took him three times to accept the call.

"Chris?" Simon asked, his voice coming out much more strained than he had intended. He looked over his shoulder to where Leo was sitting on the side of the bed, his hard cock sheathed by a glistening condom. He cleared his throat as his mouth went dry. "Chris, are you there?" Simon pulled the phone away from his ear to look at the screen. It was definitely his roommate's number, but the other end was silent.

"S-Simon." Chris' sobbing voice washed any remaining arousal away. "Can you c-come home? I need you here."

*Oh Christ.* "Are you okay, Chris? What happened? I'm on my way now." He grabbed his pants, trying to pull them on one-handed while he looked around for his shirt. And where the hell were his socks?

Chris didn't respond with anything but a harsh sob that pierced Simon directly in the gut. "Talk to me, Chris. It's gonna be okay, buddy. I'll be there soon."

Leo crossed his arms, his glare morphing into a glower.

"I'm so sorry," said Simon, covering the end of the phone with his palm. "It's my best friend. Something's happened, and I gotta go. Thank you so much for dinner. I had a lovely time." He leaned forward to place a quick kiss on Leo's lips, almost dropping the phone when a wave of heat settled back in his groin like a wildfire in the wind. Leo threaded a hand through his hair, and Simon had to force himself to pull away.

"Are you with someone?" asked Chris, his strangled voice sounding so small on the other end. "I'm sorry. I-I tried to wait until you c-came home, but then you never came and I was all alone."

"It's okay, buddy," said Simon as he finally pulled away from the tempting embrace and headed for the door. His shirt was waiting for him along the way, but his socks were gone. He shoved his feet into his shoes, cursing as they scraped against his toes uncomfortably.

He was going to have three blisters by the time he got home.

"How long until you're here?" Chris asked, his voice close to tearing Simon's heart out. Chris was such a sweet man, and even though he was six inches taller than Simon and had more hair on one arm than Simon had on his entire body, he had never tried to intimidate him or shame him for being gay.

"Um." Simon looked around to the elevator doors. There was no button in sight. And once he got downstairs, he wasn't sure which part of town he was in or if the buses would still be running to take him home.

"I'll call a cab, buddy, and I'll be home before you know it." He dreaded dipping into his bank account for the cab fare, but there was no way he was charging it on his company card. Even if he was with a client...sort of.

He glanced back into the penthouse, but Leo was nowhere to be seen. Guilt seeped into his gut, making it churn and whirl as he searched for the elevator button. Finally, he found it, tucked along the wall. He glanced down, blanching when he noticed his cock peeking through his zipper. He managed to tuck himself away as the doors slid open.

"I'll be home soon, Chris." He ended the call and stepped into the elevator, peering back into the penthouse. "Bye, Leo."

There was no answer.

# Chapter Four

Simon scrambled with the lock on the apartment door, his hands shaking as he thought about Chris' desperate call. Chris was his rock, and the last time he had cried, it was because his mother had passed away. His heart clenched painfully as he sent out a frantic hope that Chris' dad was okay.

"Chris?" He stumbled into the apartment, sweat clinging to every bit of him from the run upstairs. It was only four floors, but the stairs were narrow and steep, made for a man with a much bigger stride who could take two at a time. Chris never had a problem with them, always chuckling when he watched Simon fall up them.

"In here," said Chris, his voice deeper than usual and garbled with tears. How long had he been crying?

Simon had politely asked the cab driver to go faster but had gotten a raised eyebrow instead. He had stayed silent after that. He didn't like when someone told him how to do *his* job, after all.

He rounded the corner, his naked feet sinking into the worn carpet. Tears were streaming down Chris' face, and his eyes were pinched and swollen. At least a dozen crumpled tissues were strewn about the couch, with more around the base. The television was off, and only one light shone from a side table, exaggerating the shadows over his face.

"Oh, buddy, what happened?" Simon threw himself at Chris, settling into his lap easily and throwing his arms over Chris' shoulders to pull him close. He fit perfectly in Chris' thick arms, as he had so many times before when he was the one who'd needed comfort.

Chris looked nearly as thick as he was tall, and he was strong enough from his job that he could lift Simon with ease. His trimmed beard tickled Simon's cheek as he nuzzled close, Chris' heat soothing his skin.

It was too bad that Chris was painfully straight and so strictly on his 'off-limits' list that he had never appeared in any dreams or fantasies. Simon had even fucked a couple of *bears*, just to get Chris' type out of his mind permanently.

"I-I broke it off with Kayla," he said, choking on another sob. His big shoulders shook, a few fresh tears sliding down his bearded face. His arms, which were close to three times thicker than Simon's, wrapped around him and pulled him close, the smell of cheap body spray and tears enveloping him.

"What?" Simon drew back, his mouth dropping open. "But you guys were planning on moving in together. I thought you'd bought the ring?"

That ring had terrified Simon. It had meant that he was going to lose his roommate and best friend. But he'd hugged Chris regardless, giving him a peck on the cheek before wishing him well.

"You're going to hate me even more than she does." Chris shook his head, burying himself against Simon's neck.

Simon blamed the recent cock block for the way that his body heated, his cock perking up. *He's not my type and he's crying! Pull it together.*

"I would never hate you, Chris. I mean, you're the best guy I know, and you're *my* best guy, right?" Simon gently gripped Chris' chin, tilting his head up so he could wipe the tears from his cheeks. His skin was hot from crying for so long. If only he could have gotten here sooner so Chris hadn't had to suffer alone.

Their gazes locked and there was…something there. Simon pulled in a shuddering breath, the heat in his belly spreading and pooling in his groin. Chris' hands were suddenly unbearably hot, goosebumps peaking where his palms had settled on Simon's skin. He was so big and so broad that he could probably carry Simon, just like Leo had been able to. But while Leo was all lean strength, Chris had the body of a football player.

They were too close, and Chris was at the perfect height, with his lips so near that Simon would simply have to lean in to touch them with his own. His face flushed, and his belly erupted with butterflies. What the hell was happening to him today? This was Chris. Had it really been that long since he'd been laid?

*Yes. Yes, it has.* He actually couldn't remember when his last hook up had been besides Leo.

"I-I told her that I thought I might be gay," said Chris, looking away as fresh tears rolled over his cheeks. "I'm so sorry. I just don't know anymore. I'm with her, and I can't wait to come home to you. I want to hold your hand when we watch a movie together, and maybe even kiss you. I just don't know."

*Wait. What?* Granted, they already held hands when they watched movies together, but Simon had figured that was because Chris was only being nice. If Chris happened to put a horror movie on, Simon usually ended up in Chris' lap, hiding his face and covering his ears when the screams started. Only Chris' arms around him could make the shaking stop.

But kiss? Chris wanted to kiss him?

*Wait... Is this* my *fault?*

Simon thought back to every stolen touch and every night spent sitting together on the couch. He should have kept his distance, no matter what his suppressed feelings were. Kayla and Chris were a match made in straight heaven.

Had he forced Chris into feeling this somehow, in his effort to keep his best friend close? Every moment together jumped to the front of his mind. Best friends probably weren't supposed to snuggle on the couch or beg for a hug after a nightmare.

His face burned, his cock leaping to life as everything came rushing back to him at once. His 'off-limits' list exploded into smithereens as heat flushed through his body. What was the point of it now, anyway? *One, two...third time's the charm.*

They had touched so many times before, but this was different. Simon had never ached for his best friend like this—not with his hole still slick with lube from where Leo had smeared it over him to get him ready, not with his lips bruised from when he had kissed Mr. Mayvel.

His mouth flopped open as he gaped like a fish, not knowing if he should stand up or lean in. Chris answered the question for him as he ran his hands down Simon's shoulders, settling on his narrow waist.

He flexed his hands, as if he couldn't decide what to do, either.

"Do you hate me, too?" Chris didn't look up, his eyes wet and swollen as he sniffed. The box of tissue was empty.

"No." Simon shook his head, pinching his thigh to try to keep his cock under wraps. It throbbed, his balls aching and full from his earlier denial. "But you want to kiss me? *Me*? I don't understand."

"I'm not sure." Chris shook his head again, wiping his eyes on the back of his arm. His hair clumped as tears soaked into his skin, trickling down the dark lines of the tattoos that traced the surface. "Can I just hold you? I don't want to be alone."

"Oh, sweetie." Simon tightened his hold, pulling Chris into a hug, despite the fact that it would dig his cock into Chris' hard belly. "Let me get cleaned up real quick then come to my room. We can snuggle and talk some more."

Twenty minutes later they were lying in Simon's tiny bed, Simon playing the little spoon to hide his cock that stubbornly refused to soften. Chris hadn't seemed to notice as he crawled in behind him in his own loose pajama pants, pulling Simon close like he was the only one left on earth.

Simon let out a sigh as Chris' breaths evened and the big man fell asleep. He couldn't take any more tears from a man so strong without his own heart breaking. It was a strange sensation when his cock was so hard.

Plunging his hand into his pants, he gripped his cock, squeezing it once before wrapping his fingers around the shaft. He was so hard that it hurt, but he couldn't do anything while Chris was here with him, needing him. He pulled his hand away, leaning back into the warmth and letting himself stumble off into sleep.

*What a day…*

# Chapter Five

Simon dropped the container of cookies down on his desk, peering over at Mr. Mayvel's door. The office was still dark with the blinds drawn shut like they'd been the night before. The only difference was that the door was *closed.*

*Oh God. Oh God. Why did I come in today?* His stomach fluttered as he got closer to puking. If he did puke, he would be able to go home, even if he really didn't want to be alone. Chris wouldn't be there, and Simon had realized that he hadn't asked for Leo's number.

The pang of regret was stronger than he'd expected. He longed to go back to Leo and peel back the layers of his armor to see the man underneath. The man had had a huge cock, but that wasn't the only thing that Simon wanted to see again. He wanted to watch him cook again, moving about the kitchen like a practiced chef and elevating simple ingredients into something phenomenal.

And Chris. Poor, sweet Chris. He was so perfect and charming but so vulnerable with his walls down.

Simon just wanted to hold him until his heart surged with happiness.

Mr. Mayvel was the only one who actually made him worry. If Simon got fired, he could kiss his apartment goodbye.

He wiped the sweat from his palms and stepped up to the closed door. His heart thudded, his mind racing and sweat beginning to drip down his back. Despite the fact that he'd gotten up extra early to make a batch of cookies, he didn't think their presence would be apology enough on their own. Chris had still been sleeping when Simon had snuck out of the door, leaving a short note on the coffee maker that he had set to brew when Chris' alarm would go off.

His ultimate plan to apologize was already spiraling, because even with no sleep and forgiveness cookies, he was still sweating. Maybe Mr. Mayvel would fire him now, or maybe he'd just transfer him to a different department where everyone smelled like body odor and had casual Fridays.

He shuddered at the thought. He would accept the transfer without hesitation, but only because he didn't want Mr. Mayvel to feel uncomfortable.

Grabbing the container of snacks, he knocked on the door, clutching the cookies to his chest like a delicious shield. The last time he'd knocked on the door was on his first day, and he'd been sweating less than he was now.

A shadow moved behind the blinds before the door was yanked open. A hand reached out from the darkness, grabbing his arm and pulling him into the office. He let out a squeak as the cookies tumbled to the floor, the lid flopping open so they flung all over the carpet. One rolled all the way to Mr. Mayvel's desk before tumbling onto its side.

Darkness thrust over his eyes as the door slammed shut. At first, he thought he'd gone blind but then, as his eyes slowly adjusted, he spied the crack of light under the curtains that lined the windows. He blinked, unable to see anything in the darkness except the vague outline of *someone.*

He reached for the lights, flicking them and going momentarily blind.

"Wait!"

He let out a gasp as Mr. Mayvel's overly bright face swam into view. His beautiful golden complexion had been marred with a purple bruise under his eye and a scratch down his cheek that looked like it was from some kind of giant cat. He was still too pale, and his eyes were wide and bloodshot as if he still hadn't slept.

Simon slapped his hand over his mouth to keep from wailing. Mr. Mayvel's escort, the ones that were supposed to make sure he got home safe, had they left him too early? Had he gotten to his car safely only to have been mugged outside his condo?

"Mr. Mayvel, oh no," said Simon, unable to hold back any longer. He slid his hands along Mr. Mayvel's chin, almost crying out when he found a warm bump on his jawline. He let out a hiss, jerking his head to the side at Simon's touch.

"Did you call the police?" asked Simon, standing up on his toes so he could get a better look. The bruise under his eye looked painful, and the cut might get infected. The edges looked clean, except for a bit of dried blood that still clung to it. The skin around it was bright red and puffy.

He could call Mr. Mayvel's doctor right away to book him in for a tetanus shot, and he could have the police meet him there so he could file a report.

Mr. Mayvel shook his head, curling his lips into an ugly frown. "I can't call the police, Simon. What are you thinking? These people are dangerous. I'm lucky to be alive, but you... How did you—? What happened to you last night?"

Simon had always loved that his city was safe, but there were always dangerous people, no matter where he went in the world. He'd never had any problems in his area, but Mr. Mayvel's upscale street was probably filled with sitting ducks for thieves.

Heat flooded his face as he thought of his night, and his cock stirred at the memory of Leo's and Chris' hands on him. His stomach plunged a moment later. He should have insisted on staying with Mr. Mayvel until he was home safe. Instead, he'd followed his cock.

"I..." He paused when Mr. Mayvel's gaze dropped to his neck to the spot where Leo had left an obvious suck-bruise. Simon didn't remember when Leo had managed to put it there, but he'd gone rock hard when he'd noticed it in the mirror.

Mr. Mayvel spluttered, taking a step back and putting space between them. Simon dropped his hands to his side, shoving them into his pockets to keep from reaching out again. He refused to be ashamed of such a wonderful night and a heady experience that was second-to-none, even if it did get cut short by a bit of overwhelming news.

"But you kissed *me*." Mr. Mayvel's face fell, his eyes going shiny.

Simon couldn't take this. He couldn't have two of his favorite men fall apart within twenty-four hours—not when it was partially his fault in both cases. Thank God the memory of Leo had helped him keep himself together so far.

He couldn't hold back any longer, not with Mr. Mayvel looking at him like that. He moved closer, reaching out to hug Mr. Mayvel and fully intending to keep his lips to his own damn self.

Mr. Mayvel must've misread his intentions because he dipped down, meeting Simon's lips with his own.

The kiss was better than Simon remembered and tore the half-hearted protest right from his thoughts. Kisses with Leo were hot and possessive, and he imagined Chris would kiss slow and tentative. Mr. Mayvel was the perfect in-between, neither too hard nor too soft, but just right.

"You did it for me, didn't you? Christ, Simon, I don't deserve you," Mr. Mayvel said against his lips as he tried to pull back. Simon followed him, tasting the hint of cinnamon and bitter coffee on his lips and wanting more.

"Mr. Mayvel," said Simon, begging him to come back.

"Rubric. When you kiss me, call me Rubric." Rubric melted above him as their lips met again.

*Rubric. Of course, my kiss was for you. You deserve everything.* He had never dreamed of calling his boss by his first name. The man was leagues above him, but maybe in this situation, it was more natural.

Simon settled back into the kiss, waiting for Rubric to take control, but he never did. Despite their size difference, Rubric was the one submitting to his touch and opening his mouth when Simon pleaded for entrance.

As much as he wanted to pull back and beg Rubric to take control, he couldn't bring himself to do it. Simon was the bottom of all bottoms and detested topping in a way that most tops just didn't understand, but if this was what Rubric needed, he would do that for him, too.

Rubric was amazing, both on a business front and as a person. He was witty, attractive, seemed to be able to predict markets like he had a sixth sense and had the body that any athlete would drool for. He was leaner and more fragile than Leo, and so unlike Chris, who was built like a grizzly.

Simon cut back a moan as he dragged Rubric down to him, tasting his mouth like he'd always secretly wanted to. He threw his 'off-limits' list permanently out of the window so it could be driven over by a hundred cars below.

Rubric gripped his hips, pulling him along as he backed away until Rubric was pressed against his desk. Without looking, Rubric shuffled some papers to the side before sliding his ass over the surface of his desk and dragging Simon closer. Simon was only too happy to move in between Rubric's thighs, bringing their groins together. The desk was the perfect level, giving Simon the height advantage for the first time.

"What did he do to you?" Rubric asked as he pulled back, his eyes going dark and his brows drawing together. "I can't have you getting caught up in this, Simon. There's a reason I kept it from you. It's too dangerous."

"He made me dinner," said Simon, blushing as his voice fell away. He wasn't one to kiss and tell, no matter how amazing it had been. And he *really* didn't want to kiss and tell when Rubric's hard cock was against his.

"I want to erase his hands from you. How can I ever repay you?" Rubric eased his hands over Simon's shoulders, his grip tightening as he shook his head.

Simon was getting...confused. Despite the kiss, he wasn't exactly dating Rubric. If he wanted someone's hands on him, it was going to happen whether Rubric liked it or not. And as for payment? Well...it wasn't like he had actually been *working* late.

"I need you to get some rest. That's all the payment I need," said Simon, tipping their foreheads together and taking a deep breath. Rubric smelled delicious, even if he looked like a mess.

"I can't." Rubric shook his head. "I see their hands on me every time I close my eyes." He raised his hand to his cheek, wincing as he touched the cut.

Simon pondered Rubric's earlier words when he had begged to erase Leo's touch from Simon's skin. Maybe Rubric was the one who needed a kind hand to erase his mugger's touch.

"May I touch you?" asked Simon, licking his lower lip. His cock throbbed as Rubric nodded, before lying back against the wooden surface of his desk.

Simon extricated himself, locking the door before he returned to his spot between Rubric's thighs. He started slow, running his hands along the inside of Rubric's legs and reveling in every shiver and tremble. Each button fell away in his hands until he was tugging Rubric's shirt over his head, tossing it to the ground among the crushed chocolate chip cookies.

A second gasp stole his breath. A fist-shaped bruise hovered on the left side of Rubric's ribcage, and below that was a bruise that stretched almost all the way along his ribs. It looked like a baseball bat had come back for seconds and thirds. Another bruised line was just over the flat plane of his belly, and the third was on his hip, just above the point of his hip bone.

"Oh my God, Rubric, you have to go to the police," said Simon as he trailed his fingertips over the mark on Rubric's belly. It was black and purple with an edge of sickly green.

"I can't, Simon. Please, just drop it." He looked away, his bruised eye looking even worse as his skin paled. "Just make me forget...please."

Simon barely hesitated before he kissed Rubric's pec, letting his lips linger on his hot skin. Goosebumps broke out under his touch and Rubric let out a tiny gasp.

"Did I hurt you?" asked Simon, looking for more bruises, even as Rubric shook his head. The man must have had the pain tolerance of a woman in labor.

He moved his lips to Rubric's nipple, sucking it gently into his mouth before nibbling at the hardening bud. The saltiness of Rubric's skin rolled over his tongue, making him groan and his cock throb. *Fuck.* He wanted to come already, and he hadn't even touched himself.

He forced his arousal away, knowing he needed to take his time with Rubric and show him everything he deserved. If the man didn't think he was important enough to go to the police, Simon would just have to change his mind.

Rubric's pants fell away, and his boxers quickly followed, revealing his long, cut cock. He was narrow, but he made up for it in sheer length, jutting out with a slight curve toward his belly. There were no bruises lower than his hips, and Simon breathed out a sigh of relief.

"What did you want?" he asked against Rubric's lips, petting down his hips and carefully avoiding his cock. Rubric rocked his hips into the air as he begged for contact, but Simon shook his head, sucking Rubric's lip into his mouth. His shirt was soaked with sweat and his cock was screaming at him, but he refused to undress until he was sure what Rubric wanted.

"Fuck me?" Rubric asked, looking down through his light, fluttering lashes.

Simon held back a groan. That wasn't what he expected at all and was exactly the opposite of what he wanted. He wanted to crawl on Rubric's lap and slam himself down onto that long cock until it brushed against his prostate perfectly. He wanted to come hands-free with Rubric's cock inside him.

But this wasn't about him.

Rubric was so much taller and stronger than him, and he took control in any business situation, but somewhere along the line he had melted into a bottom. Simon's cock throbbed in confusion as his uncertainty thickened into doubt. He could refuse Rubric now, but he owed this man so much. It wasn't that much of a sacrifice to top this once.

"Do you have anything?" Simon asked, thrusting his hands in his pockets, even though he knew there was nothing there. He hadn't thought to pack condoms instead of chocolate chip cookies.

"In the desk." Rubric nodded. "Top drawer on the left."

"I never would have thought to have condoms at work," said Simon, circling around the desk and pulling open the drawer. His hands were steadier than he expected as he grabbed three condoms and the small bottle of lube that was hiding underneath. "It's a good idea, though. I always have acetaminophen, antihistamines, cold medication and lady products in case Brenda runs out again." He shook his head. That had been a day that he hoped to never live through again. There were many reasons that he was gay, and the curious mystery of lady parts was one of them.

"I've actually had them there for a while." Rubric's face tinted, his cheeks flushing bright. "I wanted to ask you a while ago, I mean."

Warmth spread through Simon's belly. Rubric was attracted to him? That was impossible. Rubric was everything, and Simon couldn't shake half a stick at his accomplishments. Simon didn't even own a car. He had to take the bus back to his overpriced apartment that he couldn't even afford without Chris.

*Oh God, Chris.* He wasn't sure if they had anything between them or not, but it had felt so good to lie beside someone all night. Sleeping with Rubric couldn't be cheating if they hadn't even kissed. Right?

And Leo. *Fuck.* As much as Simon wanted to crawl back to his penthouse, he knew it had to be a one-night stand with him. His heart ached at the thought, and he tilted his head in confusion. The feeling must've been from eating cookie dough at five o'clock in the morning.

He shook his head. Rubric needed him, even if it was only for a little while. And he looked so good spread out over his desk with his hair askew and the rosy blush on his skin that was attempting to hide the bruises. His cock was weeping, and Simon had the sudden urge to drop to his knees. But that wasn't what Rubric had wanted...what he needed.

"Turn around?" said Simon, hoping that Rubric was okay with that for their first time together. He couldn't take the pressure of Rubric watching him as he slid inside. He took a deep breath. *I can do this. It's just like college, only better.*

Rubric flipped over, leaving his ass on display. It was perfect, just like every other part of him, with just enough meat that it fit into his hands perfectly. There were cute little hollows under each hip that came from his time at the gym, but he wasn't built in the same way that Leo and Chris were.

His skin was so soft under Simon's hands, even as Rubric tensed, his ass cheeks jumping as the muscles flexed. Simon bit his lip to keep from moaning aloud as he massaged the pert globes, waiting for Rubric to relax before he dipped his thumbs along the seam, spreading him wide to the air. His hole was a perfect dark rose that clenched with each breath Rubric took. He looked so tight, and it made Simon wonder how long it had been for him. The man was always so busy... How could he even find time to date?

He wanted to get down on his knees and lick into Rubric, splitting him wide on his tongue and his fingers, but they were in the office. If someone came by and saw that the door was locked with Simon's things abandoned on his desk, certain people might start to ask questions. There was nothing that people loved more than to gossip about their boss...even if he was a great boss.

He had to be quick. His cock was on board, even if his mind was dragging behind. He slid the condom on, slathering himself with lube at the same time he coated his fingers. Rubric whimpered as the first swipe of cool lube touched his hole, his entrance winking as Simon licked his lips.

He slid one finger in deep, cutting back a groan as heat enveloped him and Rubric clamped down. Under better circumstances he would have taken his time, sliding in slow so the only thing Rubric would feel would be hazy pleasure as Simon split him apart. He hoped that Rubric didn't mind a bit of a burn.

The moment the tension eased around his finger, he slid a second one deep, staring at the space where they were connected. Rubric was so fucking tight, and there was no way that he was going to last long. From the way Rubric's cock was leaking against the desk, Simon could tell that he was close, too.

Prodding deep and curling his fingers toward Rubric's belly, he searched for the nub that would take the man's mind off a third finger. He felt the bundle of nerves and circled around it, and only hitting it as he slid a third finger all the way in. Rubric clamped down on him, jutting his ass into the air as his back bowed off the desk.

"Are you ready?" Simon asked as he leaned forward, pressing his clothed front to Rubric's sweating back. He was still fully clothed except for his freed cock, while his boss was completely naked except for his black socks. It was the strangest role reversal from the night before with Leo.

Simon shook his head. It was not the time to be thinking about Leo, no matter how much his own hole ached to be filled.

Rubric nodded, thrusting back to meet Simon's fingers and clenching down around him as he assaulted the bundle of nerves. "I think so." His voice was thick and strained, like he was on the edge of tears or orgasm. Simon hoped that it was the latter.

Slicking his cock up a second time, he withdrew his fingers from Rubric's heat, lining up his cock at the winking entrance. It had been so long since he'd topped that he had to steady himself and remind himself that he would be thrusting forward and not back to meet the force of someone behind him.

He sank his cockhead in with a soft roll of his hips before he paused to let Rubric adjust. It was tight and so fucking perfect that the only thing that would have been better was bare skin between them. Or if it had been him on the desk with Rubric behind him — that would have been true perfection.

He knew Rubric's medical history better than his own but wasn't willing to take that type of risk, and he didn't want to leave Rubric with a messy ass at work, either.

"You good?" he asked as he slowly eased forward, pausing when he was balls deep. Rubric throbbed around him as every inch of his cock was worshiped by his boss's hole. He slid his hand along the desk, pushing a pile of contracts to the side so he could reach for Rubric's hand, threading their fingers together.

"You're so fucking big," said Rubric, his voice shaking as his hole milked Simon for all he was worth. Simon cursed, clamping his hand around his base as he almost lost it, while glowing at the slightly inaccurate praise. He certainly didn't have the biggest cock out there, but he was comfortably enough above average that he didn't doubt his masculinity. He had nothing on Leo, though.

*Stop thinking about him.*

He couldn't stop, as much as he tried. He wished that Chris had chosen to call ten minutes later, so he could have felt that monster cock inside him before he had to go. He doubted he would ever see the man again at this point — not with Chris and Rubric keeping his plate brimming.

*And Chris. What would he do if he saw me now?*

Hopefully it would turn him on and answer the question as to if he was actually gay or just grasping at straws so he could leave Kayla.

Simon pulled almost all the way out, watching as Rubric's hole clung to him until just the head of his cock remained inside. He gripped Rubric's hips, dragging him back and thrusting his hips at the same time. Their skin smacked together with an obscene wet sound, and the grunt that Rubric made in response had his balls getting even heavier.

He angled his hips on the second thrust, aiming for that spot inside Rubric that would have him falling apart. He couldn't hold back now when he was so close, and Rubric was too fucking perfect. Reaching around Rubric's hip, he grabbed his cock and twisted his palm over the head before squeezing it lightly. He was so fucking wet, with pre-cum leaking all the way down his shaft and slicking the way as Simon started to jerk him off, matching the pace of his thrusts.

His own orgasm was building as a heat bloomed at the base of his cock and spine. Most guys apparently felt their orgasm approaching in their groin as a simmering burn that threatened to tip them. Simon felt it there, too, but it was weak compared to the ache in his ass. His rim clenched around nothing, and he swore he could feel his prostate throb seconds before he came. His balls hung heavy, then his cock came to life like a live wire, cum spurting from him and filling the condom.

Heat pooled on his hand as Rubric jerked below him, unable to keep still as his orgasm rocked him. He clenched on Simon, milking him for every drop he was worth and then some.

Simon's stomach sank as he pulled out, gripping the base of the condom before tying it off and disposing of it in the waste basket next to the desk.

He was definitely getting fired.

# Chapter Six

The coffee tray shifted in his hand as he pushed through the narrow glass door. Warm summer air evaporated the air-conditioned blanket on his skin, coating him in a thin layer of yuck after one step. He'd stuck with a simple thin dress shirt that morning, but it hadn't helped when he'd had to rush out for coffee for a particular client.

The client had mentioned the little coffee shop the last time they had visited the city, so of course Simon had taken note of it and what they'd had in their drink at the office. It was surprising how far the small details went sometimes. Deals had been made on less than a cup of coffee in his experience.

*If only it would rain.* Humidity clung to his skin, but the sun kept on shining. He craned his neck up, peering around for any sign of a cloud as he stepped along the sunbaked sidewalk. There was a small wisp off to the east, but it was going in the wrong direction.

With a near-silent thud, he ground to a halt as he smacked into someone. All four specialty coffees splattered against his front, sending a lance of heat across his skin. The iced cappuccino did nothing to sooth the burn of the caramel macchiato that soaked into his pale pink shirt in seconds.

"Ow, *bleep*." He dropped the tray, pulling his shirt away from his skin as the stain spread. He caught sight of dark hair out of the corner of his eye as he fanned his chest and horror spread through his gut.

"Oh my goodness, are you okay?" Simon asked, holding his shirt out. Recognition flashed through his mind and went straight to his gut when he saw Leo standing there, looking bewildered and warmer than him in a suit. Luckily Leo's clothes were still spotless.

"Did you just bleep out your own swear word?" Leo asked, a smile slowly spreading over his lips. He was even more beautiful than Simon remembered.

Simon had wondered if he was ever going to run into Leo again, and if their night had been memorable enough for Leo to recall him if he did.

Simon remembered. He had thought about Leo every night since their interrupted evening together. More than once he'd had to talk himself out of taking a cab across town.

Simon flushed, dropping his shirt and holding out his hand. It was so automatic that he was reaching to shake Leo's hand before he even realized what he was doing. Leo's smile spread wider.

"Um, yes. Sorry. I'm in work mode, and I can't swear at work." He probably could, but it wasn't professional. There was nothing worse than an assistant with a potty mouth. He looked down at his hand that was still stretched out. Coffee dripped from his fingertips and his entire arm was sticky. He drew back, flushing hotter.

"Sorry… The handshake is automatic, too, when I'm working. Are you okay, though? I didn't splash anything on you? I would hate for you to get burned because I wasn't watching where I was going." Simon looked Leo up and down once more, just to make sure coffee hadn't made its way anywhere. *Damn*, the man looked sinful with his dark hair pulled back. There were a few freckles on his face and his skin looked a tad darker than Simon remembered.

"I've been meaning to talk to you about that," said Leo, taking a step toward him. Simon took a step back as he looked down at how messy he was. He didn't want to stain Leo's clothes.

Leo took another step, and Simon felt the hot metal of a lamppost behind him. His heart started to pound, his cock perking up as if it sensed the inbound attraction.

"I was feeling pretty burned when you walked out on me, especially when you ran off to another man. Pretty fucking hard, too." Leo loomed over him, placing his hand on the lamppost and leaning down so their faces were inches apart. He flicked his glasses down his nose and Simon caught sight of his crystal-blue eyes.

Sweat dribbled down his spine, soaking into his shirt until it stuck to his back. The coffee was rapidly cooling, leaving his body overwhelmingly sticky, but he quivered in anticipation. He had missed this feeling — the instant domination that had him thinking about sucking cock and nothing else.

"I'm sorry. Chris is my…" Simon trailed off, not knowing exactly how to answer that. It had been two weeks since Chris had admitted that he might have feelings for him, but they hadn't even kissed. They had slept in the same bed twice and had cuddled on the couch like usual, but nothing else. The suspense was intense.

Not that Simon needed to get off. Rubric lay out on his desk for him every day, taking his cock like a fucking champ. His bruises had faded, but Simon still treated him like glass. The man still seemed so broken, only happy when Simon was filling him.

A coldness had been slowly spreading through Simon's core with each time he gave something that he didn't really have. To Rubric, it seemed that it still wasn't enough, even when it left Simon so empty. Without Chris, he wouldn't have been able to drag himself to the office in the morning or back home every evening. He probably wouldn't have managed to get out of bed.

"I don't like to share my things with anyone, Simon." Leo's voice pulled him back to the sticky summer day. Leo dragged his tongue over his own lower lip before he sucked it back into his mouth. Simon shuddered, imagining that tongue on his body and inside him. His cock twitched against the coffee stain that had spread down to his groin.

"I'm yours?" Simon asked, gripping the post at his back. His heart was pounding, and it fluttered faster as Leo smirked. *Oh God,* he needed to hear that more than he needed a second breakfast. The strain in his chest that had been bothering him for two weeks suddenly broke loose.

"Do you think I make dinner for just anyone? There was a connection between us as soon as we met. Don't try to deny that you felt it, too. You want my cock as much as I want your ass." Leo chuckled, slipping his hand down to the top button of Simon's shirt and flipping it open. "Ouch, baby, that looks like it hurt," said Leo as he drew his fingertips over the red burn on Simon's chest. Simon hissed at the sensation. It felt like he'd been sitting in the sun all day without sunscreen.

"Yeah, but yours? *Just* yours?" asked Simon, biting his lip. He had dated individual men in the past, but it never seemed to go anywhere. They were always so strict with what they wanted, never letting Simon switch things up and do things his way. As much as he wanted Leo, he couldn't leave Chris behind — not when Chris was just discovering a new part of himself.

"You asking me to share?" A frown tugged at Leo's lips. "I don't know if I can do that, baby." His cold eyes sparkled, even as his frown deepened.

Simon took a deep breath, getting a hint of Leo's cologne as well as the smell of his warm sweat. Any longer in his presence and he would agree to anything this man asked of him. He couldn't do that to Chris…or to Rubric.

"You're a big boy. You'll figure it out," said Simon, ducking beneath Leo's arm before his cock gave him away. The sting of Leo's eyes on him was better than any drug, sending heat directly to his groin. Leo's laugh cut through the humid air and Simon relaxed, looking back over his shoulder.

"I have to get another round of drinks. Do you want anything? It's on the house," asked Simon, trying to slip back into a professional mode as he adjusted himself.

He could barely keep his excitement contained. Leo remembered him, and he still wanted him. It was as arousing as it was confusing.

Leo shook his head, sliding his glasses up on his nose and leaning back against the lamp post. He crossed his arms, his concealed biceps bulging as he clenched his fists.

"You're going to regret that, baby," said Leo in Russian. He pushed himself off the lamp post, walking away without a single look back. Simon's heart felt like it had stopped beating.

It was a few hours later that he realized he still hadn't asked Leo for his number.

# Chapter Seven

"*National Treasure* or *Silent Hill*?" asked Simon from the couch. He leaned back into the cushion that was just a little too squishy to be comfortable but perfect when Chris was beside him.

"Depends on if I'm sleeping alone tonight," said Chris, passing him a plate with three slices of pizza on it. The smell of pepperoni made his mouth water at the same time as heat flared in his belly. His cock should have been tired from the blow job that Rubric had given him before he'd left for the day, but it always seemed to be interested in Chris now that he had possibly tossed his straightness out of the window.

"I'll have nightmares if we watch *Silent Hill*, but I'll be fine if you're beside me," said Chris as he took a seat, scooching over so his hip touched Simon's. Warmth radiated from the spot as a bundle of butterflies let loose in his belly.

Simon knew that it was probably only going to be simple spooning with clothes on, but it sounded utterly perfect. They'd hardly done anything together, and that was fine with Simon. As long as he got to see Chris at the end of the day and let the bear of a man pull him into a hug that made him struggle to breathe, then everything would be okay.

The way Chris had said it, though, alluded to more. *Is he ready?* Or maybe he was waiting for Simon to make the first move? The latter was less likely, as Chris was the epitome of the perfect top who would make the first and the last move.

Simon set his plate of pizza on the table, ignoring the grumble of his neglected belly. Chris glanced at him, his eyes going wide with a piece of pizza halfway to his mouth.

"What?" he asked, chomping down on the slice and chewing slowly. "What?" he asked again when Simon continued to stare, leaning forward enough to get in Chris' space.

"Can I kiss you?" asked Simon, only slightly grossed out when Chris' mouth flopped open and his partially chewed bite of pizza rolled out. A flush swept over Chris' cheeks and stained down his neck. It was okay if Chris said no, and Simon would respect that, but he had to know.

"I thought that…maybe you didn't want to," said Chris as he looked off to the side. "It has been a few weeks, but you didn't really seem interested, and I didn't want to push you."

Simon wanted to smack himself on the forehead and hug Chris at the same time. The big man looked so cute as his shoulders drooped.

"You can kiss me anytime you want," said Simon, hoping that he was smiling encouragingly and not panting like a bitch in heat. His cock was starting to fill, and with it, his sanity started to drift away.

Some guys lost it when they were drunk, but all Simon needed was a little bit of blood in his dick. When he was hard, he would agree to almost anything.

"But I don't know…how," said Chris, his gaze settling on Simon's lips. "I don't know how it works. I've never kissed a guy, and I was too worried about getting a computer virus to look up any gay porn."

"Oh, well, that makes sense." Simon grasped the plate from Chris' hands and set it on the table beside his own. Thank God he had said something, or they would've been at a stalemate for eternity.

"Just do whatever you want and whatever feels right. You don't have to try to put on a show for me." He grasped Chris' hand, entwining their fingers and squeezing. Chris' hands were clammy and cold, and he could feel him trembling. "You don't have to be afraid of me, Chris. You're my best friend, and I'll be here for you, no matter what—even if you're a terrible kisser."

"Do you think I'll be terrible?" Chris let out a sigh, even as he gripped Simon's hand harder. "Kayla didn't like to kiss very often because she hated the way my beard scratched her. She was always so soft and so sensitive, but I wasn't sure what you'd be like." He ran his free hand through his short beard that he had trimmed down to a few inches for the summer heat.

Simon couldn't imagine Chris' face without the beard, but he liked it best in the winter when it was long and tickled his neck when they snuggled on the couch.

"I want to get my lips on yours and feel your beard scratching against my face. I want to run my fingers through all the hair on your body and see how much there is." If his body was anything like his arms, then Simon would be in for a bit of an adventure. He'd never been with a man with much body hair and wasn't sure how he felt about it.

"My arms are the hairiest, and a bit on my legs—"

Simon cut him off with a finger to his lips. "Please, don't tell me and ruin the surprise. I want to kiss every inch of your skin and find out for myself." His cock throbbed as he said it, his balls heavy.

"Kayla never liked it." He lowered his gaze again. "She wanted me to wax it."

"Please don't." Chris was a bear in every sense of the word. Waxing him was probably against the law. "Please kiss me, Chris." Simon leaned in but left a few inches between then for Chris to close. He didn't want to pressure him if he wasn't ready.

"I'm not sure if I'm ready for more than that," said Chris, his gaze locked on Simon's lips. Simon could feel his breath against his skin, and he wanted to feel that everywhere, but he could wait. He would wait forever for Chris.

The couch groaned as Chris closed the distance between them, his lips like the wings of a hummingbird against him—so delicate, and gone before Simon had barely registered the touch. He couldn't stop himself from trying to chase Chris' warmth as he fled and the scratch of his beard against his chin. How could anyone *not* like Chris' body hair? It was softer than it looked and danced across his skin, even during the briefest touches.

Chris leaned away, his eyes wide and a blush staining his cheeks. Simon had to let out a huff. He had definitely overestimated himself. There was no one alive that could be *that* patient.

"Was it okay?" asked Simon as he realized that maybe Chris had pulled away because it had felt wrong to him. Maybe he wasn't gay after all.

"It was…short," said Chris, laughing as Simon snorted. "I don't know what to do."

"Stop thinking about what I want, Chris, and think about yourself for once. It's time to live out your fantasy of the dirtiest kiss you can imagine." Simon leaned in again, leaving the same few inches for Chris to close and letting his eyes flutter shut. Air tickled his lips as Chris panted, the smell of pizza strong with a hint of mint. He must've brushed his teeth before dinner.

A whisper of skin dragged over his lips, harder than the last time but just as brief. There was a stutter of breath, then finally Chris pressed a real kiss to his lips. It was as soft as it was sinful, and Simon couldn't get enough.

He gripped the couch with his free hand to keep from fisting Chris' hair and pulling him in harder. His beard scratched against Simon's chin, mixing the innocent pleasure of the kiss with just a hint of fire. He couldn't hold back the moan that erupted from his lips.

He expected Chris to hesitate and maybe pull back again at the sound of his moan, but instead, Chris deepened the kiss, sliding their lips together and drawing a second groan from Simon's throat. He pressed closer, until Simon was tilting back on the couch with Chris settling on top and pushing him down into the cushions.

Chris was heavier than both Rubric and Leo, but he held himself aloft to keep from crushing Simon. Simon ran his tongue between the seam of his lips as a thank you and a request. When Chris slipped inside his mouth, his world changed.

No one could kiss like that — not even people who ran kissing groups or men from his online fantasy group. Not a single one could change the world with a kiss — or even come close. But apparently his roommate was some sort of superhero.

He could hardly keep up as Chris licked, sucked and nibbled, and they became acquainted in one of the most intimate ways.

Chris leaned back, but Simon couldn't bear the loss, not when his heart was laid open, the blood ready to burst from his veins if Chris left him. He slid his hands through Chris' beard, twirling the hairs around his fingers as he touched his chin, guiding him deeper. He didn't think the kiss could get any sweeter or more possessive, but then Chris groaned, swirling his tongue and stripping Simon of all thoughts and meanings that weren't his roommate.

He was so fucking hard, and he knew Chris could feel him poking against his belly. He was almost certain that Chris' own semi was carving a spot into his thigh as the man dropped down, pushing Simon harder into the couch.

He'd never been so thoroughly possessed, and fuck, he wanted more. He would end it with Rubric and Leo now, just for another taste. The thought sent a pang of guilt through his gut and he stiffened.

No...he had feelings for them, too, and they were both intense in their own way.

"This okay?" Chris asked as he tore his lips away, dipping down to Simon's chin and scraping down his neck. Simon stiffened even further as Chris hummed under his breath, licking a strip where he knew there was a hickey. Rubric had a mouth like a Dyson and had marked Simon all over before sucking his dick like a champ.

"Have you been a bad boy?" asked Chris, all semblance of nervousness gone as he nibbled at the bruise, sucking it into his mouth gently and teasing the skin. "Who have you been fucking while I've been waiting for you to come home to me?" His voice was low, but he didn't sound angry.

Simon could barely think. When Chris had called him a bad boy, he'd barreled straight toward the edge. If he wasn't careful, he was going to come in his pants before he could even answer.

"Rubric," he stuttered out, biting his lip as Chris sucked harder, growling in his throat like an actual bear. Was Chris going to do this to every mark he saw? He hoped the answer was yes.

"Mm-m, very naughty. Do you let your boss fuck you in the janitor's closet when no one's around? Is that where you came from weeks ago, smelling like sex and lube while we cried together on the couch?"

Heat ran down Simon's spine as Chris scraped his teeth over his collar, opening the top button of his shirt. His throat bobbed as he swallowed, stumbling over his answer.

"I've only ever fucked him. But weeks ago, that wasn't him. That was Leo. He was just about to go balls deep when you called, but you needed me. He was pretty pissed when I left him hanging. He said he doesn't like to share his things." Even thinking about the possessive growl in Leo's voice made him shiver, but it was Chris' grumble that had his cock leaking.

"Good boys share," said Chris, kissing the corner of Simon's lips.

"That's what I told him."

Chris huffed out a laugh, sealing their lips again and taking his brain off line. "Of course you did. My sweet, innocent Simon. You only ever think of others but never yourself. Are you sharing for me or for you?"

It took a moment for Simon to gather the goo that his brain had become and shove it back into his skull where it belonged. He was starting to get lightheaded, his cock taking every ounce of blood in his body. At least, that's what it felt like.

"I like all of you, all three, and I would like to keep you all." He paused. "Did you like the kiss?" A flush of insecurity trickled in. None of it would really matter if Chris decided that he preferred tits to dicks.

"What do they think about each other? Leo and Rubric." Chris' voice was deadly serious, and it was enough to snap Simon the rest of the way out of his haze.

"They don't know." He shook his head. "I don't think Rubric likes Leo much, and Leo already said that he didn't want to share. I've never said anything to either of them about the other."

"Then this stops until you do." Chris leaned back, his heat withdrawing like a fall thunderstorm. Simon blinked, his vision still slightly blurry from the pounding of his heart. And *Christ*, his cock could cut diamond.

"What? But I'm…" He looked down at the tent in his pants and it was downright obscene, with a spot of wetness that had leaked through the denim. He could see the bulge in Chris' pants, too, and it looked like he might just rival Leo for size.

"I won't tolerate infidelity, Simon. By not telling them, you are taking away the option to say no. They might be okay with a shared relationship, but not if you keep it from them. Tell them now or this all ends." He adjusted his cock in his pants, wincing. "Now, was the kiss okay?" Chris' dominance dropped away as insecurity swept in. He was back to being the shy bear instead of the best kisser that Simon had ever touched.

"I think you broke me." He lay back against the couch, shaking his head as Chris laughed. "Fuck, you can kiss."

Chris laughed louder, reaching for his pizza and flicking *National Treasure* on the television. Simon cursed.

He was sleeping alone tonight.

# Chapter Eight

Simon had searched through every single cabinet and drawer in the office for a hint of Leo's name and had come up empty. He'd refused to broach the subject with Rubric, knowing that bridge was best saved for last, so he had turned to the Internet instead.

It had turned out that Leo was a popular subject in news articles, especially when it came to speculation of illegal activities. Simon had shaken his head when he'd read an article that called Leo a mafia boss. Nothing could have been further from the truth. Mafia bosses didn't offer escorts to those in need or make dinner to try to woo someone. They just ordered people around and took what they wanted while snorting cocaine and shoving a gun down their pants.

But he'd come up empty when trying to find a phone number, which was why he'd found himself bussing it over to Leo's penthouse after work.

He had to have a conversation soon, even if he was moderately petrified. Rubric's face at Simon's polite rebuff had nearly broken his heart. Chris was right, though. He'd never had conversations with either man, and secrets tended to stamp relationships with an expiration date.

His clothes were sticking to his body by the time Simon approached Leo's building. Staring up at the skyscraper like he'd done a few weeks before, he took a deep breath. He had thought that Leo would come to him and track him down, especially after his threat, but he'd given Simon his space.

Their time apart had only strengthened Simon's desire to the point that he was thinking about ice-cold eyes on an hourly basis.

The doorman somehow recognized him, as did the concierge, who looked his name up on an electronic tablet. Apparently, Simon was on some sort of list, although he was only allowed up if Leo was already home. Weeks had passed, but Leo was still welcoming him with open arms.

*Do I deserve it?* Simon's stomach flipped when he realized that there was no way to back out now. The elevator doors were already closing, and nothing short of a power outage would stop their ascent.

He licked his dry lips as the elevator rose, longing for water as his throat clicked noisily. What if Leo didn't want to see him? He would have to ride back down the elevator with the concierge eyeing him up, knowing that he had been rejected when he was removed from 'the list'.

The elevator hovered to a stop. He was finally back.

"I don't fucking care, Natalie." An angry Russian voice followed the barely audible ding that the elevator made as its doors slid wide. Simon stepped inside the condo, blinking as raised voices echoed across the flat.

He looked back, but the doors had slung shut. He was trapped.

There were four people in the kitchen, with three of them seated at the island while Leo paced back and forth. He recognized Natalie, this time dressed in tight jeans and a shirt that had more straps than fabric. One of the men was Clas, if he remembered correctly—the one who had appeared so interested in viewing the art display in Rubric's building. The remaining man was a mystery, clad in a suit that looked to be a few hundred dollars cheaper than Leo's.

"Don't blame me, Leo. You dug this hole, and you had to know that you were going to fall into it eventually," said Natalie in English as she rested her glass on the island, swirling the liquid inside around and around.

"Don't get philosophical. It just pisses me off more. Just take care of him, or he'll be the end to everything. You think that I want this?" asked Leo in Russian. Leo ran his hand through his hair, the locks sticking up in every direction. His eyes were wild, his composure lost.

Simon wished he could ease that look from Leo's eyes. He had helped last time, but he suspected it would be different now.

"Yes," she said in French, taking another sip of her drink. "I think this is exactly the excuse you were hoping for. After this, there is no going back, and that's what you want."

The way these people flipped languages like they were lightbulbs baffled his mind. How the hell did they keep up? The mystery man blinked, like he wasn't following the conversation, and Clas looked a bit lost. At least Simon wasn't the only one.

Simon had to step in before things went any further. Even if he could offer some sort of help, whatever they were talking about was none of his business. He didn't want to be any ruder than he already had been by standing silently for so long.

He cleared his throat, wilting when Leo whirled on him, his hand moving for something in his jacket. Natalie spun, reaching down toward her knee-high boot, and the other two stood from their chairs.

"Who the fuck are *you*?" The man Simon didn't recognize approached, grabbing for the glint of metal at his waistband. Simon tried to get a good look at it, but the man was wearing a suit jacket, despite the fact that it was the middle of summer. The fabric cut off his view before he could see what it was.

"Simon?" Leo blanched, rushing around the island and passing the man who was doing his best impression of a bodyguard. "What are you doing here?"

*Oh crap.* He looked pissed — like ready to yell and ban Simon from the building pissed. Simon pressed his back to the elevator's cold frame. The metal was digging into his spine and reminding him that there was no escape.

"I…well." He looked over Leo's shoulder to the others in the room. "I came to talk to you. I guess I'm on a list, but I didn't know your phone number or I would've called. I can go if you're busy or if you don't want to see me." The back of his shirt was sticking to him and he could feel a bead of sweat roll down from his hairline, itching a path all the way to his collar.

"No, it's good to see you," said Leo, looking more hesitant than Simon had ever seen or imagined him. He had always shown strong confidence without a hint of indecision. Whatever was bothering him must've been very important. Simon hoped he could help.

Leo turned away, pointing at the two men. "You two, get the fuck out," he growled in Russian, the sound sending a sprinkle of fear and desire up Simon's spine. "Natalie, we will continue this later."

"This can't wait, boss. Tell your toy to get out so we can take care of this. You know I'm right." She spoke in perfect Russian this time, and her smiling face and calm voice were the polar opposite of her words. Simon swallowed again as her green eyes pinned him to the frame.

"I can go," said Simon, his thoughts whirling as he tried to keep up. "Or I can try to help? You seem upset."

Natalie snorted, her grin widening as she took another sip of her drink.

"Oh, the little puppy thinks he can play with the big doggies. What have you been telling him, Leo? You've been filling his head with daydreams while you're supposed to be out there taking care of business." Her eyes narrowed as she spoke in Russian until her glare was nearly palpable.

Somehow, Simon was already on her bad side, even though he couldn't remember doing anything wrong. Maybe Rubric's deal had gone sideways after all and she blamed him by proxy. It would explain why he hadn't been able to find any files on Leo anywhere in Rubric's building.

Either way, it was getting a bit grating with how they kept talking about him like he wasn't standing there listening. He pushed his anger down, knowing better than to get riled up. People lashed out when they were upset, and he knew not to take it personally.

"I'm so sorry, Leo. You're obviously busy. I can go and we can chat later." Simon faltered as Leo turned back to him, his cold eyes blazing under his dark lashes.

"Whatever you have to say to me, say it now." Leo took a step forward, pinning him against the door with his glare.

For some strange reason, Simon's cock started to fill, and desire rushed into his core like molten lava. Leo's dark voice that was nearly on the edge of a growl was doing terrible and wonderful things to him.

He hadn't known what to expect, but this definitely wasn't it.

"You said you didn't share," said Simon, lowering his voice so that hopefully only Leo would hear him. Leo took a step closer, the scent of his cologne making Simon's mouth water. "But I thought maybe I could convince you to try." He glanced over Leo's shoulder and his resolve hardened. If he was going to do this, he had to be brave or he would be steamrolled by hurricane Natalie before the day was over. "I want you, Leo. I want you to fuck me hard on your bed with the sheets that are softer than heaven against my skin. I want you to bite me and mark me and make me yours. Don't hold back."

Leo's gaze darkened, his pupils dilating as he took another step. The smell of expensive cologne nearly derailed Simon.

"But I want to kiss Chris and show him what it's like to be with a man. I want him to see how wonderful he is and how great it can be. Then I want to go to work and bend Rubric over the desk and feed him my cock once inch at a time until he's begging for it, hard and fast."

He wished that it was different with Rubric and that he was the one being fucked and not the one doing the fucking, but he had to lay out the reality for Leo. He didn't want any secrets between them on his part.

He took a deep breath. Natalie's eyes had gone wide, telling him that she had definitely heard him, despite the fact that he had been trying to keep quiet. At least he had managed to surprise her. He had a feeling that was a rare event.

"You're fucking Rubric?" A frown pulled at Leo's lips, and he scrunched his nose as if he'd smelled something bad.

"Yes," said Simon. "He asked me to fuck him, and I did. Ever since that night with you, I've been fucking him." It was too late to back out now. In for a penny and all that.

"He's got a nice ass, I'll give you that," said Leo, a smirk breaking over his lips as he crossed his arms. "He's needy, too, with a tight hole that you can pound for days."

"Wait... You guys hooked up?" Simon thought his jaw might hit the floor. Fuck, that sounded so hot. He could imagine the two men fucking, Leo controlling every move and Rubric molded to the desk like the prefect clay, taking everything Leo had to give.

"Hm-m," said Leo, nodding. "It's been a while, but yeah. I understand the appeal, and I could be convinced to share—if I get to watch, of course."

*Oh God*, Simon was going to come in his pants. He revamped his fantasy until he was the one balls deep in Rubric, spreading the man over the carpet as he slammed inside. Red welts spread over Rubric's skin as the carpet marked him, and he was groaning constantly from the assault on his senses. And there was Leo in the corner, telling Simon when to go faster, and when to hold off, just to bring tears to Rubric's eyes.

"A-and Chris? He's important to me, too. I need you to be okay with him." This was the strangest conversation he'd ever had in his life—him begging one man to be with two more. His past self would declare that he was being a greedy boy.

"I'll have to meet him, then I'll decide." Leo slid his fingertips over Simon's jaw, taking his brain offline as he gripped his jaw and tugged him away from the door. "Now go to the bedroom. I'll be there in five minutes to start where we left off. I expect you to be ready."

"I can't," said Simon, shaking his head and trying not to crumble as Leo's expression turned downright murderous. Was he supposed to be this turned on because someone was mad at him? Maybe it was his childhood rebellious streak that he'd never had. It was never too late to push someone's buttons, apparently.

"You have a habit of pushing me. When you're mine, you'll come to me every time I call, and you will never leave me wanting. Your own pleasure won't matter to you, as long as I am satisfied." Leo moved in as he spoke in fluent Russian, his cold eyes pinning Simon to the frigid door before his hands were on him.

Leo wrapped one hand around Simon's neck, tracing up the sides with callused fingertips before gripping him. It wasn't enough to cut off his air, but it made Simon want to pull away and ask for more at the same time. He'd never considered asking someone to choke him, but it felt better than he could've imagined. The only thing that would have made it better was if Rubric were already on board and with Leo, laid naked on the bed.

"You wouldn't fight me, would you?" Leo didn't wait for an answer before he leaned in, dragging his lips across Simon's in a hard kiss that took his breath away.

Simon knew the answer. He wouldn't fight. Even if Leo tied him to the bed and pounded into him harder than he could stand. He would give Leo whatever he wanted, and he would love every moment.

"Goodbye, Simon," said Leo as he pulled away, dropping his hands to his sides. He reached for something in his back pocket, sliding it into Simon's hand. A phone number etched in dark ink was scrawled across the small business card. "I expect to see you soon, but if I don't…you better run fast and fly far, little birdie."

# Chapter Nine

Simon filed the third report of the day, his mind nearly numb after taking minutes during three consecutive two-hour-long meetings. He loved numbers, especially when they went up and not down, but that many numbers with no break had his head swimming. It was really too bad that he didn't like coffee, because it was probably the only thing that would get him through the rest of the day without a migraine.

He lowered his head to his desk, wrapping his arms around his face to block out the light. He focused on the sound of his breaths and the beating of his heart, relaxing his shoulders until they settled to their regular level.

It had been two days since he'd left Leo's apartment with a phantom handprint on his neck and a cock that was harder than silicon carbide. Work had been so busy that he had hardly seen Rubric outside of meetings, let alone had time to corner him in his office. It was almost like the man was avoiding him.

And Chris…*fuck*. He craved another kiss worse than fuzzy peaches on a hungry day. Chris refused to touch him or even sit next to him on the couch, probably knowing that Simon would sprawl on him like he always did.

He greeted Simon with the same smile as usual, but everything else had changed. His lovable, huggable best friend had withdrawn, and the wrath from his recent breakup had finally started sinking in.

Simon wanted to help, but Chris was beyond reach, tucked away until Simon fessed up to Rubric. He had to set up a time for Leo and Chris to meet each other, too… There was so much to do.

"Simon?"

Rubric's voice had him shooting upright and blinking the spots from his vision. The dark circles under Rubric's eyes were back. It wasn't enough for any clients to notice, but Simon knew Rubric almost better than he knew himself. And ever since he'd turned Rubric down that last time, he had acted like a spurned lover.

"Rubric, can I talk to you?" He slid his hands over the hard wooden surface of his desk, accidentally nicking his finger on the edge of a stack of papers. Just another contract that had to be closed that afternoon— and so many more numbers.

"We should have a few minutes before the next round," said Rubric, glancing at his watch as he plastered a false smile on his face that didn't even come close to reaching his eyes. Maybe Simon could stay up late to make another batch of cookies for Rubric to try to cheer him up? White chocolate macadamia nut would hopefully do the trick, even if they were a pain in the butt to make.

He followed Rubric into his office, letting the door click shut behind him before he took a deep breath. Rubric was facing away, looking out of the window with one hand on the desk. He almost appeared at ease, until Simon spotted the tension in his shoulders and the way his foot was cocked awkwardly to the side.

"Rubric, I'm not really sure how to say this." It had been so much easier with Leo and Chris, but Rubric's presence took his breath away, leaving his mind a blank slate that refused to cooperate. How could he be open with someone who was so far above him?

"Simon, it's okay," said Rubric, shaking his head without turning around. "I completely understand if you want to end things. It probably shouldn't have happened, anyway. You're too sweet and too kind to get mixed up with someone like me." Rubric let out a sigh, drooping his shoulders and sliding his hand along the desk.

"But that's not it at all," said Simon, taking a step toward the desk but shoving his hands into his pockets to keep from reaching out. He needed to talk *before* he touched. "I really like you, Rubric, and I can see our relationship developing outside of a quick office liaison, but I need you to know that I'm interested in someone else as well…two someones, really."

"What?" Rubric spun around, his eyes narrowing with confusion. "I don't understand. You don't want to stop what we're doing, but you want to see someone else?"

"Well, yes, I mean…the three of you are so different, and I feel connected to each of you in such opposite ways. You're my quiet Rubric, who needs someone to take control so you don't fall apart. Chris is my lost best friend, looking for someone to show him the way. And

Leo? He's…well." *Dominant, possibly kinky, possessive and delicious.* "He's Leo."

"Wait." Rubric took a step back, his face going pale. "You *want* a relationship with Leo?"

"Yes, and Chris, too—and you." Simon bit his tongue. He was screwing it up, he just knew it. Why was this so much harder with Rubric? Maybe because Rubric was the only man he'd ever tried to impress. No, not tried. He *had* to impress him or he'd be out of the job.

"Leo is a monster, Simon," Rubric roared, his nostrils flaring as he stood to his full height. "Why would you want to fuck him? Do you know who he is, and what he's done? He's the head of the fucking mafia, for Christ's sake, and you want to sleep with him? *Willingly?*"

"But *you* slept with him," said Simon, as his mind blanked. He took a step back as Rubric's face flushed bright red. Simon couldn't believe everything he read online, especially when the man whom the articles described was nothing like Leo. Rubric was a trusted source, but he had disliked Leo from the beginning.

"I slept with him so he would finance this company," said Rubric, grabbing a stack of papers and tossing them toward Simon. Simon sidestepped the hundreds of papercuts before they reached him, his heart pounding. "I slept with him because it was either him or the bottom of a dumpster. He's a fucking animal, Simon, and he wouldn't hesitate to kill you." A vein throbbed at Rubric's temple, and for a moment, Simon wondered if he was about to be punched. Rubric had never yelled at him before, and it felt like a physical hit to the gut.

"But that's not Leo at all. He may be a bit controlling and possessive, but he's considerate," said Simon, sniffing quietly as his eyes started to burn. He had begged Leo to take him without prep, but Leo had stalled, asking him over and over if he was sure. A monster wouldn't do that. "I understand if you guys have some bad history, but I'm sure he was just trying to help you. If he hadn't given you the money to start this company, then you wouldn't be one of the richest men in the country. He was only trying to help."

"Not everyone is a good person, Simon." Rubric deflated like a spent cock without the pleasant after tingles. "Some people are just…evil. And he's one of them. If you stay with him, he'll hurt you, and I don't want to get a call from Chris to identify your body. It would kill me." He leaned back against the desk, his voice going quiet.

"Rubric, I…I think I should go," said Simon as he finally lost the battle to keep his tears from spilling over. He knew that once the floodgates opened, he wouldn't be able to stop until he'd sobbed his heart out. He could only hang out in the bathroom at work for so long before someone started to think that he'd died.

He couldn't do this. He couldn't keep being the strong person for Rubric without Chris to back him. He couldn't keep thinking about Leo and how it had felt to be laid out on his bed, with the silken sheets caressing his skin. He couldn't give Rubric his all without becoming nothing himself.

"Simon, please, listen to me." Rubric took a step toward him, but Simon shook his head before wiping his tears on the back of his hand and squaring his shoulders. "Okay, don't listen, but promise me that you'll never see him again," said Rubric. His hand trembled as he reached out for Simon, his voice pleading.

"I promise you won't see me again, Rubric. Please don't call me."

# Chapter Ten

Simon stumbled from the office, making it onto the bus before he couldn't hold back his sobs any longer. The woman in the seat beside him gave him a startled look as the first noise let loose from his chest, before she stood and shuffled away to a seat at the front of the bus. Simon couldn't blame her. Crying in public was as humiliating as it was horrible, and he would hate to be a witness as much as he was a participant.

When he arrived at the apartment, Chris was standing just inside the door, unlacing his ridiculous boots that he insisted on wearing to work. He had claimed that they gave him traction during a pursuit and that they had saved his ass on more than one occasion. They were still cleats, though.

Chris' uniform was damp with sweat, but the buttons were open, displaying the soaked tank underneath that barely stretched over his huge frame. Dark hairs curled through the fabric, giving Simon a peek of what he craved. The uniform was one of the sexiest that existed, exceeding both fireman and male nurse.

Chris' police career had almost sent him into a spiral of depression before he had taken a step back and cut his hours in half. After that, he hadn't been able to afford an apartment on his own, but he'd become a new person. He hadn't been ready to move in with Kayla and had stumbled upon Simon, who had been looking for someone to share his expenses and do his dishes every once in a while.

Chris looked up as Simon entered, his smile dropping away as Simon sniffed and wiped his cheeks with the back of his hand. He knew he was just smearing his tears around instead of hiding them, but he didn't want Chris to see. His face was hot and swollen to the touch, and he could only imagine what he looked like. He didn't have the skill to cry while still looking beautiful.

"I'm gonna kill him. Was it Leo or Rubric who did this to you?" Chris stood, one cleat still clinging to his foot as he wrapped his arms around Simon. The smell of fresh sweat and summer air engulfed Simon, and he sank into the warm embrace, letting the tears flow.

"It doesn't matter," said Simon, his words muffled by Chris' chest. The fabric was stiff and scratchy against his sensitive eyelids, but he didn't want to draw away. "Besides, you actually carry a gun on you, and I don't want you to follow through on that threat." He tried for a joke, which fell utterly flat from the way Chris' arms tightened around him.

"Will you tell me what happened?" Chris murmured into the top of his head. The distant scratch of his beard had Simon swallowing a fresh round of tears. No matter what happened, Chris was always there for him, and that wasn't about to change now.

"Rubric, he um… He didn't take my request well." Simon let out a huff at the massive understatement. "He and Leo have a history, I guess, and Rubric wanted nothing to do with him. He told me to stay away from him, too, or I'd end up in a body bag." He still couldn't quite believe that Rubric had said that. His life wasn't a movie, after all.

Chris stiffened, his arms going tight. He kicked off his remaining cleat, uncharacteristically letting it smash into the wall, spreading dirt over the crisp blue paint. He moved them to the couch, shuffling Simon into his lap.

"Why would he say something like that?" Chris asked softly, combing his fingers through Simon's hair.

Despite the grief pulling at Simon's chest, he started to relax. Chris always seemed to know exactly what he needed, even if Simon didn't. It was one of the things that had drawn them into being best friends so quickly after Chris had moved in. Perhaps there had been more there than friendship from the very beginning and neither of them had seen it.

"He said that Leo was the head of the mafia," said Simon, shaking his head as he breathed in Chris' scent. "But stuff like that doesn't happen in real life. There's drug dealers and stuff, but there isn't a mafia anymore." Simon peered up into Chris' face, hoping for confirmation.

If anyone would know, Chris would. Before he cut his hours, he was on a special task force that dealt with drug, human and fugitive trafficking.

"You're so sweet, Simon, but so naive." Chris' face was grim, which definitely wasn't a good sign. Simon's stomach tightened. "There is a mafia…many in fact—not just here but all around the world in places you would least expect. I spent years of my life near the edge, trying to track them down and send them to prison, only for them to find their way out again a few days or years later."

Simon felt the color drain from his face as his blood started to rush through his ears. He trusted Chris, but he had to be wrong. This city was safe—one of the safest in the world—so there was no way there was a mafia here.

"But hey." Chris let out a sigh, a small smile tugging at his lips. "That's the reason I like you so much. You keep me thinking positive when the world has gone to shit. And as long as your Leo isn't Leo Zoya, then you're in the clear."

*Zoya.* That was the name that Leo had used to introduce himself in Rubric's office.

He'd been holding Rubric by the throat, hadn't he? Simon had thought it had been a contract gone wrong, but looking back, maybe it was a threat.

Then Rubric had appeared with bruises after his *escort…*

They had *beaten* him.

He wanted to wither away to nothing. He had been so stupid. He slapped a hand to his face, crumpling into Chris.

"Holy fuck, your Leo *is* Leo Zoya." Chris' face was unreadable, his lips set in a firm line.

"Yes." Simon cringed, waiting for Chris to toss him away so he could curl up in a ball to hide from reality. Chris would probably throw him out if he found out how much the growl in Leo's voice had turned him on.

*Fuck*…the glint of silver he'd seen a few times and the way Leo had reached for something in his jacket when Simon had arrived unannounced… Had that been a gun? He was going to be sick.

"Okay," said Chris, tugging him closer. Simon choked on a sob as acceptance soaked into him, instead of the rejection he'd feared. Chris was too good for him. How could he understand, even when Simon had been so blind?

"It's okay, Simon. You can cry. Let it all out for me. I'm not upset—a little concerned—but not upset. You can't help who calls to your heart, just like I can't help that I'm in love with you."

Simon choked on a sob, looking up at Chris, who's eyes had a glimmer to them. "Don't cry, please," said Simon, his heart already breaking.

Chris shook his head, lowering his hands to Simon's hips where he squeezed softly and settled his thumbs against the bone. "Things aren't going to be easy for you if you choose this path, Simon, but I'll be here for you, no matter what.

"Shit." Simon buried his face again as another round of sobs racked him. He half expected Chris to tell him what to do, just like Rubric had. But now, a rush of freedom washed over his body and stripped his fear away. The only one he could disappoint now was himself.

"Can I call him?" asked Simon when he found his voice again. "He gave me his number the last time I tracked him down, and he wants to meet you."

He should be pushing Leo away from his thoughts, but he wanted him more than ever. The thought of never seeing him again gave him the same feeling as thinking about losing Chris. Losing Rubric was a dull knife in comparison.

"Technically, we've already met, but we can try under better circumstances," said Chris, his voice dropping into business mode. Simon shivered. He hadn't spoken to 'Chris the cop' much, but he would have to make a point of doing it more. Maybe just in the bedroom, though, because now was not the time.

"I'll call him." His hands shook as he dialed the number that he had memorized as soon as he'd typed it into his cell phone. He pressed it to his ear, sliding his eyes shut when he heard the line connect.

"Who is this?" Leo asked, his voice gruff with the edge of violence. Simon shuddered. He knew that the danger wasn't a false threat and that Leo *was* dangerous, but that didn't make his heart hurt any less.

"I-it's Simon." He cleared his throat, his voice garbled from so much crying.

"Little bird," said Leo, slipping between English and Russian seamlessly. "I was hoping to hear from you sooner. I was starting to worry that I was wasting my time waiting for you."

"Why did you wait?" asked Simon quietly. He needed to know if this was one-sided before he got any deeper. He reached for Chris, squeezing his hand.

"Because I believe you are worth the wait. You're a fascinating man, Simon." His voice dropped into a rumble. "All I can think about is those moments you were dragged away from me, and what was left unfinished."

Simon's cock twitched just thinking about it, but he needed more.

"When it's finished, will you stay or will you be out to find someone more interesting to pass the time? I need to know before I see you again, so I can be prepared either way." Simon took a deep breath. He was so glad that Chris was there with him.

"You shouldn't speak of yourself like you're some trifle. It's disrespectful." He heard Leo inhale, letting his breath out slowly. "But it's a valid question worth an answer. I have no desire to end our relationship after one night, even if it means *sharing* you."

"T-That's actually why I'm calling you —"

"Please don't tell me there's another name already." Leo let out a huff. "I haven't even met this Chris yet or heard Rubric's answer. My limits can only be stretched so far."

"No, there's no one else, and Rubric? Well, he wasn't a fan of the idea." He felt the burn at the back of his eyes and waited for his lip to stop trembling before he continued. "Chris wants to talk to you, so I was wondering if you can come over."

"He can bring a friend if he is more comfortable," said Chris, his voice quiet, but, from Leo's scoff, he must've heard it.

"I'll be there in…ten minutes," said Leo after a brief pause. "And I'll be coming alone."

"Wait! I didn't tell you my address," called Simon, sensing that Leo was about to hang up. Leo chuckled, the sound deep and dark.

"I know where to find you, little bird."

# Chapter Eleven

A knock sounded at the door nine-and-a-half minutes later, and Simon jumped from the couch to answer. Chris had disappeared to shower and change while Simon waited and fanned his face, willing his tears to dry. He had stopped crying, but his face was still puffy and red, his eyes sore and a headache throbbing behind his temple.

He didn't even want to know what his headache would become when he started thinking about a job search and rent that was due in nine days. He had enough saved up to stretch a few months, but the job market was next to impossible, and no one wanted someone *else's* assistant — not unless they were looking for the inside scoop, which Simon would not provide.

He took a deep breath at the door, gazing through the peep hole to see Leo standing there, looking even more handsome than he remembered. He was wearing a suit again today, but the top buttons were open and his tie was slightly askew as if he had been starting to change before he'd rushed over. His straight dark hair was fluffy from the humidity that still clung to the air.

He cracked the door, then swung it wide as Leo looked up. A frown tugged at his lips as he looked Simon up and down, his eyes glowering behind his sunglasses.

"Rubric?" he asked, waiting for Simon's nod. "He's not worth tears, Simon." He placed his hand on Simon's shoulder, squeezing softly. "But I'm here for you if you need me for anything at all." He paused and Simon wanted nothing more than to pull him in for a hug. "Can I come in?"

"Aw crap, sorry!" Simon stepped back to let Leo past. "It's nothing special, but it's home." It was a two-bedroom closet compared to Leo's place, but it had more character than any other building in the area — if broken elevators and leaky pipes counted as character.

"It's just your name on the lease, but you don't live alone," said Leo, glancing at the boot tray that contained two collections of very different-sized shoes.

*Shit*, and Chris' cleat was still leaning against the wall. He grabbed it, setting it back into its appropriate spot.

"I sublet," said Simon. "It's the only way I can afford this neighborhood." It wasn't exactly a legal option, but he figured that he had a free pass because Chris was a cop and he'd never mentioned having an issue with it.

"Hmm-m, it is a nice neighborhood. Very low crime rate." Leo toed off his shoes, sliding his sunglasses on top of his head. It pushed his bangs back, displaying his forehead that had too many worry lines for a man of his age. Simon wondered how old Leo actually was. He couldn't narrow it down more than late twenties to early forties.

"Low crime is good," said Simon, biting his tongue when Leo looked at him sharply. *Why the hell did I say that?*

He followed Leo into the living room and sat on the couch as Leo peered around the room, stepping up to a photo on one wall. It was of Chris' parents and his sister when they had gone on a cruise together. Chris had been the one taking the picture, so the sun was glaring into the camera lens, but the smiles were genuine.

"Your family or your roommate's?" Leo tapped the frame.

"Chris' family. He's just getting cleaned up, but he should be out soon." Simon clasped his hands, rubbing them together awkwardly. His heart was pounding and his palms were sweating, despite the air conditioner humming away in the window.

"I know it's not much — this place — but it suits us. Your place is just wow," said Simon, searching for anything to break the silence that had descended. Leo's place probably had more zeros than he would see in his lifetime.

"You'd think that you would be able to afford this place on your own with what Rubric is paying you," said Leo, turning back around to face Simon. His glare had the edge of an interrogation. "And your roommate, is he unemployed?"

"No," said Chris, appearing in the doorway that led to where the bedrooms and bathroom lay. "I'm a cop." He had donned a pair of jeans that were fastened at the waist by a thick leather belt, but that was it. Every inch of his chest was on display, his hair still damp from the shower, and heat clung to his skin. The fresh scent of body wash made Simon's mouth water.

"Chris Fuck'n Denver," Leo cursed, an accent appearing as his body went rigid. He reached into his jacket, and suddenly there was a glint of steel in his hand with a gun barrel pointed directly at Chris' naked chest.

Simon's heart stopped when he saw the gun for what it really was. It had been there every time he had seen Leo, hadn't it? And now it was in his hand, making him look like the lethal devil that everyone was telling him that he was.

He couldn't breathe. He couldn't even stand from the couch to intervene. His legs and arms had locked up, stealing every wisp of power from his bones.

"Is this some kind of set-up?" asked Leo, his gaze flickering to Simon's paralyzed form, his forehead furrowing. His glasses slipped from his head, the lens popping from the frame as they crashed to the ground.

"Do you think you could take me in a fair fight, *boy*?" asked Chris as he took another step into the room, drawing Leo's attention.

Simon let out an involuntary squeak. Was Chris insane? He should be running, not moving closer.

"You're aiming a gun on an unarmed man," said Chris, holding his arms wide in surrender. "That's pretty low, even for a slippery fucker like you." His chest rose and fell rapidly, the only sign of his fear.

"A fuck'n cop." Leo shook his head with a snarl. "I shoulda known that it was too good to be true." He glanced back at Simon, his eyes going cold. "How long have you been planning this, little bird? What do you get for taking down the big bad mobster? I hope it's worth your life."

Simon swallowed, his tears prickling as his world spun. The gun moved, until he was looking down the thin-threaded barrel. The relief that he should have felt for Chris' safety was blasted away by a rush of self-preservation. The gun looked so much bigger than he remembered Chris' looking, with a barrel that seemed to stretch forever.

*A silencer*, his mind whispered. He had watched enough television that he should have known immediately. There would be no noise, so the neighbors wouldn't even know to call the cops if a bullet ripped through him, taking his life from his body.

"Stop," Chris growled low in his throat. For a moment, he seemed more dangerous than the loaded gun. "Simon is the only one in this room who defended you and believed that there was a shred of good in you. He refused to believe you could be a bad person, no matter what anyone said. When he told me who you were, I was ready to kill you myself. But I had to *know* this person who had made their way into his heart. That" — he motioned to the gun — "doesn't belong to the same person Simon told me about."

Leo paused, confusion etching into his features as his stance wavered. He flexed his hand on the grip of the gun, his fingers perilously close to the trigger.

"Please don't kill each other," said Simon, finally able to muster up his weak voice. "If you aren't okay with each other, I'm not going to choose. It's either both or nothing. So, please don't fight." He was shaking so hard that he could hardly speak, and his hands had gone numb where they gripped the couch.

"Fuck," said Leo, sliding his gun back into his jacket and pinching the base of his nose. "Simon, just…fuck."

"Hmm-m I agree, *boy*," said Chris as he crossed the remaining distance to Leo before holding out his hand.

"But I don't think we are there yet. For now, I won't fuck you over, and I expect you to do the same."

Simon flushed as his mind jumped to sleeping with both of these men. Would they be okay with taking him at the same time? *God*, could he even take that? A guy could dream.

They shook hands, their grips more aggressive than they probably should have been, but Simon was finally able to breathe a sigh of relief. He had a feeling that that could have gone so much worse. It almost had.

"Don't fuck'n arrest me," said Leo, dropping his hand back to his side. His voice was slurred with an accent that Simon had never picked up before. Leo's defenses were obviously down, and his soul was bared to the room.

Chris arched one brow before he crossed his arms. "Then don't fucking shoot at me, *boy*."

# Chapter Twelve

Simon sighed and lay back on his bed. His eyes were nearly glued shut with exhaustion and his limbs were heavy, but his mind buzzed, refusing to let sleep take him. The distant hum of the air-conditioning scratched against his skull but sweat trickled down his forehead, nonetheless.

Someday, he would be able to afford central air and not just a window shaker that was very adept at keeping one room cool while the others stayed sticky.

Leo had stayed for hours, speaking quietly with Chris on the couch while Simon had tried to keep up, his mouth hanging open as he'd waited for the guns to come out—*again*. They had more history than Simon had realized, including several close calls with each other's lives.

Despite the newfound easiness in the room, Leo had never said anything that could have been remotely incriminating. He had chosen his words very carefully, apparently pondering for several minutes sometimes before he had answered.

Simon's heart was going to burst. He'd known that he had been starting to fall in love with Leo the moment he'd walked out of his penthouse for the first time. Longing like that came with a hefty side dish of feelings, no matter how much he tried to suppress them.

And Chris... When he looked deep within himself, he realized he had been in love with Chris since he had knocked on the door with his bags in hand, ready to move in.

The men weren't the only thing on his mind, unfortunately. One particular thing kept turning over in his head, setting seeds that were quickly sprouting into doubt and uncertainty.

Leo had casually mentioned that he should have been able to afford a nicer place for what Rubric was paying him...but this apartment was the best he could do. There were no other expenses that he could cut, and he already lived as cheaply as he could. He even waited for clear-out sales to get his new suits and shirts, which was why they didn't fit him perfectly sometimes.

How much should he have been making? He'd never really thought about it too much. He'd always been able to make ends meet, and he'd enjoyed his job...for the most part. Rubric had always been fair, if not a bit demanding—especially when their relationship strayed from strictly professional.

Perhaps his low wage had been because he had been banned from staying late, so he couldn't rack up any overtime. That had to be why. As demanding as Rubric was, he wasn't cruel.

He rolled onto his side as he heard a knock at his door, forcing his eyelids to open. He'd left his lamp on by accident, and the room was flooded with unnatural light, casting shadows that created monsters all over the curling walls.

"Come in?" It was strange that Chris was even knocking, let alone waiting for an answer, before he just opened the door. Then again, Simon didn't usually have the door all the way shut. But he'd needed to be alone. His heart and mind had been laid open in the living room, and he was still counting to make sure he had all the pieces.

"Hey, you okay?" Chris stuck his head in, his voice soft and low. His face was drawn, and he looked as exhausted as Simon felt, but there was a brightness to his eyes. "I just wanted to see if you needed a snuggle buddy."

Simon patted the mattress behind him, scooching closer to the edge so Chris would have enough room. He was going to have to invest in a new mattress if Leo started staying over. He had a feeling the man had never slept in something smaller than a king.

Chris circled the bed, shedding his reading glasses and placing them on the nightstand before he clicked the light off and pulled the covers back. Simon waited until warmth settled against his back before he let out a sigh.

"I thought he was going to shoot you," whispered Simon, reaching for Chris' hand as Chris wrapped his arm around his waist. Chris shifted until his broad chest was pressed to his back, his warmth welcome, even in the stuffy room.

"So did I," said Chris. "But I had hope. I knew you saw something in him…something more than a killer." He leaned down, his breath tickling Simon's nape.

Simon shifted his hips back, needing to feel Chris completely. So far, they had kept everything above the belt and had only shared wonderful kisses and heated looks. Simon longed to feel Chris' cock against his ass. It didn't even have to be hard.

"What do you think about what we said? Is it going to work for you?" asked Chris, seemingly oblivious as Simon snuggled closer, grinding just a bit to get comfortable. Chris' grip tightened, giving him away.

Simon honestly couldn't remember a single thing that they had talked about after the gun had disappeared. He'd suffered a massive adrenaline crash, and his brain had gone offline for the most part. He knew they had made plans. Maybe for dinner? But he couldn't remember when or where. He did hope it was soon, though.

He heard Chris sigh softly as he gave in, grinding against Simon's ass as his cock started to fill. Simon clenched his cheeks, trying to get a sense of the size and shape as it stiffened against him, but it was no use.

Chris' lips at the sensitive spot under his ear had him gasping. That spot never failed to make his knees weak and his cock hard, especially when Chris dragged his talented tongue across it.

"Is Leo okay if we do this? Just with us, I mean?" Simon asked as he cut off a groan, drawing in a breath when Chris dipped lower along his neck, chuckling as he went.

"You really weren't listening," said Chris before he sucked Simon's neck, probably bringing a bruise to the surface. Simon arched into the touch as it skittered along the edge of pain.

"I tried, but I couldn't." He groaned as he felt Chris' teeth touch him.

"It's okay. I think you were in a little bit of shock."

"I thought you were going to die. I was so scared." He shook at the memory of Leo's cold eyes and the steel cruelty he'd held in his hand. Inexplicably, his cock filled out, his balls going heavy between his legs.

"Are you okay? Do you still? I mean… If you have a problem with Leo, I'll take care of it. You don't have to be afraid of him." Chris paused his kisses as he asked, letting Simon think clearly before he answered.

"I… Is it okay if I kind of liked it?" The fear he wasn't a huge fan of, but the rush of adrenalin was enough to make him hard. And Leo had looked so fucking sexy with that wild look in his eyes and his hair fluttering down when his glasses crashed to the floor. He could see why he was the head of the mafia. No one would cross him and expect to live.

Chris chuckled again, smoothing his hands down Simon's sides. "It's very okay. And yes, Leo is okay with it, and so am I. We talked about dating separately and together, and our thoughts were to start with whatever feels right at the time. You promised us that you would tell us if you felt pulled in one direction or the other and that we would talk about it as a group if there was a spark of jealousy."

Simon didn't exactly remember making that promise, but he would try to keep it. It would be hard to focus on his own feelings instead of soaking up the ones around him like he had with Rubric.

"Did I make any other promises?" Simon asked quietly, tilting his neck to give Chris better access and beg for more kisses.

"You promised me a blow job tonight." Chris moved his hands lower, gripping Simon's ass with his large palms.

Now, *that* was a great promise. He could do that...twice, if Chris would let him. Hell, he would suck him all night if he wanted it, then hold him in his mouth after he'd gone soft, just so he would never have to let go.

*Well, that's new.* His inner slut must've been rearing its head. It always seemed to choose the most random moments.

"I can do that," said Simon, starting to sit up before Chris burst out laughing, rolling onto his back.

"I was kidding," Chris wheezed, wiping his eyes as Simon's mouth dropped open in horror. Horror at himself, not Chris. "Tonight is about you, and we are gonna snuggle the fuck out of each other then go to sleep. Tomorrow is going to be a crazy day. It's a full moon, too, so it'll be fucked before it even starts. All the loonies call nine-one-one on a full moon."

"And I'll start the job search tomorrow," said Simon, shuddering as he thought of all that that entailed. He hoped there was someplace out there that was desperate enough to take him on. At this point, he would be fine with picking up dry cleaning or running for coffee, which was something he did for Rubric anyway.

"You could come work with me," said Chris, snuggling close before going lax. "I've always wanted a service dog, although you seem like you'd be more like a Chihuahua than a Shepherd."

And *that* was exactly why he loved Chris. Even though he'd just had a gun shoved in his face, the man still managed to make him laugh.

# Chapter Thirteen

Simon looked up as the door slammed shut, rattling the picture frames on the living room wall. He glanced at his watch, setting his cell down on the couch beside him, the screen glowing with one of hundreds of help-wanted ads. There were a lot of companies looking for new workers, but their list of required qualifications made him regret not getting a second college degree.

It was only ten in the morning, and the summer sun was glaring in the east-facing window and heating the apartment up, despite the air conditioner humming away. Chris shouldn't have been back until at least four, though, and it could only be him slamming the door that hard. No one else had the muscle to do it.

He pushed off the couch before rounding the corner into the front hall, blinking in the sudden darkness. Something flung its way toward his feet, slamming into his toes with the force of a sledgehammer.

"Ah." He flung back, tripping over his own feet and slamming onto his ass as his toes throbbed. He glared at the culprit—a large cardboard box that was brimming with what looked like picture frames, papers and a few coffee mugs.

No wonder his toes felt like they might be broken. The coffee mugs were the thirty ouncers that he'd gotten Chris as a gag gift for Christmas, and they probably weighed almost a pound each when empty.

"Ah shit, Simon, I didn't see you there. Are you okay?" Chris knelt down, pushing the box to the side so he could grip Simon's throbbing foot.

"Oh, ouch. Ouch! I think my toes are broken," said Simon, trying to pull away. Chris held tight, peeling the sock from his foot and looking over his reddened toes. Simon flushed and looked away, trying not to wiggle his toes in discomfort.

What if his feet smelled? It was summer, after all, and he hated walking around in bare feet and collecting all the bits of stuff on the floor that the vacuum missed.

"I think you're okay, but I'm still sorry. I didn't see you there before I tossed the box, and it was getting heavy." Chris pulled his other foot close, stripping the sock off before lining them up, side by side. The crushed toes were noticeably red and swollen, but not by as much as Simon had expected.

"Why do you have a box with all your stuff?" Simon peered at the box again, spying one of the frames on top. It was a degree certificate, one that he knew Chris was proud of. It didn't belong inside of a cramped box, unless…

"You quit?" asked Simon, spluttering at the idea. Chris was a cop through and through. Even if he only did it part-time, he loved it.

"I got fired," said Chris as he shook his head, a small smile on his face. He looked like he could hardly believe it either.

He snorted, slowly setting Simon's foot back on the ground. "Did you know that they don't value part-timers much, especially if they put in for a transfer? I guess it's not worth their time trying to *accommodate* a slacker like me."

Simon tried to speak, but although his jaw moved up and down, no sound came out. Chris was the best man he knew, and he was worth more than a little accommodation.

"That's what I said," said Chris, motioning at Simon's gaping face. "And they didn't seem to like that, either. I guess I was supposed to take it like a man, with dignity and all that crap."

"But why did you ask for a transfer? Are you leaving?" Simon's heart plunged past the floor and into the sewers below the city. He couldn't do this without Chris. Well, he probably *could*, but he certainly didn't want to. And there was only one reason that Chris would want to leave. "I'm so sorry!" Simon shouted, before Chris could speak up. He threw his arms around Chris' neck, burying his face into his neck. "This is all my fault. If I wouldn't have thrown myself at you, then you wouldn't have felt obligated to have Leo over. Then he wouldn't have pulled a gun on you and made you worried about going into the field. *Oh God*, I'm fucking everything up."

"Yes and no," said Chris, hugging Simon close. "I couldn't be in that department if I have anything to do with Leo that isn't remotely professional. I thought the best thing to do was to clear the air and ask for a transfer. They thought the best thing was firing me. That's not your fault."

"But I brought Leo here." Simon bit his lip. He was not going to cry again. He had cried enough for seven men in the last few days, and he had had enough.

"And I decided that your happiness is worth more than them." Chris leaned back as he slid his hands along Simon's face, cupping his chin. "I think this has been a long time coming, buddy. I punched my ticket the day I went part-time. It was just the excuse they had to find. Their minds were already set that I couldn't be a cop if I didn't devote my life and sanity to it."

"Oh." Simon didn't know what to say. It still sounded like it was his fault, at least partially.

"On the plus side, did you already start looking for new jobs? We can look together." Chris dropped his hands, leaning down to pick up his box before he carried it off to the kitchen.

"Aren't you upset?" asked Simon, following him like a lost puppy. "I cried like crazy when I quit, but you...you don't seem to really care. Sorry." He felt himself flush. Of course, Chris cared. He just didn't wear his heart out in the open like Simon did.

Chris dropped the box on the slim counter in the galley kitchen, opening the cupboard with a hum. He shifted the resident mugs to the side, stacking a few on top of each other so he could fit his giant ones. They were almost too tall for the space.

"I care, trust me, but I don't get upset. I just get pissed off," said Chris as he slammed the cupboard door shut, the mugs tinkling inside from the force. His arm bulged as he curled his hand into a fist, thumping it once on the counter.

Simon tried to look away, but he was lost. He watched Chris flex his arm again, his bicep stretching the thin material of his uniform. He had more strength in one arm than Simon probably had in his entire body. His mind dropped to the gutter, and he licked his lips.

"What?" Chris asked, turning to face Simon before looking down at himself. "Do I have chocolate on me or something?" He stretched his shirt away from his body and the top button burst from its loop, a bit of his chest hair peeking through the space.

Simon wanted to see all of him and worship every square inch with his tongue. He wanted to comb through his soft chest hair, tugging on it as he rode Chris to climax, before feeling him come inside. He trembled, imagining Chris so deep that he could hardly breathe.

Chris shifted before tugging on his shirt. Another button pulled free, revealing tanned skin and soft, dark hair. The lines of one of his tattoos were like a beacon. He was one of the hairier men that Simon had ever thought about in his dreams, but he found himself more turned on by it than he had expected. He was so much better than fake muscles and someone so high maintenance that they waxed every bit of their body from top to bottom. Chris was all natural, and fuck, did he look delicious.

"I'm starting to get worried. Is it worse than chocolate? I swear, it's probably chocolate. I ate three bars on the way home," said Chris, tugging at his shirt harder and releasing another button. Simon couldn't tear his eyes away from the rise of Chris' pec — and the nipple, already hard as the air-conditioning caressed it.

"It's not…" Simon trailed off and licked his lips. He honestly had no idea what the hell Chris was talking about, but he hoped that whatever it was, he would keep stripping. He spied one lighter hair among the sea of darkness in the middle of his chest, and it made his cock twitch.

He wanted to defile Chris and show his cuddle bear that there was so much left out there to explore. Would he make love the same way he kissed, or would he suddenly become unleashed and ravage Simon like a wild beast?

He was so fucking hard, and he knew his sweatpants would do nothing to hide it from Chris' perceptive gaze. Luckily, Chris was still talking as he looked down at himself, pulling his shirt as he looked for an invisible stain. Every tug pulled his uniform a little closer to freedom. It was almost halfway undone now, with his navel so close to view that Simon's mouth started to water.

"Are you fucking with me?" Chris' words finally punched through Simon's haze, his breath stuttering as their gazes caught. Simon knew that he had to look like a mess, standing in the kitchen, chewing his lip with his face flushed and his cock hard. He couldn't help it. Chris' display of raw strength had him hooked.

"No?" Simon asked, flushing hotter as Chris finally noticed his situation, his eyes going wide.

"Are you *hard* right now?" Chris asked, incredulous. He crossed his arms, concealing the view of his built body and allowing Simon's brain to temporarily come back online.

"I can't help it," said Simon, biting his lip harder. Chris' arms looked even thicker when he crossed them, his biceps bulging and his forearms flexing.

"You've seen me naked before, but you've never done this," said Chris.

"This is different," said Simon, tearing his eyes away. "You weren't available before, so I couldn't look at you like this, but now..." He let the call of Chris' body drag him back. "You're so fucking hot."

"Fuck, Simon," said Chris as he reached out, closing the distance between them. He leaned down, and Simon surged up, crashing their lips together with every ounce of his repressed desire.

He vividly remembered the day that he had seen Chris naked. Kayla had been over, and Simon had spent an hour pretending that he hadn't heard them fucking in the next room, but he had finally given in, throwing his bedroom door open and heading to the kitchen. He had needed a cool glass of water to simmer himself down and to get the sounds of female pleasure out of his head.

He had stood there with his head against the cupboard and the cold glass in his hand, letting the hum of the fridge take him to another place. Then Chris had appeared, completely naked with sweat prickling all over his body. His cock had still been half-hard and glistening with cum and slick. It had twitched when Simon had looked at it. Chris had burst out laughing, apologizing as Simon fled the room with a flush on his cheeks.

He had refused to think about that before, but with Chris' hard body against his, he couldn't help himself. He pushed his tongue deep into Chris' mouth, and Chris responded by sucking on him like he was the perfect cock. Did the man even know what he did to him?

Chris slid his hands down Simon's body, cupping his ass then lifting him, as if he weighed nothing. Chris' chest tensed under his hands, going rock hard as they started moving. Their tongues continued to battle as

Chris bypassed the couch, heading straight for Simon's room.

"My room?" Simon breathed out when his back touched his firm mattress. "Your bed is bigger." It was also a better height for fucking, but Simon kept that to himself. He was more than ready to go all the way, but he didn't want to rush Chris into anything, especially with so much on his plate already.

"I don't have any stuff," said Chris as he climbed over Simon, covering his body with his own. "I figured that you would have what we need."

Oh God, they were doing this. Simon couldn't get any harder, not even when Chris skimmed his lips down his neck, sucking a bruise along his throat. He arched into the touch, fisting Chris' short hair as his beard scratched along his collar.

"I did some research with a crappy computer," said Chris as he pulled Simon's shirt over his head, leaving him bare, with his nipples peaked and ready. He dropped his mouth lower, cupping Simon's pec and sucking his nipple into his mouth. The suction was intense, but gentle, as Chris kneaded him. "That's different," said Chris before he moved back in, tonguing at Simon's nipple as he pinched his neglected one gently. "They're firmer than I expected." He flicked the bud and Simon gasped, pulling Chris closer.

"Fuck, harder," said Simon, tugging Chris when he didn't comply right away. He pictured Chris doing his *research* and wondered what he had found in the bowels of the Internet. One could never rely on the Internet being close reality. Not everyone could take a cock like a porn star, even if Simon wanted to try sometimes.

"I love it when I make you swear," said Chris, blowing over Simon's wet skin. Simon let out a second curse. How was Chris so calm? Simon's cock was twitching and leaking on the inside of his sweats, turning him into a slick mess. He could feel Chris' intimidating hardness through his uniform, but the man seemed to be able to maintain control easily. He was so fucking gentle, more than anyone had ever been with Simon.

"Chris, I want you to fuck me," said Simon, trying to pull Chris back up for a kiss. His hole clenched around nothing as he longed to be filled. It had been too long since someone other than his own fingers had been inside him. He needed it.

"Only if you can keep from coming," said Chris, before he leaned in for a chaste kiss. "I read that guys can get really sensitive after they come, and I don't want to hurt you."

*So. Fucking. Considerate.* Simon was not going to survive him. He'd had lovers that only wanted to take and others that were okay at giving, but in the end, they had always been after their own pleasure — especially men like Rubric.

He pushed that thought away as his stomach went cold. He was *not* thinking about Rubric right now.

Chris moved, sliding his warm hands down Simon's sides before dipping in each groove between his ribs. He moved so slow, like chilled molasses, each touch sending a streak of fire into his gut. He bit his lip, trying to calm down, but Chris was too good, turning him to jelly as he tickled across his groin. His hands were so big, like the rest of him, and Simon was almost dreading the size of his cock. *Almost.*

"Your skin is so soft," said Chris, making another pass over Simon's belly. Simon flushed, looking at the peek of tanned skin through Chris' uniform. Chris was so strong, the top of his six-pack visible through the half-buttoned shirt, but Simon was slimmer. He had muscles, but they were buried beneath the few millimeters of chubbiness that had plagued him for his entire life. Some said it made him look like a twink, and others called him fuckable, but he'd always imagined that he would have looked better with cut abs.

Chris flicked Simon's drawstring open, dipping his fingers into his track pants. "And here. You're coarser here than I thought you'd be, but you're still so fucking soft." Chris nuzzled against the same spot, taking a deep breath before letting it out to dance over Simon's prickling skin.

"How do you imagine I taste?" asked Simon, suddenly needing to know. Some guys loved the taste of cock, just like Simon did, but others refused to ever put a cock in their mouth. He twitched as he imagined Chris wrapped around him, his lips stretched wide as he tongued at the head.

"Like me, only sweeter," said Chris, edging the waistband down. "I've tasted myself before, and it was nothing special, but you? I imagine you taste like fucking sugar. Can I put my mouth on you the same way I've imagined doing? The way I've longed to do ever since I looked up how to do it online."

"Oh God," Simon chanted. "Do it. Fucking do it, Chris. Put your mouth on me and suck me deep. Tell me how I taste." He humped the air, but Chris pushed him back to the bed with a firm hand, holding his hips still as he pulled his pants off with one mighty tug.

Simon gasped as his cock touched the air without any barriers.

When Chris touched his cock with just a tentative press of his fingertips, Simon almost came. He flushed a violent purple as his toes curled, barely keeping back from the edge. He wasn't going to last. He just couldn't do it.

"You're cut," said Chris, with a small frown that disappeared before unease could sink in. "I've always felt bad for guys who are cut. Felt like they were missing out on the full experience." Chris palmed himself through his uniform, a dark stain against the front of the fabric.

Chris followed his exploring fingertips with his tongue, lapping at the head gently as the rest of his body stilled, keeping a single-minded focus that Simon rarely saw. Pre-cum welled up to replace the amount that Chris had just licked away.

"I'm gonna come," said Simon, gripping Chris by the hair and trying to pull him away. "Don't make me come. Please fuck me." His hips twitched, even as he begged Chris to stop.

"Just a taste. I need to see how sweet you are." Chris lowered him mouth down Simon's shaft, taking him farther than Simon thought possible. The man was obviously made for sucking cock if he was this good on his first try. Chris' teeth scraped on the underside, sending a bolt of pain to mingle with the pleasure.

"Shit! Shit, I'm gonna come. Fuck, Chris, please." He didn't know if he was begging Chris to go deeper or pull off, but Chris must've taken it as the former. He plunged down until Simon hit the back of his throat before gagging violently. He pulled off, coughing as Simon hung on by a thread.

"How do I make you fit in my mouth? I want you all the way inside," said Chris as he cleared his throat, looking up at Simon through hooded lashes. There was a tear at the corner of one eye and his pupils were blown black.

"Practice. Lots of practice," said Simon, gripping the base of his cock to hold himself back. "It took me years before I could deep throat without gagging." His mouth watered. Chris would probably still make him gag. His bulge looked huge through his uniform pants.

"Kayla didn't like giving head, but I think I do. You're heavy and sweet in my mouth—but salty, too. I just wish I could fit all of you." Chris glared at Simon's cock, as if being slightly above average was a fucking sin.

"I can show you," said Simon, reaching for Chris' cock. A big hand stopped him, pushing him back onto the bed.

"I think I can figure it out." He plunged back down, taking Simon as deep as he could without hitting the back of his throat. Spreading his big hands over Simon's hips, he pushed him down into the bed. He sucked harshly, his teeth scraping a second time.

Simon had hoped that the pause had pushed him far enough away from the edge that he would be able to stay in control. He was so wrong. The second Chris' lips hit him, he was unraveling like a bowstring that had been shot without an arrow. He called out, trying to warn Chris as his balls drew up, going tight as he started to shoot.

Chris grunted when the first shot splattered over his tongue but didn't pull back until the second one. Simon whined as the heat left him, his cock throbbing near painfully as he emptied himself over and over. He caught the gleam of his cum on Chris' lips and his orgasm stretched on, taking his breath as he painted the man's face and chest. Chris watched it all, his eyes wide and fascinated and so fucking dark that he was nearly predatory.

"Oh," said Chris as Simon went limp, his muscles going slack as he floated toward unconsciousness. "Oh fuck, Simon."

Simon watched through lowered lids as Chris tugged at his zipper, freeing his uncut cock. He was fucking massive. Leo was huge, but Chris had managed to surpass him in every way. His purple head peeked through the hood of foreskin, winking at Simon.

Chris jerked himself harshly, leaning over Simon's body and panting as he came seconds later, painting Simon white with his cum. He groaned with a low rumble in his chest as his cock continued to shoot, claiming Simon's exhausted body.

Chris collapsed to the side, pulling Simon close and kissing his sweaty neck. Simon grunted, hardly able to process anything after the erotic sight that had his cock trying to rise.

"Simon?" Chris asked, his breath still coming in harsh pants.

"Mm-m." Simon turned, shoving his face into Chris' neck and looping his naked leg over his hips. A shock went up his groin as their bare cocks aligned, both still slippery. Chris humped closer, leaning down to speak into his ear.

"I think I'm gay."

# Chapter Fourteen

"I can't *make* pizza. Are you kidding me?" said Simon as he stormed back to the living room where Chris was sitting on their couch. "The dough alone would take two hours, and we don't even have any cheese."

The tiny, molded nub of cheese stuck in the door did not count. There was a point that even he refused to just cut off the mold and eat the bit underneath.

They had both woken from their unplanned snooze, starving for something packed with calories. The sun streamed through the uncovered windows, making the apartment stifling *before* turning the stove on. It would be torture trying to cook with sweat pouring down his face.

"But I want pizza. And we can't afford to order in because we are both out of work. You've been off longer than I have, so you've had more time to look up recipes between interviews. Ergo, you make pizza."

Chris crossed his arms, looking Simon up and down. A few people might be frightened by the massive and miffed form that was Chris, but Simon knew better. He could see past the beard, thick muscles and the scowl to the teddy bear underneath.

The teddy bear who could suck cock like a champ.

"Don't get hangry with me. It's not my fault that you blew me into unconsciousness," said Simon as he stormed back into the kitchen. The cupboards were bare except for a can of soup and one can of olives. Could he make a meal out of olives? Probably, but it wouldn't exactly be edible. The fridge wasn't much better off, but at least they had milk.

"I'll just order the usual, Chris. We have to go shopping tomorrow anyway." They always shopped together on Tuesdays, so they could get the best deals before the new flyers hit stores on Wednesday.

*Why am I just realizing that I'm in love with Chris? We're like an old married couple.*

"Idea," said Chris, popping up on his elbows. "Call Leo. You said that he made you the best dinner ever, so *he* can make us pizza. I'm starving to death over here, Simon. All I've had to eat all day is a bagel and three chocolate bars."

"We can't take advantage of him just for food, Chris. I want a relationship with the man, and I can't start that by mooching." Simon shook his head, picking up the can of soup and peering at the label. It was peeling, so the seam of glue was barely holding on and it expired in three days. There was probably enough salt in it that it could last through the next ice age. "Ew, clam chowder. No wonder this is still in here." The only thing worse than the smell of fish was the taste.

He tossed it into the trash before staring at the remaining can of olives. They were starting to look better and better. He couldn't remember the last time that he'd eaten black olives. Maybe back in college? He would have been desperate enough.

"*Sure*, we can mooch. Call it payback for him pointing a gun at me. And it's kind of his fault I lost my job, too. In fact, I think he owes us dinner," Chris argued, grabbing Simon's phone from the couch and unlocking it without hesitation.

"How do you know my password?" asked Simon, smiling as Chris shook his head before muttering '*cop*'. "I have him saved under Leo Zoya."

"No shit," Chris grumbled before he clicked the contact, holding the phone to his ear. For such a kind man, he sure got pissy when he didn't get food within ten minutes of getting hungry.

Simon rolled his eyes, perching on the edge of the couch. The first time he'd encountered a hangry Chris, he'd almost gone looking for a new roommate, but after the tenth time, he'd learned not to take it personally. Low blood sugar was a real thing.

The line connected and Simon heard the soft rumble of Leo's voice from his spot on the couch. Warmth spread through his chest, even if he couldn't hear the words.

"I'm not…whatever you call Simon. I don't even want to know. It's Chris." He spoke abruptly into the phone and Simon flushed, smacking his hand to his forehead. "No, he's fine, but we're both starving, and as of today, we are both out of a job. Will you make us pizza?"

Simon didn't hear Leo's answer, but Chris' spreading smile was answer enough. He ended the call, his smile broadening as he looked at Simon. "We are headed to his place in five." He paused, a flush rising on his cheeks. "We should probably pack an overnight bag, too."

\* \* \* \*

The penthouse was just as grand the third time that Simon saw it, but he noticed a few new things this time as well. He'd been so awestruck and distracted the last two times that he'd completely missed the chandelier that hung over the island and the balcony that led off the living area to a surprisingly spacious outdoor space.

The place smelled heavenly when they arrived, with garlic and spices floating in the air. Unfortunately, much to Chris' grumbling chagrin, it did not smell like pizza.

Leo waved them inside after the concierge escorted them up, turning to head back to the kitchen before Simon could utter a proper hello. Simon's smile dropped away, and Chris stayed blessedly silent as he assessed the mobster.

His shoulders were tense and bulging beneath the crumpled layer of his dress shirt, and his back was stiff, like he'd just sat through three consecutive meetings. From the glimpse that Simon got of his face, he had looked drawn and exhausted.

Simon stepped into the kitchen and reached for Chris without looking. His hand met empty air, and when he looked back, Chris had already crossed the room to look out of the window, his brows nearly hitting his hairline at the beautiful view. There was even a sliver of lake that could be seen beyond the endless rows of city streets.

"Thank you for having us over, Leo," said Simon as he toed his way into the kitchen, making sure to keep well back to stay out of Leo's way. "I'm sorry about Chris' behavior. He can be very abrupt when he gets hungry, and I think he's really, really hungry."

He tried for a smile, but only got a nod from Leo as he stirred something in a pan that sizzled on the stove. His mouth watered as he looked down at the concoction.

"Can I help?" Simon stepped closer, reaching for the lid on the nearest pot that was simmering away. "Maybe I can give you another kitchen tip?"

Lifting the lid, he waited for the steam to clear until he spotted rice in the pot that was bubbling away on medium heat. He snapped the lid back down, lowering the heat to low before the rice could seize permanently to the bottom of the pot.

"You okay? Did I do something? Please let me know if I did...or Chris." Simon held his breath as Leo let out a sigh, shaking his head.

"Just work stuff. I can't talk about it." His gaze cut over to Chris who hadn't moved from the view. "I'm glad you're here, though...both of you. I was already making too much food to begin with to try to wind down, but at least now I have someone to share it with."

Simon moved slowly, wrapping his arms around Leo before leaning against his chest, so he put himself between the man and the stove. He felt the tension drain from Leo's body as he moved his hands down his back to his waist, pulling him closer.

"You can always talk to me if you need to, Leo. I know I may not agree with what you do for a living, but any leadership job can take a toll on someone mentally. Please let me know if you need any help. I have lots of time on my hands nowadays. Nobody is looking for a PA who doesn't have three university degrees and a master's in business." He tightened his grip, resting his head in the dip between Leo's collar and pec. The man's chest was rock hard and carved like marble beneath his shirt.

"You day sounds worse than mine, then," said Leo, moving his hand up to Simon's hair to play with the strands as the stove sizzled on.

Simon shook his head. "Chris' day was the worst. He got fired. That's so much worse than quitting." Getting fired was like the pinnacle to a terrible life, where you'd sunk everything into it, only to find out that your offshore accounts had been seized and you didn't have enough money to get out of the country.

Leo's head snapped up to Chris, his voice carrying across the open space. "What the fuck do you mean you got fired?" The tension was back, so Simon hugged him tighter, keeping him close as he listened to his heart.

"I asked for a transfer," said Chris, without looking away from the window. "They showed me the door. You have a nice view here, by the way. Very romantic."

Leo snorted, muttering in Russian under his breath. "You guys are unreal if you think I'm going to believe this...this fucking ruse. You can't get me. I won't fucking let you."

"I understand your hesitation, Leo," Simon whispered back in Russian, hoping his accent wasn't nearly as bad as he thought. "I really am falling for you. And as for Chris? Once he makes a promise, he'll never go back on it."

He looked up at Leo's face. The man had blanched, his ice-blue eyes like two beacons in the dark.

"What the fuck? You speak Russian?" Leo backed away, freeing himself from Simon's grip. The pan spattered behind Simon as something started to burn, the acrid scent sinking into his clothes.

"I know five languages," said Simon, nodding. Of course, no one was looking for *that* kind of quality in a PA right now. "French, Spanish, Russian, I'm passable in Mandarin and English, of course." He flushed as he counted them off. He didn't like to brag, but that was one part of his education that he was proud of.

"But I've spoken around you in Russian before. When we first met, then when you came here unexpectedly…" He trailed off, looking over to Chris, who was watching the interaction from his spot by the window. "Why didn't you report me? Or call the police?"

"Oh, well, I didn't know you were part of the mafia then, for one." Simon flushed bright. He was the only one in the world dense enough not to see that. "And your business isn't my business. If you need to threaten someone, then you do you, but Chris and I are off limits."

"The mafia doesn't make threats, Simon," said Chris from the window. "When they take care of someone, that means they kill them. End of story. No loose ends." He crossed his arms, turning to watch them with his back against the window. The sunset blazed behind him as another day washed out.

"Oh." Simon looked down at his hands. They were shaking and his skin had gone clammy. "When you were talking about taking care of someone when I came up here? Did you kill them?" He glanced up at Leo and the look in his eyes was enough. He was a killer through and through, and more dangerous than anyone that Simon had ever encountered. But the thought of losing him was too much to bear.

Leo stayed silent.

"You won't hurt me or Chris, right?" Simon asked, his voice trembling. He glanced down to Leo's waist where he had seen the glint of a gun in the past. There was nothing there right now, but Simon had missed it before.

"Are you going to call the cops?" He looked up to Chris again, his face going grim.

"Um, no," said Simon, his vision blurring. He probably *should* go to the cops. Hell, Chris should have been on the phone with them right now before he zip-tied Leo's hands behind his back.

"I can't trust you," said Leo, breaking Simon's heart just a little more.

Leo reached out, grasping Simon's hand and bringing it to his chest. His heart was pounding beneath his skin with steady even thuds. His hands were so warm as they cradled Simon's.

"I don't trust anyone," said Leo. "It's not just you or Chris or the police. I don't trust them because I can't. It doesn't matter what my feelings are. My business is a matter of life and death, and I won't risk myself or anyone else. This will be the last time we discuss this, but I will let you ask one question. Ask me one question and we can put this all behind us and move on."

"Are you going to kill Rubric?" asked Simon. As much as Rubric had hurt him and pushed him to do things that he wasn't exactly comfortable with, somehow he still cared for the man. He didn't deserve to die over money.

"I have no plans to do that...as long as he behaves himself," said Leo seriously, turning to Chris who had slowly made his way to the kitchen, before leaning his elbows on the marble island. "Chris, I can't wait to hear your question. I'll answer as honestly as I can."

"I don't have one," said Chris, his lips pressed into a thin line. He hunched his shoulders as he leaned on the surface of the marble, his muscles bulging with strength.

Leo snorted. "Now, *that* I don't believe for a second. You're a cop, and you can't think of a single burning question that you are dying to know?"

"They fired me, remember? I don't want to know because I won't be able to do anything about it. I can't bring back the ones you've killed or warn the ones you plan to. I'm not a snitch, and I'm not a coward. As far as I'm concerned, you work for a multinational import-export business that just happens to deal with drug source companies."

"You can't expect me to believe this bullshit," said Leo, his voice dropping to a snarl. "Are you wired? Is that it?" Smoke poured from the stove, but he ignored it, even as the air started to fill with a thick haze.

"You're the one who offered the question, *boy*," said Chris, pushing his way between Leo and Simon. He was taller than Leo by a few inches, and his bulk made him look like a bear getting ready to maul.

"You're manipulating me. You're using my feelings for Simon to try to expose me," Leo growled right back, his voice like a dull knife on tissue paper. He stood to his full height, reaching for his gun that wasn't there.

"You leave him out of this, *boy*," said Chris, his voice rising into a shout. "This is about you and me. If you don't trust me, that's fine, but don't try to drag me into your shit. I'm a good guy. I'm not the best, but I do what I can, and I pay my taxes on time. I can't make myself forget who you are and what you've done, but I might be able to find a man underneath all the shit—someone who's worth losing everything for."

Leo's eyes shimmered with emotion as he swallowed with a loud click. He looked like he was somewhere between denial and joy, but Simon was too terrified to speak up and ask. He wasn't terrified of Leo, or of Chris, but of losing them both if they suddenly realized that there was no way this was going to work.

"Dinner's burning," said Leo as he grabbed the smoking pan from the stove, dousing it into the sink and sending bits of burned food bouncing everywhere. He dropped the pan with a sigh, running his hands through his hair before he faced them again. "Pizza, you say?"

# Chapter Fifteen

It couldn't have been real pizza. The bread, tomato sauce and cheese were somehow melting in his mouth and pushing his tastebuds beyond anything he'd ever imagined. He didn't even know that pizza could be this good. And he *wanted* to eat the crust. There had to be some kind of witchcraft involved.

"This is good pizza," said Chris, echoing Simon's thoughts as he took a large slice before chomping on it with a groan. Simon hadn't been able to hold back his own moan at his first bite — or the second. Leo was the only one who remained silent, watching them more than the movie that was playing on the massive television screen. He took delicate bites, wiping his hands on a napkin in between each and licking the grease from his lips.

Simon and Chris were seated on Leo's living room couch facing the television that was displaying an action scene where a helicopter exploded into nothing. It wasn't a new movie, but it still managed to be one of Simon's favorites. Leo seemed to have every streaming service available, and Simon's mouth had watered at the sheer possibilities.

Simon shifted on the couch, carefully adjusting the puzzle of napkins all around him. The couch was stark white, but Leo had insisted that they eat there, instead of at the island. Simon had grabbed a dozen napkins, covering himself and every stretch of couch around him to try to keep the sauce from tainting the surface. It had worked so far, saving the arm rest from a pepperoni when it slid off his slice.

Simon moaned as he took another bite, licking the sauce from his lips and sucking a bit of grease from his fingertip. If pizza was sex, then this was some five-star action—like a double orgasm, a cream pie and a partridge in a pear tree kind of sex.

When he looked up, both Chris and Leo were staring at him, Leo's eyes dark and Chris' pizza frozen inches away from his open mouth. Leo shifted on his armchair, his napkin fluttering to the floor.

"Good?" Leo asked, clearing his throat and setting his slice back onto his plate.

"So good," said Simon, his voice on the edge of an orgasmic hum. Was he hard? It kind of felt like it, and, honestly, he wouldn't be surprised. This was the best pizza he'd ever had, and he ate pizza once per week.

Leo leaned back, patting his leg. "Can I try yours?"

"Of course," said Simon, jumping from the couch in a rush of falling napkins. They'd all ordered their own mini-pizzas at Leo's urging, so Simon had picked his favorite toppings without fear that his green olives would taint Chris' slice. "Can I try yours, too?"

He stopped in front of Leo, who was seated on his own single armchair that was next to the couch which Chris still occupied, along with a battlefield of napkins.

Simon held his slice awkwardly, cupping his hand just in case the sauce started to drip. It was still hot enough to burn, but he was not going to let himself stain Leo's penthouse. He should have brought his plate.

Leo patted his knee again and Simon flushed, slowly lowering himself to sit on Leo's leg. He glanced over at Chris, who hadn't moved, his pizza still paused in front of his mouth.

"Here." He turned the crust end of the pizza to Leo so he would be able to grab it. Leo shook his head, a smirk settling over his lips.

"I want you to feed me, baby."

*Oh fuck. Oh Christ.* Simon was definitely hard now, and his track pants were not going to conceal that. He had wanted to get changed into something more concealing before they came over, but Chris had been too hungry and had barged out of the door.

He lifted the slice to Leo's lips, feeding the tip in slowly before Leo grasped it in his teeth, tearing off a chunk. He chewed slowly, letting out a small groan that Simon could just barely hear, before his eyes fluttered closed and he swallowed.

"You're right. That *is* good." Leo leaned in, lifting the rest of the slice from Simon's hands and depositing it on his plate. His hands settled on Simon's hips, pulling him closer.

"Do I get to try yours?" Simon asked, his voice just above a whisper. Leo crooked his finger until Simon leaned in.

"Come get a taste, baby." Leo closed the distance, his lips searing as he grabbed Simon's hips and spun him until Simon wrapped his legs around his waist. Leo slid his hands down his ass, kneading his cheeks and pulling them apart until the seam of his track pants tickled his crack, teasing his most sensitive place.

Simon gripped Leo's hair, tugging as his mouth was devoured and plundered. Leo's kisses were so different from Chris' and the delicate way the ex-cop consumed him. Leo took every ounce of control, leaving nothing for Simon to do but hold on and allow himself to be taken.

"I've never seen someone kiss like that," said Chris from behind him, his voice breathy and hoarse. Simon tore his lips away to look at his roommate, whose eyes had gone dark with lust. The tent in his pants looked absolutely massive.

"What have you two done together?" asked Leo, tugging at Simon's ear lobe before sucking it into his mouth and soothing it with his tongue. "Did you stretch his tight hole out around your cock already? I've never had the chance myself."

Chris shook his head. "I didn't want to hurt him. I was hoping maybe you could show me how. He's the only man I've been with."

Simon groaned as they talked over him as if he weren't there—as if he was just an accessory to their pleasure. It made his toes curl and his spine tingle as he ached to be filled. All he wanted was to serve these two men and give them everything they desired.

Leo gripped his ass harder, standing from the couch with a grunt. He was strong, and although he looked to be nowhere near as strong as Chris, he could still lift Simon without too much effort. Simon clutched his neck, holding on as Leo led the way to the bedroom, before tossing him on the king-sized bed.

He landed in the silky sheets that were even softer than he remembered. He had dreamed of those sheets and the way they had felt all over his naked body. His cock wept at the memory.

"You good, baby?" asked Leo as he bent over him, tucking a stray bit of hair behind his ear. It was getting too long for him again, and he would need to cut it before he even thought of going for an interview. He couldn't stand the way it would tickle his ears when it started to grow out. "If you need us to stop, just say so." He leaned in for another kiss, taking Simon's breath away.

Leo moved away, grabbing an armchair from the corner of the room and pushing it next to the bed. He sat down with a flourish, motioning for Chris to step closer to Simon. Chris sent him a questioning look, hesitantly moving to where Simon was waiting for him with his cock aching and his mind whirling.

"Take your shirt off, Chris," said Leo, leaning back in the chair with an air of nonchalance.

Simon's breath stuttered. Was he really going to watch…and *direct* them? He watched as Leo raised one of his brows, clearing his throat when Chris didn't immediately start moving.

Chris gripped the bottom of his T-shirt, looking between Simon and Leo one last time before he pulled it over his head. His chest was rising and falling rapidly, his abs and pecs straining with each breath. His tanned skin looked almost golden in the warm light of the bedroom, and the hair all over his body only accentuated the cut lines.

"Fuck, that's good," said Leo, gripping himself through his dress pants. Simon agreed, nodding numbly as Chris smiled shyly, his confidence forgotten as he was seemingly flooded with nervousness.

"Your pants next. Let's see that pretty cock of yours." Leo licked his lips, leaning forward as Simon did the same. Simon had only had a glimpse of Chris' cock, but he was ready to see it on display in all its hard glory.

When the track pants slid down Chris' hips, Simon couldn't stifle his moan. He was so fucking big that the sane part of Simon was wondering if he was going to break tonight. He wouldn't be able to take Chris as hard and fast as he wanted, that was for sure, but he had a feeling Chris would want to slide into him real slow and do his best to treat him right.

"Fuck," said Leo, his stoic façade fading. "You're fucking huge. Where have you been hiding that package all my life?" He let out a groan, looking back at Simon, who was trembling from suppressed need. "We're going to have to take this real slow, baby. No ramming it all in there, just because you want to."

"I wouldn't," Chris stammered, a blush forming on his cheeks.

"Not you," said Leo. "The last time I was in this bedroom with Simon, he begged me to take him without any prep at all. He wanted me to tear him apart and fuck him hard. Not today. We're going to make him wait until he's begging for your cock to fill him nice and slow."

Simon let out a groan, dropping his hand to his clothed cock and pinching the head. Leo's gaze zipped to him, his eyes narrowing until Simon removed his hand, dropping it back to the bed.

"Undress him," said Leo, leaning back in his chair.

Chris' hands were steady as they pulled Simon's shirt over his head, then dropped to his waist band. He played with the band, looking up to meet Simon's gaze with a silent question.

Simon nodded, his stomach fluttering with need and pride. Chris was so new at this, but so fucking good at it already. He had the potential to melt hearts and burn panties simultaneously.

His pants slid past his hips, and he lay back against the bed at Chris' gentle urging. Chris gripped his ankle, slipping his pants over his ankles and dropping them to the ground. He moved his hands up Simon's inner thighs, making his cock twitch and leak against his belly. He hadn't worn anything underneath.

"Such a gentleman," said Leo with an approving nod. The mobster slid his tongue over his lips, making them glisten as he stared at them with a single-minded focus. "Put him on the bed with his head near that side and kiss him."

Simon felt the flush paint his skin as Chris' lips descended on his, following the directions to perfection. Instead of shuffling him backward to the edge, he simply hefted Simon up, cradling him against his body until he could lay him out against the cool sheets in the new spot. His heavier body settled on Simon, sending his mind into overdrive.

Simon wanted to curse and come at the same time. It was perfection wrapped up in heaven's bow with Chris' gentle lips on him, plundering him deep with the cool sheets slithering against him. Chris cradled his hips and scraped up and down his sides with each undulation. The hair on his chest tickled Simon's nipples, bringing them to needy peaks as he whined low in his throat.

Leo's eyes burned into him at the same time, controlling them both, even though it felt like he was a world away. He emitted power with the way he spoke, as if Simon couldn't even hear him, and as if he knew that Chris would follow his direction without questioning. He was not a man who was used to being disobeyed, and Simon had no intention of doing so. Chris was obviously on board, with his huge cock throbbing between them and leaving a cooling trail wherever it lingered.

"Spread his legs."

Leo's voice boomed above them like a soulless angel encouraging their depravity. Simon spread his legs eagerly, inviting Chris to grind against him and push him into the mattress with his weight. Chris thrust gently, their cocks meeting with perfect pressure, just like their lips.

"Wider. Let me see his hole."

Chris pushed his knees wide and back to his chest until the stretch was almost too much to bear. Chris shifted on top of him, pulling himself up so that Leo could see past him to where Simon's entrance lay. Simon could feel the weight of their stares on him, his hole twitching in desire and humiliation.

"He looks so tight, doesn't he?" said Leo, leaning forward to get a better look as Chris pushed Simon's legs even wider, displaying him like a wanton slut. "He wants you to fuck him just like this, splitting him wide and tearing him open to carve a spot just for you inside him...but you won't. You're going to make him beg."

It was like Leo could read his mind, right down to his dirtiest secret and most depraved thought. He groaned as Chris hummed, his eyes blown and his cock weeping steadily.

"Here," said Leo, holding out a bottle of lube that he had pulled from God knew where. "Slick your fingers up on your right hand. Simon, hold your legs wide. I want to watch him finger you open."

Simon grabbed the back of his knees, keeping himself bent in half while Chris popped the bottle open and coated his fingers. His heart pounded and he tried to slow his breaths, but it was no use. He was so firmly trapped between these two men, and he never wanted to escape.

"Slide your finger over his hole. Get him wet."

Chris' finger still shocked him when it slid over his crack a moment later. The lube was cold, and there was enough of it that it dripped down to the bedsheets below.

"Did you want me to grab a towel?" Simon whispered, afraid that if he spoke too loudly he would destroy the mood. "I don't want to ruin your sheets." They were slippery and soft, probably silk or something else exotic. Definitely more expensive than his flannels.

"Baby." Leo shook his head. "I don't think you get it. We are going to destroy you tonight. The last thing you should be worrying about is the sheets."

Simon's cock flexed and he took a deep breath. He tightened his grip where he was slipping, pulling his knees to his chest again.

"Put more slick on him. I want him dripping," Leo continued as if Simon had never interrupted him — as if no one could change his carefully constructed plans.

Chilly lube slid over his balls and back farther until he was sure that the sheets were a mess. He groaned when Chris cupped his sac, massaging him with the slick oil until he thought he might burst.

"Please," he said, unable to even rock his hips with how contorted he was. Chris moved behind his balls, slipping over his seam, but never getting close enough to his hole. His gut clenched as his sac grew heavier, his cock leaking steadily.

"Please." He couldn't take it. This was fucking torture. There were two men here and neither of them were inside him or touching his cock. He ached so much that it had passed the point of pleasure and had dipped into sizzling pain.

"Give him a finger, Chris. Slide it in real slow and feel how tight he is. Can you feel him gripping you and begging you to go deeper?"

"Yes." Chris nodded as he pushed in all the way to the last knuckle. Simon gasped as he was split wide. Chris' finger was so thick that it was almost too much. The stretch was perfect and the familiar feeling of fullness that he loved and had missed so much made it all worth it.

"Do you think he likes it?" asked Leo, his voice going even deeper.

Chris groaned, flexing his finger inside and forcing another gasp through Simon's lips. "I don't know, boy. He isn't begging anymore. Maybe I should stop."

"Don't you fucking dare," Simon cried. They were both so cruel, ganging up on him like this and pushing all his buttons except the one inside. "Deeper, Chris. Fucking make me come."

Simon's eyes flew open as a warm hand wrapped around his neck. He looked into Leo's ice-cold eyes that had gone suddenly hard. Leo flexed the hand on his neck, lighting up the sensitive nerves and massaging them into submission.

Leo's hair was hardly out of place, and his tie hung down into Simon's face as he gripped just hard enough to make a threat but not cut off Simon's air. It still made his head swim and his chest heave.

"That didn't sound like begging to me," said Leo, stroking his hand up and down Simon's neck before gripping him again. "You must really not want anything inside you. Does it hurt, baby? Do you need Chris to stop?"

He smirked when Simon nearly lost his breath as desire flooded him, pushing him so close to the edge that a single touch could send him over.

"Please, Leo. I'm sorry. Please, I want you inside of me. Both of you. Make me come." Simon babbled, loosing track of what he was saying when a second and third finger sank inside of him. Leo hadn't moved back to the chair and was hovering over him instead, directing Chris and tweaking Simon's nipples.

"I'm going to come," said Simon, his toes curling when someone's hand brushed against his cock. Someone else gripped him, bringing him off with a few quick jerks. He clamped down on Chris' fingers as Leo leaned down for a kiss, stealing his breath. The hand on his cock kept going, pushing him through his orgasm and beyond. In response, his cock refused to shrink, smacking against his belly when it was released, still fully hard as he shuddered.

"Beautiful." Chris' voice cut through his haze as his fingers withdrew all at once. Something huge and blunt lined up instead, easing inside so slowly that it made Simon keen. His body throbbed, and his cock was still so hard.

"Fuck him slowly, Chris. Make him beg."

Chris' cock kept going, splitting Simon wide as it went on and on, never seeming to end. His rim ached from the stretch, and he swore he could feel Chris all the way in his gut, but the man still hadn't stopped moving yet. By the time his hips settled against Simon's ass, he could scarcely breathe.

"Fuck," Simon screamed as he tipped closer to his breaking point. It was so fucking good, and Leo's hand on his neck and Chris' kisses along his chin made it bearable. "Move! Please, fuck me hard."

His hips jerked on their own as Chris started rocking, his cock glancing against his spot with each movement. He clamped down on every inch of Chris inside him, feeling it so deep.

Usually, he hated the feeling of getting fucked after he'd already come. His control would slip through his fingers, leaving him open and aching. But, for some reason, it was exactly what he wanted with Chris and Leo.

"You feel him asking for your cum? Every time you hit his spot, he's begging for it hard. Give it to him." Leo pinched Simon's nipples one last time, biting his chest and pulling back as Chris started to slam deep. Simon could only moan and keen, scrambling for purchase at the edge of the bed but finding none.

Someone grabbed his hair, pulling his head back toward the edge. His mouth opened automatically and something slid between his lips. Musk landed over his tongue, salty and sweet and only making him harder. He had nearly forgotten how good Leo tasted, but he couldn't avoid it now, as the man slid his cock all the way to the back of his throat.

Leo paused, as if he were allowing Simon to adjust, but Simon wasn't having it. If he could suck a cock every day of the week, he would. That's how much he loved it. Leo was big and thick, and it would be a challenge, but that was where Simon thrived.

He gripped Leo's hips, still clothed with only his cock peeking through his lowered zipper. Material bunched under his hand as he tugged, pulling Leo until his cock was all the way down his throat, with Simon's nose against the hem of Leo's pants that still clung to his hips. Chris thrust at the same moment, pushing Leo that much deeper into Simon's throat.

All three men let out a groan as Leo gripped Simon's neck, fucking in and out of his throat with a rapid pace as Chris slammed deep. Simon tried to keep from gagging, although he almost lost composure a few times. Leo gave him that extra second, letting him get a breath before he was back, stretching Simon's lips and throat wide.

Chris' pace stuttered, his cock jerking as he slammed inside one last time as he started to shoot. Simon swore he could feel Chris' cum painting his hole and marking him. It was enough to make him clamp down, coming again without a single touch to his cock. His groan sent vibrations along Leo's cock, making the man gasp and pull back.

Leo jerked himself quickly, shooting across Simon's face as he hit his limit. Simon's eyelids fluttered shut after the first drop made its way into his eye, stinging his nerve endings and making tears flow.

Simon was still breathing hard when Leo retreated, heading to the en suite and returning with two warm cloths. "Clean him first. The second one is for you." He tossed both cloths to Chris, who caught them easily, swiping at Simon's face first, before he moved down to his chest. He still hadn't pulled out, and Simon could swear he felt wetness seeping around Chris' softening cock.

"Did you come inside me?" Simon asked softly, not sure if he was okay with it or not. He loved the idea of being claimed by Chris like that, but he also wanted to be safe, especially if he was with more than one man and they hadn't had the exclusive talk yet.

"No." Chris chuckled and shook his head. "I may have gone a little overboard with the lube. I squirted a bunch inside you before I put the condom on, and now it's everywhere."

He pulled out slowly, leaving Simon empty and longing to be filled again. After what they'd done, it probably wouldn't be too extreme to ask for a plug, but he didn't want to keep just lube inside him

"One day, when you both come inside me, I want you to plug me up to keep it there…to keep me full." Simon reached down between his legs, running his fingers through the slickness.

"Fuck," Chris cursed, pausing as he swiped over Simon's sack. A hand on Simon's chin tilted him back and Leo's mouth smashed against his own, claiming him more than the cum on his face.

"Fucking beautiful…both of you."

# Chapter Sixteen

Simon sprawled on Leo's couch, watching Leo work in the kitchen yet again. The man seemed to have a passion for cooking, among other things. Whatever he did, he seemed to do well. *Cooking, murdering, fucking.*

He was so accomplished. Simon was nothing to him. *Christ,* he couldn't even get a job.

It's not like he hadn't had interviews. He'd managed to find a few good fits in the stack of wanted ads smeared all over the Internet. The interviews had gone well, at least from his perspective. One had even gone as far as to ask him if he had been okay to start right away and had said that they would call him the next day with more details.

No one had called. And when he'd made a call to the office to inquire after the position, he'd been transferred endlessly to voicemails that were probably never listened to. After two inquiries and two voicemails, he had given up.

It wouldn't have been as dire if their rent hadn't gone up for the third time that year. In January it had increased its usual five percent, but then the owner had tacked on an extra five when they'd claimed that some repairs had to be completed. Nothing had been repaired to date, but that hadn't stopped them from raising it by another ten percent shortly after Simon had lost his job.

He let out a sigh, rolling onto his back to stare at the ceiling. Maybe he was just unemployable. He hadn't listed Rubric as a reference, just to be safe. Troy had been more than happy to offer a reference…and Simon trusted that he would keep the bits about him fucking his boss out of it if he was aware of what had happened.

"When will Chris get here?" asked Leo from the kitchen as he stirred something that smelled of citrus, raspberry and chocolate. He had insisted on making something special in celebration of Chris' first day at *his* new job. It had taken him four interviews before he'd found a place that he liked enough to consider working for. That it happened to be a strip club made Simon blush.

"I think he works until seven," said Simon, reaching for a newspaper that had been thrown over the coffee table. Maybe there would be something in there that would suit his skills.

Everyone that mentioned languages seemed to need a written translator, but no one wanted a verbal one. He could speak Russian fine, but there was no way he could tackle their alphabet.

"I could also call the club and ask them to let him off early," said Leo with a smirk. It was only after Chris accepted the job that he had told them where it was. Leo had snorted with laughter, shaking his head. Leo *owned* the club.

"Nah, he doesn't like favors—not that kind, anyway," said Simon, flipping past three depressing news stories and straight to the classifieds. There was a sudoku puzzle that was definitely worth pursuing in the near future.

There was a position for a truck driver and a librarian, both which required things that he definitely didn't have. Or maybe he could work outside of the city as a chicken catcher.

That sounded terrifying. He'd never actually seen a chicken in real life before, other than on his plate or as a headless and featherless version in the grocery store.

"Any more leads in there?" asked Leo.

Simon had already told the mobster several times that he didn't want any favors for himself, either, even if it was getting tempting as hell. He tried to keep his mouth shut as hopelessness crushed him.

"If they would just return my calls, then I would already have a job," said Simon quietly. He cringed when Leo paused in the kitchen, his sharp gaze cutting sideways.

"What does that mean?" The metal spoon scraped over the bottom of the pot as Leo twisted it too hard, a bit of reddish chocolate dripping over and onto the stove with a hissing sizzle.

"Nothing. It's nothing. I'm just a little frustrated, that's all." He set the newspaper neatly back on the coffee table, pulling himself up so that he was sitting. He glanced down at the soles of his feet. They looked clean, but he didn't think they would ever be clean enough to put them up on a white couch.

"You'll find something, baby," said Leo.

Simon smiled at the nickname. What had started in the bedroom was now his name all the time, and he loved it. A warm fuzziness settled into his belly. He knew Leo would take care of him, but being called 'baby' just hammered that home.

He wandered to the kitchen, taking a deep breath. The air was thick here, with so much chocolate smell that he was almost drooling. Leo smelled even better as he plastered himself to the man's back. Leo was too tall for him to be able to peek over his shoulder, so he looked around his arm at the mouth-watering mixture swirling around the pot.

"What is it?" he asked, moving around Leo and dipping his finger into the pot. "Ow, that's hot!" He shook his finger, blowing on it until the chocolate went from molten lava to pleasantly warm.

"It's on the stove." Leo chuckled. "And it's pudding." He stirred it again, the mixture coating the spoon perfectly.

"Yum." Simon sucked his finger clean, searching for any lingering taste with his tongue. His finger was stained with reddish chocolate as well as a hint of a burn. "Corn starch or egg yolks?"

"I love that we speak the same language," said Leo, his gaze going to Simon's mouth as he slurped loudly, searching for more chocolate on his finger. "Chris can't cook to save his life. He doesn't even know what *cordon bleu* is."

"Nope," said Simon, looping his arms around Leo's chest. "But he could probably catch the chicken for it. He has his skills and cooking is not one of them, but that's what he has us for."

The smile on Leo's lips was one that Simon hadn't seen before. He looked so relaxed, so content, as if life would never catch up with them or drag them down. It made Simon's stomach flop and his limbs go fuzzy.

"Can you stir this for me, baby? I have to mail a package," said Leo, handing the spoon over and stepping away. "You can't stop stirring or the eggs will cook— "

"And the starch will curdle. I know." Simon waved him away. He expected Leo to walk toward the door, but instead he went farther into the penthouse. "I thought you were mailing a package?" asked Simon, shouting so his voice carried across the space.

"I have to take a shit," Leo yelled right back, cackling as he disappeared.

Simon shook his head, snorting. *God*, he could be so clueless sometimes. He bit his lip, stirring the pudding as he stared at the grain on the marble countertop. He only hoped that he wasn't kidding himself about their relationship. Everything was working so perfectly, and he dreaded the moment it all fell to pieces. He would never be able to pick himself up again.

# Chapter Seventeen

He'd only been stirring for thirty seconds when his ring tone cut through his musings. He jumped, the spoon slipping from his fingers and sliding to the bottom of the pot. The ring was *loud* — so much louder than he remembered setting it — and he didn't remember leaving his phone on the counter either.

He accepted the call, flicking it on speaker as he grabbed two new spoons to try and lift the lost one out of the pot. The pudding was thick, and the missing spoon grated along the bottom as he searched for it.

"Hello?" He tried to force his voice into a professional mode as he grabbed a fourth spoon when he dropped another. Maybe tongs would work better?

"I need to speak to you urgently. I'm downstairs." The male voice was unfamiliar and speaking in perfect Russian.

Simon gulped, looking back at the phone as a smear of chocolate found its way up the handle and onto his fingertips. It bloomed red where it touched his skin.

"I'm so sorry, but I think I answered the wrong phone," he replied in English, his mind too jumbled to even attempt Russian. When he looked at it again, he noticed that Leo's phone was a tad bigger than his, and a bit cleaner too, with the shiny edge of something new. He'd had no idea that they shared a ringtone.

"Who is this? How did you get this phone?" the man asked in rapid and accented English that Simon only understood because he had dealt with so many overseas contracts.

"It's Simon," he said, wondering if he should add his last name, but the man was already moving on.

"How did you get this phone? Where is Zoya? You will tell me *now*."

Simon's hands trembled and more pudding smeared over his palms. He wiped them on his shirt, spreading a red stain that made him gulp.

"He's not available," he said, barely keeping the tremble out of his voice. The line went silent for a moment before there was a scraping sound as if someone had dragged their hand over the speaker. The signal crackled with static.

"You will put him on the phone *now*." The man's voice was practically dripping with rage and contempt. "I know who you are, Simon, and I know your family. Your sister has two children now and she's having trouble making ends meet. You would know that, too, if you talked to her more than once a month."

A blind panicked rage consumed Simon, unlike anything he'd ever known. He had managed to keep a cool head when multimillion-dollar deals went bust and when ancient businessmen tried to grab his ass. But no one was allowed to talk about his family like that.

There was a noise behind him, but he ignored it. Hopefully it was Leo coming back to the kitchen right now so Simon could apologize for answering the wrong phone. Apologize, then hang up on this man.

"I... You can't speak to me like that." Simon wanted to curse, but he knew it wouldn't do any good. He wouldn't give this guy the satisfaction of his anger.

Simon went stiff when he felt something behind him. It was only a brush of air against the back of his neck, but it made every hair on his body stand on end. Leo would have announced himself by now or asked what Simon was doing.

He tried to turn, but he was too late. Brutal hands grabbed him, pulling him back against a hard chest. He was enveloped by the strong scent of expensive cologne, so similar to Leo's but with an edge of stale cigarettes. A hand closed over his mouth as something cold and sharp pressed to his neck, scraping a line of heat where it carved too deep. It took him a moment to realize that it was a knife.

"Scream and I'll cut your throat," the man breathed against his ear, sending a shiver down his body. It was the same man from the phone, the one who had claimed he was downstairs but now had Simon in a chokehold with a knife to his neck.

The man's body was like steel, his arms immovable, even as Simon struggled. The knife dug in deeper, and something dripped down Simon's neck to the collar of his shirt. His knees went weak.

"Where is Zoya?" the man growled at him, lifting his hand from Simon's mouth. Simon took a deep breath, gasping as his body quivered and terror sank into his belly.

"I'm not telling," said Simon, his voice weak. He tried to come across as strong, but he sounded more like a toddler to his ears. The cold marble stung his bare feet, such a contrast to the temperature of the man behind him.

The man chuckled, an unearthly sound with no humor at all. "You have no choice. You tell me or you die." His accent was thick, the anger in his voice making him even harder to understand. The knife dragged across Simon's throat, a threat that sliced into the outermost layer of his skin, but no farther. Any pressure on the knife and the man could kill him.

Simon felt himself flush then go cold, his body fluctuating between temperatures so quickly that his mind could hardly keep up. His palms were suddenly slippery, and he clenched his hands into fists. Was Leo worth dying for? It only took him a moment to come up with the answer.

"I don't care. I'm not telling you where he is." He couldn't let this man hurt Leo, no matter what tortures he threatened. He prayed that Leo would somehow hear the commotion and stay in the bathroom where he would be safe.

"Suit yourself. He will reward me generously." The tip of the knife dug into Simon's neck and a fresh drop of blood welled up. The man flexed his arms, holding Simon secure and gripping the knife hard.

This was it. The end.

"What are you doing?" a familiar Russian voice asked, sending a rush of warmth back into Simon's body. He had never been so happy to hear Leo sound so angry.

The knife paused, twisting against his flesh as they both looked up. Leo was standing at the end of the kitchen, his hair wild and haloed by the lights, and his pants barely clinging to his hips. His silver gun was in his hand, the barrel pointed straight at the intruder's forehead. He was Simon's own personal avenging angel.

"Taking care of your loose ends, brother," the man replied in Russian, the knife dipping into Simon's neck. Simon's knees wobbled as a gush of warmth dripped down into his shirt.

"He is not to be touched," Leo replied in Russian. "He is mine and under my protection." His grip never faltered on the gun, even as his trousers slipped on his hips, the fly and button both undone and his briefs crooked underneath.

"You've been blinded." The intruder shook his head. "This one here has betrayed you. While you let him suck your cock here, he is out there letting another fuck him—a cop. And they've gathered enough support to put out a hit on you. They want you dead, brother. But I can kill him for you, so your conscience will be clear. Unless you want the honors?"

Leo gripped the gun, his knuckles going white as his gaze flicked from Simon to the intruder. His jaw tensed, and his eyes darkened, and Simon knew in his heart that he was going to pull the trigger. He just didn't know who the gun would be aimed at.

"S-stop," said Simon, clutching at the intruder's hand that held the knife. His grip turned slippery as he accidentally touched the blade. "Don't shoot him, Leo." It was suddenly so clear. "He's only trying to help you."

"Listen to him," said the intruder, grabbing Simon's hands and forcing them down.

"I will blow your fucking brains out, Mikeal. Drop the knife." Leo's voice never wavered and neither did the gun. He was a cold, steady killer, ready to destroy his brother. Simon's stomach churned.

"I'm gonna puke." Simon could already feel his stomach starting to protest as his diaphragm contracted. Mikeal released him a moment later and he dropped to his knees, spewing all over the marble floor. Ugh, he was never eating pastrami again.

When Simon looked up from the floor, with his stomach still contracting and his sides aching, he thought he might puke again.

Leo hadn't put the gun down. Instead, he'd moved close enough to press the barrel directly to Mikeal's forehead. They were almost the same height, and although Mikeal was much broader, he seemed to melt under Leo's gaze. The knife clattered to the floor.

"Explain. Quickly." Leo tapped the barrel against his brother's skull when he didn't start speaking right away.

"You threaten your brother?" Mikeal took a step back, his face going pale. "You choose this loose slut over family?"

Leo swung his arm back, slamming the gun into the side of his brother's head and sending him to his knees. Simon gasped in horror when Leo put the gun back to his brother's forehead, his lips pressed into a thin line and his eyes burning with rage.

"Don't ever question me," he said, continuing in Russian which Simon scrambled to follow through his muggy thoughts. "Your life is mine, and if you would like me to keep it, then explain quickly."

"There's a hit out on you, boss," said Mikeal, switching back to thickened English and holding his hands up by his head in a placating gesture. "Someone wants you dead."

Simon's stomach plummeted and his sides heaved. He scrambled to do something — anything — to protect Leo, but he was frozen on the ground, with the remains of his lunch soaking into his knees.

"Hazard of the job," said Leo, a cruel smirk etching across his features. He should have looked terrifying, and to Mikeal he must've, because he looked like he wanted to piss himself. But Simon couldn't see past *his* Leo to the mobster and killer. Even with a gun in his hand, Simon still trusted him.

"Who put out the hit?" asked Leo, slowly lowering his gun and letting it rest at his side. He cocked one hip, the picture of relaxation.

"We don't know," said Mikeal, his gaze cutting to Simon before flipping back to the gun. "We have a source saying that it was him and his lover." The knife lay between them, the blade shiny and red. Simon's stomach churned.

"*I* am his lover," said Leo, setting his gun on the island. He ran a hand through his dark hair as his icy eyes blazed.

"You've been deceived." Mikeal shook his head, glaring at Simon with a snarl. "This one. Our source was certain that he is fucking the cop."

"I know. He is my lover as well. The three of us are together." He looked at Simon for the first time, his façade falling away. "There is only one other person who knows that, though."

Mikeal surged to his feet, nearly slipping in the mess. "I don't understand." His gaze dropped back to Simon, his face contorting as if he was looking at a piece of shit stuck to the bottom of his shoe. "You with another man is something I have come to terms with. We all need our toys. But two men? This cannot be right. And a cop? Where is your head, little brother?"

"Next to my heart." From the way Leo's lips snapped shut, Simon knew that he hadn't meant to say it.

Mikeal's face twisted further, his arms bulging as he clenched his fists. He wasn't quite as bulky as Chris, but he could probably give him a run for his money.

"There is no heart in this...in men. You know this. Father would never forgive you for this—"

"Then it's a good thing I blew his brains out." Leo shook his head. He reached for the gun, his hand tapping on the handle. "You will be silent on the matter or you will join him. Now get the fuck out."

# Chapter Eighteen

The elevator closed behind Mikeal and Leo turned back to Simon. The gun was gone — put somewhere that Simon couldn't see. He was still on his knees, the smell of his sickness permeating his nose and making him even more nauseated. He could hear himself breathing, harsh and deep, but it never seemed to quite fill him, each gasp leaving him breathless.

A minute ago, there had been a knife to his throat and a gun had been inches from his head. He had been trapped in the room with two killers while he was between them, small and helpless.

Mikeal's presence had left a gaping hole of uncertainty in its wake. The cold ebony cupboards sucked the light from the room, and the marble drained the heat from his body. He was lucky that he had only ended up with a few scratches. The pudding had dried to a near-crimson color, reminding him of what else he could have lost.

"I'm sorry you had to see that." Leo strode back to him, calm and collected as if he hadn't just held a gun to someone's head and threatened to blow their brains out all over his white marble.

He was every inch the mob boss that Simon had first met in Rubric's office. The moment that Mikeal had rushed out of the door, fleeing with a confused scowl, Leo had grabbed his gun, ripping the clip from the base and freeing a bullet from the chamber. The bullet had dropped to the floor, rolling to the edge of Simon's vision before it had been plucked from the ground.

Leo's movements were exact and precise, like they'd been performed a hundred times in the most exhausting of moments. Leo's face remained hard, his gaze almost unrecognizable.

"He was only trying to help you," said Simon, his eyes downcast. At some point he was going to have to stand up and relieve his aching knees, but the room was spinning. He would need to clean the floor until it was spotless, then himself. It would take a lot of water before he felt clean again.

Leo paused, as if he'd only now noticed that Simon was on the ground, his knees soaking and stained with the smell of acidic bile in the air. His face softened, the angry furrow in his forehead smoothing until he looked a bit more like the man Simon knew.

"Come here," said Leo, holding out his hand. He crouched down when Simon shook his head, his chest tight. "Simon, I won't hurt you." His voice dropped to a whisper.

Of course Leo wouldn't hurt him. He'd had more than one chance to put a bullet through his head, but something had stopped him every time.

"I know you won't hurt *me*, but you'll kill for me?" He tried to hold back his tears, but he wasn't sure if he was succeeding. His adrenaline was draining quickly, leaving an empty shivering shell behind.

He was starting to wonder if the shaking was only going to keep getting worse. He heard the quiet shifting and hum of the elevator as it went to another floor, delivering an unrelated executive. He'd never noticed the sound before, but now it was like he was hypersensitized to it. He hadn't even heard the elevator or the dinging door when Mikeal had slipped into the penthouse — not until there was already a knife to his neck.

"I would. And from what I heard, you'd die for me, too." A small smile flickered over Leo's face before it disappeared again.

If killing meant nothing to Leo, then what did it matter?

It still mattered to Simon. He could never imagine pulling the trigger and watching someone's life drain from their body, but if he could prevent someone from getting hurt, he would every time.

Simon nodded. Even now, even after...that, he would still do the same thing. If the cops stormed Leo's penthouse in that moment, he would have lied and told them that he'd never seen a thing. He would stand in front of Leo so that the officer's bullet would hit his own chest and not Leo's.

"Then I'll kill to keep you safe," said Leo, his voice brutal and thick. His eyes were glowing with more than just rage. There was excitement there, too.

*He says it like it's the easiest thing in the world — like killing means nothing to him.*

"He's your brother, and I'm...just me." He looked at his hands and the red stain of pudding across his palm. There was more on his shirt, and something brighter —

something that looked much more real. His head swam.

"Stop. Don't put yourself down. You do this all the time. You think you are so useless, so stupid, but you forget that you are one of the smartest men I know." Leo finally reached out, his warm palm resting on Simon's shoulder. The touch burned.

Simon shuddered at the contact. "I can't see people for what they are—not until it's too late."

"You see the best in them. You see the best in me and in Chris. I've never been as happy as I am now, and I've never been willing to kill for anyone but myself." Leo slid his hand down to Simon's, cupping his palm and turning it up to the light. There was a thin line of blood from when he had grabbed at the knife. It was no bigger than a papercut and had stopped bleeding, but it was still wet and tacky.

"I think I love you," said Simon, letting Leo pull him close and wrap his arms around him. He took a deep breath of Leo's smell, letting it wash over him.

He didn't expect Leo to say it back. It was too soon, after all. Simon knew he fell hard and fast, spiraling out of control when his past partners hadn't even considered going steady yet. It had shattered him before.

"I care about you more than anyone I've ever known. Is that love? I've never felt it before, so I wouldn't know," said Leo as he pulled him closer, apparently not caring if he stained his shirt.

"I don't know." Simon couldn't imagine an existence like that. Love was what made him whole. Even if it was only a bit, it kept him going. "Do you feel that way about Chris?"

"Hmm-m, Chris and I have a few things to work out. He can be a bit much sometimes...a bit dominant. It will take us a while to get along." His arms tightened around Simon, pushing more of his dark thoughts away.

"Would you kill for *him*?" asked Simon, leaning away from Leo's chest so he could look into his placid blue eyes. He was harder to read that anyone Simon had ever met. He was always guarded, always hiding—because he had to.

"I don't know." Leo looked off toward the elevator door, his eyes unfocused. "I didn't know that I would kill for you until I saw Mikeal with a knife to your throat. I couldn't let him take you from me. I would have done anything to stop him, even if that meant ending his life."

*That's a lot to unpack.*

"Do you trust us? You told me that you've never trusted anyone." Simon had to pry a little deeper. He had to see under the impenetrable shell that was wrapped around Leo. He needed a glimpse of who he really was, even if it broke him in the end.

"I don't think you put a hit out on me, if that's what you mean. You don't have the heart for it." Leo let out a soft sigh, looking down at the mess on Simon's clothes.

"That's not what I asked," said Simon, going stiff as Leo tried to pull him back in. He didn't want a hug right now. He wanted answers. He needed to know before he let his heart break. He needed to know if he had to get out.

"I don't trust anyone. Nothing in the world will change that." Leo's eyes went hard, his lips thinning as he scowled.

"Then you don't love me," said Simon. "Until you trust me, you can't love me."

It didn't hurt. Okay, maybe it stung a little, but his chest loosened and he let himself fall back into Leo's embrace. He couldn't force someone to have feelings that didn't exist, but he could demand honesty. If Leo was going to lie, he would have already.

"Are you upset?" Leo had dropped his hands, as if he didn't quite know what to do with them. Simon knew the feeling.

"No." He was surprised that it was the truth. "I can't force you to feel something that you don't, but I can tempt you." He looked down at himself, then the floor. "But maybe when I'm clean."

"Then let me clean you, baby."

# Chapter Nineteen

Simon let Leo carry him to the shower, even if it did make him feel a little less manly. He wasn't *that* tiny. It just so happened that his boyfriends were freaking built.

"I want to call you my boyfriend. I hope that's okay," said Simon, leaning into Leo's chest as he was lowered to the shower bench. The room was much larger than it had any right to be and had two sinks, a claw-foot tub and a massive shower.

The bench in the shower was the definite highlight, though. Benches were perfect for putting your leg up on to scrub the hard-to-reach bits, but they were the best for fucking.

Leo disappeared as Simon started the shower. He waited for steam to start to rise before he stepped under the stream, gasping as a line of fire carved across his throat. Every little nick that the knife had left behind ached, even if they were tiny.

Leo was at his side in a moment, throwing the curtain back to look at his hands, then his throat. Water poured over him as he inspected Simon, soaking into his dress shirt that was probably dry clean only. Simon gasped as Leo touched his fingers to his throat.

"It shouldn't scar all the way across. Maybe just here," he said, pressing gently on the ragged edge where the blade had twisted. "He was close. Too close. I should still kill him, just for marking you." His eyes blazed with fury and Simon melted beneath the stare.

"Don't," he begged. "He's your brother."

"I'm adopted." Leo snorted, as if it were his own inside joke.

It would explain why the two men looked nothing alike and Leo's affinity for languages. Some adopted children had to learn a second language, just to fit in with their new families.

"Still counts," said Simon, brushing Leo's dripping hair back from his face. "Join me instead. Make it better." He didn't usually give orders during sex, but he needed Leo. He needed to remember the good in him before he got lost in a spiral of doubt.

"Let me finish cleaning up, then I'll join you." Leo pecked him on the forehead and retreated through the curtain. Simon flushed, hanging his head as he thought of Leo cleaning up his mess. That sounded a lot like love to him.

He let the water rain down, waiting to grab the soap until the sting had faded into a tolerable throb. He gargled until the taste of bile had long since disappeared, leaving only the memory of its grossness.

The water did more than wash away the blood and the sticky pudding from his hands. It centered his thoughts and pushed the last of his fear away. Someday, when he sprouted a spine, he would be able to fight back for himself. *Someday.*

"What are you thinking about?"

Simon jumped when Leo's voice came from right behind him. A moment later, his naked chest pressed against Simon's slick back. Leo's soft cock nestled between his cheeks, already showing signs of life when Simon pushed back against the touch.

"Seducing you," said Simon, flushing when Leo ground against him.

"Accomplished. What's next?" Leo chuckled as he grabbed the soap and leaned away to wash himself. Simon stepped to the side, letting Leo rinse when he was ready, before he moved close again.

"I was thinking that you haven't been inside me yet, and I want to feel how deep your cock will go," said Simon. He bit his lip, surprised at his own bravery. Usually, his desires stayed buried deep—unless he was hard. Then all his self-control went out of the fucking window.

Leo shot up his brows before a smirk carved across his face. "I should be a little worried that you aren't more upset, but you are too sexy for me to care. Let me rinse, and I'll meet you in the bedroom."

Simon shook his head, his gaze dropping to his toes as his face flushed hotter. Suds swirled around his feet, circling the drain before plunging down. His bravery fell away, lost with the last of the soap.

He *was* upset. He was fucking terrified—but not of Leo. He'd never felt safer than when he was with Leo and Chris. They wouldn't let some guy gut him or slice his throat. *He hoped.*

"What did you want, baby?" Leo asked, following Simon's gaze. "You don't want me to fuck you in the bedroom?"

Simon shook his head again, convinced that if he waited another moment, Leo would never fuck him properly. He needed him to erase the feeling of foreign hands on him and to take his hurt away. He bit his lip, sucking it into his mouth. Leo's hand on his chin forced him to meet his icy gaze.

"You want me to fuck you in here?" Leo's eyes sparkled as Simon's cock twitched, giving him away in one motion. "I could push you against the wall and you could wrap your legs around my waist so I could pound you hard and fast."

Simon shook his head again, his gaze snapping to the bench. Leo followed, his smirk going downright predatory.

"Get on the bench on your knees," said Leo, his voice deadly serious. A shiver ran down Simon's spine as he scrambled to comply. The bench was harder than he'd expected, digging into his kneecaps and into the bruises that had already started to form. Cool water had pooled on the surface, making him shudder.

Leo moved in behind him, pressing his hand between his shoulder blades until Simon was bent over with his hands coming up to brace on the shower wall. He widened his stance, trying to relieve the pressure on his knees. They still ached from dropping to the marble floor, and they would probably hurt for a while.

Leo slid his hands over Simon's ass, gripping his cheeks and pulling them wide until Simon could feel Leo's breath on his rim. He clenched tight, his hands sliding on the slippery wall.

"You look so good like this for me, baby — so open, but so fucking tight. How did you ever take Chris in this little hole?" Leo scraped his nail over Simon's entrance, pulling a gasp from his lips. "So fucking sensitive for me, baby. Are you going to beg me for it? You begged Chris so well."

Simon shook as he lowered his head. His cock was jutting between his legs, nearly touching his belly as Leo continued to speak. No one had ever spoken to him like Leo did.

"You have to say it, baby." Leo teased his entrance, never sinking inside. "I need to hear how much you want me to split you open."

"Please." A finger sank into him. The drag was harsh, slicked only by the water, and it made him ache immediately. Leo was so big, and he knew he would need something to ease the way so he didn't tear. Body wash was out of the question, not unless he wanted to tingle and burn for the next two days.

"Lube." Simon cried out as the finger withdrew, leaving him empty.

Leo chuckled, moving closer until his cock slid between Simon's slicked cheeks. A dribble of fear trickled into Simon's core. Leo wasn't going to? Was he? He was right there, his cock prodding Simon's entrance and about to push inside. His breath quickened and he leaned back into the touch.

Simon should have urged him away or said no. But he wanted it. He wanted Leo to slam his way inside and split him wide, pulling him back onto his cock until he could barely breathe. He wanted to experience the real Leo—the rough one who had no mercy.

"You really think I'm going to fuck you in the shower, baby?" Leo rolled his hips, his cock straining against Simon's hole. "You want me to make you mine and make you ache, so you can't sit for a week without thinking of me? I could ruin you." He ground harder, his cock almost breaching the tight ring.

"Do you trust me now?" His voice was a growl and his grip turned brutal, one hand digging into Simon's neck and searing along his wound.

"Yes," said Simon, tilting his head back and sinking into the touch. He was so fucking hard, and the pressure on his throat just made it better. If it would have been anyone else, he would have struggled to get away, but with Leo...it was perfect.

Leo's heat disappeared along with the pressure from his ruthless cock. The water suddenly stopped, and Simon was plunged into a misty world where the only sounds were his ragged breaths and the slap of Leo's feet on the slick ground.

"Turn around," Leo growled, his voice carved with rage.

Simon shook, his knees the consistency of tapioca as he lifted his head and looked back over his shoulder. Leo was on him in an instant.

He was lifted as if he weighed nothing, slipping against Leo's chest as he was carried from the shower and out of the bathroom into the frigid air-conditioning of the bedroom. Leo tossed him on the bed like a pair of discarded pajamas and he bounced once before he landed on his front on the softest mattress in the world.

He scrambled to get to his hands and knees, but Leo descended on him, pushing his chest down into the mattress until his ass swung in the air, completely open and ripe for the taking. Simon shuddered, his cock dripping and twitching every time Leo applied more force.

Leo's blunt cock pushed against his entrance a moment later, only this time it was wet and dripping with lube. Tension drained from his body as Leo slid between his cheeks, creating a slick channel for himself.

Simon was so ready to be taken, and he had no desire to fight. He wanted Leo more than anything.

"You're mine, Simon," said Leo as he pressed down on his shoulders, forcing him into the mattress. "I won't break what's mine, not even if you ask nicely. You deserve so much better." He grunted, rolling his hips.

Simon's body resisted, his hole clenching tight, despite the fact that he welcomed the intrusion. His body simply didn't understand what his mind wanted. He was so tight — too tight — with only the memory of Chris inside him.

Leo persisted until the head of his cock pushed through the delicate ring, and he sank into Simon's body. He pierced him deep, sliding all the way in, despite the way Simon's body protested and clamped down automatically. It hurt so fucking much, but he wanted more.

"This ass is *mine*." Leo slid all the way out and slammed back in, leaving no time for the burn to fade or for Simon to adjust. "This body is *mine*." He pulled Simon's hips back to meet him as he snapped forward. His cock slammed against Simon's prostate and a scream caught in his throat.

"Every time you think less of yourself or put yourself in harm's way, you are putting my property at risk. I won't fucking tolerate it. You're *mine*." His voice dropped into a low growl as he fucked into Simon hard and fast.

Simon cried out, his voice strangled between an apology and a scream. It was so fucking good, and Leo was so big. His strength was mind-blowing, and his control was unlike anything Simon had experienced. He clamped down, wanting to feel every inch, and the mobster grunted, reaching up to tweak his nipple.

"Tell me what you want," said Leo between thrusts, his breath coming in harsh pants.

"Harder." Simon clawed at the sheets, tears dripping from his eyes as Leo possessed him, sending him to a place that he had never been. He was fucking soaring and aching perfectly from both pleasure and pain. Nothing else mattered but Leo's cock and the way it throbbed inside him, pushing him closer to the edge. His own cock was forgotten, even as his prostate was assaulted.

"No." Leo stilled his hips, grinding slow and soft until he was as deep as he could go. Simon keened at the stretch, wondering if he would be able to feel Leo if he touched his belly.

"I'll take you how I want, baby." He slipped out, gripping Simon's hips and turning him over. When he slid back inside, their lips lined up and he pulled Simon into a kiss. Their tongues twined as he slowly ground into Simon's body, the pain easing away to nothing.

This was different. Simon could feel Leo's racing heart where their chests were touching and taste the sweetness of his mouth. All he could smell was Leo — the saltiness of his sweat and the musk of his cologne.

Leo plunged his tongue deeper into his mouth, his thrusts slowing until they were nothing more than a gentle rock. He grazed against Simon's prostate, until the pleasure hummed under his skin. The pain was gone, and Simon could only feel and hope that he could hang on for an eternity.

"Don't ever do that again," Leo mumbled against his lips. "You will *not* die for me."

They moved together like the tide, one falling as the other one rose, their mouths and their bodies as one. Simon's peak snuck up on him as a gentle wave that made him thrum with something new. Leo followed, with a groaning breath the only sign of his orgasm before his hips stilled.

Simon took it all, wishing there were no barrier between them. He wanted Leo's cum to drip out of him and stain the sheets. He wanted Chris to lick it from his hole, pulling his cheeks wide, even as Simon burned with shame.

He whined when Leo pulled out, reaching between his own cheeks to feel his hole. It was tender and swollen, despite the lube, and his finger slid readily inside. He was slick with excess lube, but he could imagine that it was something else if he closed his eyes.

"I want…" Simon slipped a second finger inside. He couldn't be empty right now, not after they had made love. And that was exactly what it had been. He knew in his heart, even if Leo didn't yet.

"I've got you, baby," Leo whispered, kissing Simon's cheek gently before holding something cold and hard to his entrance. Simon slid his fingers out, gasping when they were replaced with something much bigger and more satisfying. It wasn't much of a stretch, but he could feel it inside, especially if he clamped down. He could imagine all the lube that was being held inside him, wishing it were something more.

"Soon, baby." Leo ran a hand down his back, seeming to know exactly what Simon needed. "I think Chris will be on board if we all want to be exclusive. We'll get tested, then we can both fill up that greedy hole. We'll make sure it never goes hungry."

Simon's cock stiffened again, his body milking the plug. The results couldn't come soon enough.

# Chapter Twenty

Simon was back on the couch by the time Chris arrived at the penthouse. He absently scratched at the gauze around his neck, looking up at the soft ding as the elevator doors opened. His heart pounded at the sound, his phone falling from his hand. Who thought an elevator could be so terrifying?

He'd have to ask Leo about installing an intercom or something if he was planning on spending more time at the penthouse. His heart couldn't take any more surprise visitors.

Chris' bulky shoulders wrapped in a long-sleeved Henley were the first thing he saw. His beautiful face was etched with both exhaustion and satisfaction, and he looked more relaxed than Simon could every remember seeing him. Their eyes found each other and concern marred Chris' perfect face.

Leo moved seamlessly from the kitchen, grasping Chris' shoulder and leaning close to speak in his ear. The two men couldn't have looked more different. Leo was dark everywhere that Chris was light, and the mobster was all lean muscle where Chris showed his strength visibly.

The furrow on Chris' face deepened and his gaze locked with Simon's. He nodded once at what Leo said before he pushed past him, making his way to the couch. He knelt down, sliding his hands over Simon's face and cupping his chin before examining the gauze that Leo had wrapped around the wound on his neck.

"It doesn't hurt," said Simon, ducking his head as Chris gripped his hands, turning his palms up before running his finger along the healing lines down the center. The cuts really weren't deep and were more annoying than anything. They only hurt when Simon opened and closed his hands, and they were clean. Leo was certain that there would be no scars on his palms.

"Are you okay?" asked Chris as he placed a kiss in the center of Simon's palm. The warmth of his touch spread, making his fear fizzle away to nothing.

Simon nodded. He didn't trust himself to speak right now. He'd thought he was all right, but now that Chris was in front of him, his face etched with concern, he wasn't so sure.

"I'm sorry," said Simon, not really sure what he was apologizing for.

"You should have called me, Simon," he said, pulling him into a tight hug. He smelled like aftershave, but with a hint of alcohol and cigarette smoke that he only used to have when he'd had an encounter with a drunk.

"I didn't want to ruin your first day."

"You wouldn't have. I would rather know if you need me, so I can be there for you." He ran his fingers through Simon's hair. "Leo told me what you did for him and how brave you were." He pulled back, forcing

Simon to meet his gaze. "I need you to tell me if you want to leave. We will both be here for you either way, but I don't want you to be afraid. I can take you home if you want. Leo understands if you don't want to see him anymore." His eyes were so warm, so pure.

"What? No, I want to stay. Please, Chris, it wasn't his fault." Simon shook his head. He gripped Chris' Henley, then smoothed his hands over the material, feeling the muscles bunch under his touch.

"It will probably happen again, though not the same thing. Leo is going to address his security concerns, but he is a dangerous man living a dangerous life. He can't guarantee your safety." The honesty was so plain that it broke Simon's heart.

*We will never be safe, but I love them.*

"I know," said Simon, pulling Chris close. "I accept the risk. I'd do the same for you, you know. You're both worth it." He had to bite his lip to keep his tears back. He didn't want to cry right now. "Besides, Leo said that he knows who has put the hit out on him."

"Who?" asked Chris, stiffening under Simon's grasp. Simon shrugged. Leo had very expertly avoided that question and answer.

"The only person who knows about our mutual relationship." Leo spoke up from across the room. "He's also the same person who has blacklisted one of my boyfriends." Leo's gaze snapped to Simon. "No one will return your calls, and you can hardly get an interview. There's only one person who can benefit from that."

"Rubric?" Chris asked, his eyes going wide. "I know you don't get along with him, Leo, but I don't think he's the bad guy here." He sat down next to Simon, pulling him close. Simon could barely breathe through his shock.

What did Rubric have to do with any of this? Simon had been the one to leave, not Rubric. If Rubric hated him, he would have fired him.

"Simon, this isn't going to be pleasant, but I need you to be honest with us," said Leo as he moved closer to the couch. His voice was quiet, and nothing like the mobster that Simon had seen earlier.

"I think Rubric's been using you for longer than just a few weeks, and for more than sex. Did he ever force you?" Leo knelt down beside Chris.

Simon's heart thudded in his chest as he shook his head. The thought of that made him sick. Rubric wasn't a rapist, and he wasn't a bad guy just because he had a lot of money. Their relationship hadn't been ideal, but Simon had never said no.

"Good," said Leo, smiling gently. "You are doing so good, baby." He swept a tear away from Simon's cheek before it could fall. "How many hours were you working? I know you said that he wouldn't let you do any overtime."

"Oh." Simon lowered his gaze to Leo's chest. He could see a peek of pale skin and a tuft of hair through his dress shirt that had the top two buttons undone. Even after fucking, Leo had still got dressed back up.

"Maybe ten hours per day. I got there around eight and left at six sharp." There were a few days that he had gone in early when work had piled up, but his paycheck had never changed.

"Hmm-m." Leo kissed his forehead. "That's overtime, baby."

"No. It's different for assistants," said Simon. He remembered when Rubric had explained it to him on his first day. Personal assistants were in a different category, a lot like bartenders. Their wages were different by law, and so were their working hours. It was expected that they would have longer hours and longer days.

"It's okay," said Leo, cupping his chin. "None of this is your fault. How much did you make per year, after taxes?"

"That's private and confidential." He echoed Rubric's words in his memories. "I don't even care about the money, anyway. I just want a job where I could use my skills. I have a degree, but it's nothing fancy. I'm just good at languages." There were so many people in the world who were multilingual. He was nothing special.

"You managed all his legal clients. That's hundreds of millions of dollars," said Leo, an edge seeping into his voice. Simon cringed, refusing to read between the lines. *I didn't even know about his illegal accounts.* The tiny lines at the corners of Leo's eyes creased, giving him the appearance of a man who was five years older.

"Yeah, but—"

"Tell me, Simon," said Leo, his voice almost a yell. Chris gave him a sharp look, but Leo shook his head, refusing to back down.

Silence hung in the air as Simon swallowed. His wage had nothing to do with the size of his dick, and it didn't even matter. His stomach exploded with butterflies as insecurities from the past five years suddenly emerged.

*I'm just a glorified coffee runner, and that's why I know what every client prefers to drink.*

*I'm closing contracts that are way above my paygrade, but that must be covered under the 'other duties as required' clause.*

*Mr. Mayvel just landed enough in commission in one day to buy a yacht, but I'm the one who closed the deal...or maybe I didn't? I'm just a PA. I don't want to bother him and ask for a raise. He's just too busy.*

"Maybe thirty thousand a year?" He tried to picture his last round of income tax paperwork that had also been managed by Rubric. He'd offered to do his taxes as a perk, and even had a financial planner who helped Simon out.

Rubric had managed everything from the moment Simon was hired. He'd helped him find his apartment and recommended a bank that would take care of his finances. He'd gotten Simon a deal on his phone and Internet for his new place, and set up all of his bills for auto-deposits. Every penny that he made went through Rubric somehow.

Rubric was a billionaire, so why was it a bad thing to take his advice? Simon chewed his lip. He'd never thought to second-guess it.

Not even when Rubric had offered a spare room at his place when Simon had mentioned the yearly increase on his rent. Simon had declined, stumbling on Chris a week later.

Not when things hadn't seemed to add up each month. He had blamed it on ordering too much take-out. He'd always thought he would do better the next month.

He might have dealt with millions of dollars in a day, but it left him too drained to look after his own account. It would take care of itself. Right?

Chris had gone deathly silent, his grip going near-painful on Simon's wrist.

"Did you have any benefits like dental...or a pension?" Leo's voice went soft, despite the way his eyes had gone cold. Simon gulped, looking from Chris' stony gaze and back to Leo's terrifying one. His stomach dropped and he flushed, wondering if he was lower than the piece of gum that refused to come off the bottom of his shoe.

"I know it's not a lot and I don't have much to bring to the table in this relationship, but I really am trying to get another job. Worse comes to worst, I can always pick up a job at a coffee shop for a while. I could probably even get you a discount on fancy coffee." He tried for a smile, but both men were unmoved.

Chris swore, pulling away from him and standing from the couch. He gripped his hands into fists, his arms going taut with every muscle on clear display through his Henley.

"Leo," Chris started, then shook his head and ran his fingers through his beard. "You know what? Do whatever you need to do." He gnashed his teeth, marching to the kitchen and throwing open the fridge.

"I'm sorry." Simon crumpled. "I didn't think you guys would care about the money." Especially Chris. Chris never cared about any of that shit.

He could slip out now and wander back to the apartment. Everyone had their priorities, but money wasn't one of his. As long as he had a bed to lay his head down on, the rest would work itself out. Why couldn't they see it the same way as him? Why did it have to matter?

"Hey, baby, what's going on in your head?" Leo cradled his cheeks, wiping away the fresh tears that blurred Simon's vision.

"I-I'm not enough. I'm just not good enough." A sob burst from his throat and his chest ached. He hadn't been good enough for the entirety of his life, but he'd finally thought that it was getting better.

The warm ache from his ass was suddenly too painful, and he was uncomfortably full. "I have to go." He pushed Leo away, tripping on a pillow that attempted to send him back down onto the couch.

"Simon, stop!" Leo called out, grabbing his wrist when he continued marching to the door.

They'd finally realized that Simon was nothing more than an idiot. Couldn't they let him lick his wounds in peace?

Chris was in front of him, his arms circling around him in a hug that Simon could hardly endure. It was so warm, so soft and comfortable and perfect. He wished it would never end.

"Simon," Chris whispered into his ear, shushing his sobs, "how much do you think I make, honey? Come on. It's okay. Don't run away."

"I don't know. It doesn't matter." Simon pushed his face into Chris' chest, shuddering when Leo pressed against his back. They wrapped him in a warm impenetrable blanket. He was safe.

"I make more than that, and I work five hours a day and I'm off on weekends," said Chris, kissing the top of his head. "Rubric was taking advantage of you. You should have been making at least double that."

"More than that," said Leo, his voice still soft but his grip tight. "Rubric's a fucking billionaire, and Simon has spent the last five years practically running his legal business."

"He needed my help," said Simon, his voice muffled by Chris' shirt.

"He's your boss, not your friend. If he was your friend, the help would go both ways." Chris cut off

Simon's thoughts. "Don't cry for him. You've got us now, and we aren't letting you go. You're so special to us, Simon, and you don't even realize how much."

"I'll take care of it," said Leo, his voice suddenly hard. Simon didn't want to think about what that meant, but he had to.

"Don't hurt him. Please." Simon turned, looping his arms around Leo's neck.

"I might not have a choice, baby." Leo's lips quirked. "He's got a hit on me, too, remember? But don't worry about that now. Chris and I are going to take care of you. Go show Chris his present, and I'll clean up."

With a final kiss, Leo retreated to the kitchen. He probably had to scrape yet another round of his pudding off the bottom of the pan. It seemed to be fate that he would continually be distracted while trying to make the dish. Simon couldn't help but feel a bit bad. It *was* a waste of food.

"I love surprises," said Chris, his deep voice pulling a grin to Simon's lips. For such a big man, it was the little things that he seemed to live for.

Simon nodded, flushing as he thought of what the surprise was. He took a deep breath, pressing his palms over his eyes until he was sure that his tears weren't coming back. He was done crying over Rubric and any other asshole who wanted to ruin his day.

"It was Leo's idea." As if that made it any less embarrassing. "But it's something I've thought of before."

He grabbed Chris' hand, leading him to the bedroom with his heart thrumming for a different reason. The last few weeks had been an emotional roller coaster, and he couldn't remember the last time he'd cried so much. Hopefully it was out of his system for a while.

"How do you feel about getting tested?" asked Simon, his flush going fiercer. "I mean, I want to make love with nothing between us—not even a condom."

"What about Leo between us?" Chris asked with a chuckle. Simon peered back over his shoulder to Leo's form in the kitchen. He was dumping another round of pudding into the trash, but he looked at ease again. Simon would have to remember to show him how to use a metal sieve to try to salvage the pudding next time.

"I don't think Leo bottoms," said Simon. He could imagine it, with Leo's face pressed into the pillow, biting his lip as Chris slid inside. That was a pretty fucking picture. His cock went rock hard, tenting the track pants he had thrown on.

"I would bottom for him," said Chris with a shrug. Simon's eyes bulged as he looked Chris up and down.

"But you're so…" *Big. Handsome. A beautiful bear. Dominant yet sweet.*

"I'd try anything once. I'd bottom for you, too, Simon." He tapped his finger against Simon's nose as Simon's mouth flopped open.

"I—I. I don't…wow." A smile brimmed on his face. He had absolutely no desire to top Chris, but the gesture meant more than anything. "Come on. I have to show you your surprise."

He pushed Chris down onto the edge of the bed with his feet flat on the floor. The sheets were messy from their earlier activities and there was a dried stain near the middle of the bed. Chris looked at it, a smirk rising onto his lips.

Simon dug his toes into the soft rug, rocking back and forth, and generally stalling until Chris let out an impatient huff. The cuts on his hands stung as he pulled at the drawstring of his track pants, but he shrugged it off.

"You stripping for me?" A smile spread over Chris' face. "It's a nice change from all of the naked women all day. I mean, I like pussy, but not that much. And some of those bitches were just nasty."

Simon pulled at his shirt. Even if he were desperate, he would never go to a strip club. Unless…

"Do they have a lady's night?" Most of the guys would be straight, but there was always one in the bunch who didn't mind giving a lap dance to a guy.

"Nope. We'll have to speak to the owner about that." He snorted, grasping Simon's hands as he struggled with the drawstring. "It was a good shift, though, and rewarding. I love being able to throw a drunk punk out on his ass and not worry that the captain's gonna lose his shit because it's his nephew. Let me help you."

He tugged the pants over Simon's hips, letting them fall to the ground. His hands bracketed Simon's waist, so much bigger and darker against his pale flesh.

"You look so good under my hands." Chris squeezed once. "I've wanted to touch you for so long, but I was afraid to give in. I would catch myself looking at you and wanting to hold you for no reason at all."

Simon dipped down, pressing his lips to Chris'. He could taste a hint of his mint gum and a bit of chocolate that he must've snacked on during his break. He delved deeper, groaning as Chris took gentle control, before guiding Simon to straddle his waist. He was so sweet, but so consuming, like nothing Simon had ever encountered. He could never get tired of this.

"What's my surprise?" Chris asked against Simon's lips, manhandling him as he shifted back on the bed. His cock swelled under Simon's ass, a reminder of his aching hole and how full he still was.

Simon flushed, ducking his head. He couldn't say it.

"I'll find out. I'll kiss and lick every inch of you until you tell me all of your dirty little secrets." Chris' confidence shone in his voice, and he was so much more relaxed this time, as if he just needed to know what he was doing for him to be comfortable.

Chris flipped them, and Simon let out a sigh as his back struck the mattress. He peeled Simon's shirt from his body and promptly attacked. Chris' desire was so much gentler than Leo's lust had been, but no less insistent.

Chris worked his way down, skipping Simon's bandaged neck, and only lingering to suck on each of Simon's nipples, flicking the buds with his tongue while pressing his teeth against the rigid flesh. When he found a hickey that Leo had left, he chuckled low before sucking Simon's skin into his mouth, making the spot so much darker.

Simon whimpered and cried out, lost between the ache of Chris' mouth and teeth, and the throbbing of his groin. His belly tingled with the start of his orgasm, still far off, but rushing straight into his balls.

"I love your cock," Chris whispered as he lowered himself to the head of Simon's cock before licking the bead of pre-cum from the tip. Simon's hips jerked violently as the scrape of teeth followed, the sensation almost too much. "It's such a lovely thing. Nice and thick, and the perfect size to fit in my mouth." He sucked Simon deep before popping off the head once more to tongue at the slit. "I like how you're cut — so open and neat. And your taste, fuck. I could lick it up all day." He groaned, sucking Simon hard, as if he could simply suck the cum from his balls.

"Ah, oh God." Simon's hips stuttered with an unsteady rhythm. But Chris wasn't done. He reached down to play with his sac, rolling his balls in his hand before scraping his nail softly down the seam.

"I'm not sure what to do with these, to be honest." Chris rolled them again and Simon gasped. "Do I suck them, lick them or just play with them? I usually don't pay mine much attention. My cock was always more sensitive, anyway."

"Yes. Yes." Simon arched as Chris tugged on his balls.

"You are so sensitive for me, Simon. So fucking perfect. I love it here, too." His hand dropped down, his eyebrows rising as he found Simon's surprise. "Oh, honey, I fucking love it."

Simon had gotten a look at the plug's base in the mirror after Leo had slid it inside of him. It had a green jewel that shimmered every time the light hit it. It looked so slim, never revealing how wide it stretched him inside. He wanted to wear it all the time, but he wanted to be filled properly first.

"So pretty." Chris spread Simon's legs wide, tugging at the plug. Simon tightened as it started to withdraw, splitting him open from the inside as it tried to escape his tight hole. When Chris let go of it, it slid back into his hole automatically, settling deep as he clenched around it.

"I wanted to be ready for you." Simon hummed, gasping as Chris tugged again, going almost to the thickest part of the plug before he let it go. His body sucked it back inside, all the way to the narrow neck.

"Look at you, fucking yourself on it for me. How big is it inside?" Chris tongued at Simon's cock, presumably waiting for an answer.

"It's big. I'm so full, Chris." It was borderline uncomfortable, but not more than Simon could take. And besides, he ached to be filled more.

"Not as big as me," said Chris. It wasn't a question. Chris obviously knew he was massive and had no shame about it.

"No," said Simon, gripping Chris' hair as he sucked him deep again. "I'm gonna come." Simon bucked his hips, pushing deep into Chris' mouth. The man choked once before he seemed to get control. He hummed, sucking like a fucking Dyson as he pushed at the base of the plug.

It was too much. The plug scraped over Simon's spot at the same time Chris' tongue swept over the head of his cock. He couldn't have held back, even if he'd tried. He jerked, his hips spasming as he lost his control, tipping over the edge and shooting into Chris' mouth.

Chris grimaced, jerking Simon's cock so the rest landed on his chin. "I'll never get used to that taste, though." He swallowed, grimacing again.

"I kind of like it," said Simon, laughing at Chris' expression as he panted for breath. "I like the feeling of pulling someone apart with only my mouth until they can't hold back anymore. Them coming in my mouth, when they can't even warn me? That's the best." It wasn't the taste he loved as much as the power of it.

Chris crawled up his body and their lips met. Simon could taste himself on Chris' tongue and the headiness of it made him shudder. Okay, maybe he liked the taste of it, too.

"I want you inside me," said Simon, biting at Chris' lip. Chris reached for the side stand where they both knew that Leo kept the condoms. He grabbed Chris' hand, dragging him back.

"I want you inside me bare. I want to feel your cum dripping from my hole before you plug me back up again. I trust you." He pulled Chris back into a kiss, even as he stiffened.

"Not until we get tested." Chris shook his head, pushing Simon back to the bed before reaching for the condoms again. "After that, good luck trying to keep us from filling your hole. Between the two of us, we're going to make sure that you are always bursting."

Simon groaned, rubbing his hand over his belly. He could imagine being so full of cum that he could feel the stretch under his hand. The plug would keep it from escaping until one of them needed him again. They could fuck him over and over, pushing him to his limit before they replaced the plug. He would be bursting and so well claimed that he would never be able to doubt himself again.

"What are you thinking about?" Chris leaned back over him, slicking his lubed fingers over Simon's awakening cock. "Something hot if you're getting hard again so quick."

"I'm thinking about your cum inside of me," said Simon, his face flushing. "And Leo's. So much of it that I can't take it anymore. I would be able to see it here — and feel it." He smoothed his hand down his flat belly.

"Shit." Chris grabbed himself, clamping his hand down at the base of his covered cock. "Warn a guy. I never even knew that I had a kink like that, but man..." He shook his head, teasing the base of the plug.

Simon whimpered as Chris pulled, the plug stretching him wide before slipping out and leaving him empty. He felt the dribble of lube from Leo follow it, and he clenched tight, the ache fiercer than he expected. Leo had rammed him harder than he'd thought. It was a good thing Leo hadn't listened to his begging to take him even harder — and dry at that.

He moved to roll over, so Chris would have the best view of his sore and probably reddened rim as he sank inside.

"No. I want to watch your face when I push inside." He grabbed Simon's legs and pressed his knees against his chest, leaving him open and on display. "You're red here." He dragged a slick finger across Simon's entrance, sinking the tip inside and sending the nerves alight.

"Leo." It was the only explanation he could give. Chris hummed, thrusting his finger inside to the last knuckle, and curling it so he prodded Simon's prostate head-on. It was like he had memorized Simon's body after their time together, and either he was a quick learner, or he was just a natural.

"He should be more careful with you." Chris nibbled the inside of Simon's thigh as he sank a second finger to the knuckle. "You're not as tight as last time, but you're so fucking warm. Is that because of the plug?"

"Yeah." Simon gulped as a third finger speared him. "You don't have to prep me with the plug, 'cause it stretches me out for you." He still forgot that Chris was new at this, especially when he played his prostate so perfectly. "And even if you didn't prep me, I could still take it. I like the stretch, and I love it harder. I begged Leo to go harder, but he wouldn't."

"Because I know you're reckless and that you don't think of the consequences of your actions." Leo's voice cut through their bubble. He was standing in the doorway to the bedroom, his shirt unbuttoned and untucked from his slacks. His arms were crossed, a smirk on his face. "By all means, please continue." He waved his hand at them before he cut through the bedroom, heading for the bathroom.

"That is so hot," said Simon under his breath. "He could be watching us at any time or join in. It makes my skin feel like it's on fire."

"You *are* a kinky little shit," said Chris, quirking his brow. He lowered his voice. "But I don't mind the interruption, either."

Chris withdrew his fingers and the blunt head of his cock pushed against Simon's rim, sinking inside with the barest hints of resistance. The ache was fierce, but it was what Simon loved most about sex. It pushed his limits, giving him an equal share of pleasure and pain that kept him somehow balanced.

"Fuck, you're still so tight," said Chris, groaning as he sunk to the hilt.

Simon clamped down, feeling every inch of Chris' rigid cock inside him. It was so fucking deep. "Move. I'm ready for you."

Chris didn't doubt him this time. He pulled out, then slammed himself deep in one hard thrust. It pushed the air from Simon's lungs. The man was so powerful that he could shatter Simon without even trying.

Simon tried to let out a strangled yelp, but someone's lips were on his that weren't Chris'.

He heard Chris' curse at the same time Leo took utter possession of him, driving the last of his lust-filled thoughts from his head. Leo had lain along the head of the bed, his body aligned with the row of pillows that had grown since their relationship had begun. Simon only remembered a single one the first time he'd come to the penthouse, but now there were three.

Chris leaned back, tugging on Simon until he was upright and straddling Chris' broad thighs. His cock shifted deeper, hitting his spot dead-on. A jet of pre-cum spread between their slick stomachs.

"C'mere, *boy*." Chris beckoned Leo, who sidled up behind Simon, pressing his naked chest to Simon's sweat-slicked back. Leo gripped Simon's hips, pushing him down farther onto Chris' cock at the same time Chris threaded his hand through Leo's hair, pulling him in for a kiss.

The kiss was so loud right beside Simon's ear, but it was the most erotic thing in the history of mankind. He had a front row seat in the owner's box to the two sexiest men alive competing for dominance, while one man was balls deep in him and the other was humping against his ass.

"Fuck, you can kiss." Leo licked his lips before winding his own hand through Chris' shorter hair and tugging their lips back together. They sandwiched Simon tight, their heat engulfing him and the scent of sweat and sex heavy in the air.

Then, somehow, Chris began to move. He rocked his hips, gently at first, then harder when Simon lifted up, balancing on his knees between them. Simon fucked his cock against Chris' sculpted belly, letting his ass grind against Leo's cock behind him.

Leo gasped in a breath, breaking contact with Chris and planting his lips onto Simon's shoulder instead, before sucking the spot so fiercely that it ached. The position made his cock drop lower, until the tip bumped the spot where Simon and Chris were joined.

"Oh, fuck," Simon cried out, slamming himself down, just to feel Leo rub him there. There was no way that he could take them both, not without some serious prep, but that didn't stop him from wanting it.

"Put your finger inside of me, Leo. Stroke Chris' cock as he fucks me deep." His fantasies were laid bare, and all three of them groaned.

Leo didn't hesitate, even as Chris' hips stuttered. Leo's finger circled where they were joined, whispering profanities into Simon's ear before he slowly sank inside.

The pressure was intense and so fucking painful, but Chris' groan made it all worth it. Simon bit his lip, blinking to hold back the tears as they threatened to spill. He didn't remember Leo's fingers being that big, but they had obviously grown.

"You're so fucking tight here, baby." Leo flexed his finger, stroking Simon's walls and probably Chris' cock at the same time. "I just want to ruin you and see how much you could take. You're a slut for it, baby — for me and Chris. Just for us."

Simon nodded, the term 'slut' burning over his skin and setting his nerves alight. He was their slut, and he would do anything for them.

"Make me take it," said Simon, shuddering as Chris starting fucking him in earnest, Leo pulling at his rim and massaging him inside.

"You take it so well, baby. Just imagine both of our bare cocks inside of you, filling you up at the same time. You'd be so full and stretched. I'd have to slap that hole just so you could keep our cum inside you."

"Fuck. Fuck. Fuck."

Simon wasn't sure who was cursing, but he whole-heartedly agreed.

"You're gonna make Chris come, baby. Can you feel him getting harder for you?" Leo's hand disappeared from Simon's hole. He must've done something to Chris, because a moment later Chris was jerking and coming, his hips snapping up almost painfully.

There was barely a breath between the time that Chris finished to when Simon was suddenly being jerked off his cock and slammed down onto Leo's. There was a fleeting moment of disappointment when Simon realized that Leo had found a condom at some point, but the disappointment was squashed the moment Leo went to work.

He pulled Simon back to meet his thrusts, pushing him between his shoulders until Simon's face was pressed against Chris' spent cock. Chris was still mostly hard, the tip of the condom filled with his spend that would slowly start to leak out soon. Simon didn't want to miss out on his treat.

Scrambling for his senses as Leo reamed his ass, Simon jerked the condom off Chris' cock and tossed it to the floor, hoping that it didn't make a mess of Leo's rug. He hungrily sucked Chris into his mouth, taking him down to the base as he started to shrink.

The taste of latex nearly made him gag and the spermicidal lube wasn't any better, but he pushed past that, seeking out his favorite salty treat and sucking until his cheeks hollowed out. Chris gripped his hair hard, spasming when Simon didn't let up his relentless assault.

Chris was definitely the one who was chanting curses now, his hips twitching as if he didn't know if he was going to get hard again or try to pull away.

Leo's hand on his cock finally forced Simon to the edge of his orgasm and beyond, making him gasp around Chris' cock as he came. Leo's hips stuttered a moment later, and he held himself deep, his cock twitching and flexing in the most delicious way.

Chris tugged Simon off as he tried to start sucking on his cock again, still searching for the saltiness he craved.

"We have ourselves a cum-slut, Chris." Leo chuckled and eased out, tossing his own condom and guiding Simon to his own spent cock. Simon sucked him to the back of his throat, forcing himself to ignore the tempting foreskin that looked so fun to play with. He could only imagine how sensitive it would've been.

"I get really sensitive after," said Chris, rubbing a hand down Simon's spine and through the rapidly cooling sweat.

Leo grunted as Simon dropped all the way to the base, tonguing at Leo's balls and licking along the seam.

"Go gentle, baby. It feels like you are about to suck my dick off." Leo laughed as Simon let out a sigh, making himself slow down. He held Leo in his mouth, trying not to suck as saliva gathered in his mouth. The urge to swallow built, until he couldn't hold back any longer.

"That's better, baby," said Leo, reaching for Chris and pulling him in for a kiss. "You hold me as long as you need, baby. We aren't going anywhere."

Simon tongued the weight of Leo's cock in his mouth, humming with contentment. The moment seemed to stretch for an eternity, as if everything else had been banished from his worried mind. He was protected. He was loved.

# Chapter Twenty-One

Simon wiped his sweaty palms on his pants for the third time in the last ten minutes. The slacks were made of tightly-wound fabric that looked expensive but didn't absorb moisture worth crap. His track pants would have been so much better, but he refused to meet with Leo's — whatever he called them — in track pants.

He glanced at his watch, but almost no time had passed since he'd last looked. Leo was still in the shower after another glorious round of fucking. Simon still ached, clenching around the plug that sealed everything inside him.

He shuddered at the thought, but his cock stayed limp. There was no way he could come again. Leo had already rung three out of him before he had fucked him in earnest, coming deep inside.

Fuck, it had been good. He should have let Leo pull his 'strings' so they would've got their test results back the same day. Instead, he had waited for what seemed like forever. He had shoved his results in Leo's and

Chris' hands, stripping and heading to the bedroom. Before he'd posed on the bed, he'd grabbed the condoms, which promptly went in the garbage, and a plug, which he'd set on the bedside table.

That had been the best round of fucking that Simon had ever experienced. They had passed him back and forth, taking their time and wringing every bit of pleasure from his body until he felt completely owned and loved.

But reality had unfortunately called. Leo had summoned his underlings to deal with Rubric, and Simon had insisted that he attend. He couldn't sit by idly in his apartment while his boyfriend was defending him, even if that sounded romantic.

Chris had disappeared. He was a good man, one who couldn't stand to see Leo's dark side so blatantly. He wasn't in the same place that Simon was, where his heart had overruled his conscience when it came to Leo. That might never happen with Chris at all, but the man was trying.

And watching them kiss was better than any porn…including the stuff he had to pay for. If scientists figured out how to bottle it, no gay man would ever need Viagra again.

"They'll be here soon," said Leo as he stepped out of the bedroom and across the living room space. His hair was still damp from the shower, and he fiddled with his cuff, struggling to fasten it with damp fingers. "They are never late."

*Ten minutes.* Simon took a deep breath, smoothing down the front of his shirt. There was a persistent wrinkle right near the middle, but it was too late to iron it now.

He glanced at his arm, squinting at the fabric. Was that a stain or just a shadow?

"You look fine," said Leo, cupping Simon's chin and tilting his head back for a kiss. "Are you sure you want to be a part of this? This isn't like dipping your toe in a pool to see if it's warm enough. Once you're in, you're in. There's no going back. You're going to hear things and probably see things that you wish you hadn't, and there's nothing you can do about them."

"As long as you're there to pick up the pieces. You and Chris are all I need." Simon blinked, knowing in his heart that it was true. Their relationship was still new, but he'd never felt so whole. Thinking about Rubric and how he'd been manipulated made his stomach churn, but the idea that he could be doing the same thing to someone else was what had settled the deal.

Leo seemed to think that Rubric was obsessed with Simon, as if he were interesting enough to draw that kind of attention. It still didn't make sense to Simon. Rubric could have anyone he wanted, so why would he target him?

*Because I'm vulnerable.* He swallowed the lump in his throat. *Not anymore.*

"You are a good person, Simon." Leo kissed him, sweet and slow. "Don't let me change that." He looked so hesitant, so unsure, and it was exactly how Simon felt. At least he wasn't alone.

"Maybe I'll change you," said Simon. Leo snorted, turning away.

"I killed my foster-father in cold blood and many others after him. I have more money than anyone in this city, and most of it is from illegal activities. I won't stop at anything to keep this city under my control, and no one will stand in my way." His voice was so dark that it sank straight into Simon's soul, leeching the color from his thoughts.

"That's quite...bleak," said Simon, swallowing. "I don't expect you to change for me, Leo, or for Chris. We are who we are. That doesn't stop me from loving you." He crossed his arms, staring at Leo's strong back. There was a spot of moisture along his spine where he'd obviously missed when drying off. That alone made him look almost like a normal guy.

"You're too good for me," said Leo, a real smile breaking over his lips as he turned back to Simon. His smile disappeared as his phone buzzed. "They're here. We will speak mostly in Russian, as it will be easier for some of us that way. Try to keep up."

The protest died on Simon's lips as Leo tapped something on his phone and the elevator door shuffled open. He spun to face the newcomers, his mouth going dry. He recognized almost all of them. Clas and Natalie were there, along with the other man who had been in Rubric's office the day they'd met.

Trailing the pack was Mikeal—the man who had put a knife to his throat. Simon's scar throbbed as he swallowed, healed but still sensitive. Leo had told him who to expect, but knowing and seeing were two very different things.

The doors slid shut with a swish, locking them together in the penthouse. He hoped this wasn't like one of those panic room horror movies where only one of them got out alive.

Maybe he should try to grab a knife from the drawer, just in case? He glanced at the nearest cupboard. The only things in it were a few butter knives and one plastic fork from when they'd convinced Leo to try

Indian take-out. The mobster had been unimpressed with the lack of cardamom in his korma.

Mikeal's eyes went wide as he spotted Simon, and he froze before he looked to Leo — as if Simon would be standing in Leo's kitchen without his permission.

The man's doubt grated under his skin, like a sliver jammed under his nailbed that was festering but too deep to reach with tweezers.

Mikeal was attractive, with chiseled features that were almost pleasing without a knife in his hand. In another life, Simon might have made a pass at him if he'd wandered into the right kind of bar.

Simon bit his lip before his gaze and mind wandered. Leo was counting on him to pay attention, but his thoughts were already taking a stroll. He had to keep his focus, for himself and for Rubric.

"Do we have to watch you fawn over your pet while we discuss business now?" Natalie spoke in Russian, probably thinking that Simon couldn't understand her. He tried not to bristle at her words, letting them roll off him instead.

Maybe she had a point. He was wearing a plug, keeping Leo's cum inside of him right now. And he loved Leo's hands on him.

"Let's talk business," Leo replied, sticking with Russian, as he told Simon they would.

The others circled the kitchen island, some standing while others slid into their seats. Leo and Mikeal were both in pressed suits, but the others were in jeans and T-shirts. Natalie's jeans were skintight, and he could see her bra through her T-shirt. He wondered if they represented some kind of a street crew.

*God*, he was such a shitty mobster boyfriend. He knew literally nothing about the mafia except for what he'd seen in movies.

One by one they pulled their phones from their pockets, dropping them into the middle of the table. Leo slid his into the middle last, so five nearly identical phones sat in the center. How they didn't get them mixed up was beyond him.

He flinched as a thick arm moved into the edge of his vision, and familiar cologne engulfed him. Mikeal was right beside him, only inches away from his stool where he was perched at the island. He swiveled, staring at the man head-on and refusing to turn his back. He was not going to be taken by surprise this time.

"I am sorry," said Mikeal in his thick-accented English that Simon could hardly understand. "For the misunderstanding." He spoke slowly, choosing his words carefully.

The gaze of every person in the room settled on Simon, and he wanted to wilt away. He pushed the fact that they probably all had weapons on them to the back of his mind and straightened in his chair, ignoring the way the plug shifted inside him. He had stared down perverted billionaires before. He could rock this.

"Thank you," said Simon, subconsciously reaching for the small scar on his neck. He knew that the line was still pink and bright, and so freshly closed that it felt like it might split open at any moment. Leo had taken such good care of it, cleaning it daily for him and wrapping it in gauze until the edges had pulled together.

Mikeal nodded, focusing his gaze on the table and utterly dismissing Simon. When Simon swiveled back around, everyone was still looking at him. Natalie was scowling, her face not quite as attractive when she looked like she wanted to murder him.

Leo cleared his throat. "Put your phone on the table, Simon — no eyes, no ears and no ring tones."

Simon patted at his pockets, searching for his phone, His hands were still sweating, leaving small damp spots wherever he touched. He should have been cooler with the air-conditioning set so high.

His pockets were empty except for a quarter that was jammed so low that he would likely never get it out. There was a bit of crunchy fuzz there, too, like he'd accidentally left a candy in his pocket the last time he'd worn the outfit.

"Um." He bit his lip, trying his back pockets next, but they were empty too. "Oh, wait." He leaped from the chair, causing more than one person to reach for their hips, which was supremely disturbing.

On the couch, jammed between the two cushions, was the pale blue of his smudged phone case. He'd been reading the paper again, continuing his endless search for a job somewhere where Rubric hadn't thought to blacklist him. He hadn't gotten very far before another sudoku puzzle had distracted him.

He grabbed his phone, running back to the table and tossing it down in the center with the other phones. It looked like an ancient dirty telegram next the rest. He still had no idea how he could have mistaken Leo's phone for his own. The cases were the same color, but that was about it.

The woman snorted and shook her head, quirking an eyebrow at Leo, who looked like he wanted to face palm.

"You could have just said that it was in a different room," said Leo, a very faint flush on his cheeks.

"Oh, sorry," said Simon, forcing a smile to his face as his stomach dropped. He was already playing the part of the fool, and they hadn't even begun. "It just seemed very ritualistic, and I didn't want to mess with it."

"Moving on." Leo faced the others, staring at them each in turn, before switching to Russian. "Some of you know why you are here, and others"—he turned his glare on Mikeal—"are outside of the loop for one reason or another. I need all of you on this now, so drop whatever else you are doing."

"You name it, and we'll nail it, boss," said Clas, an eerie smile on his face. For someone who seemed to have such an interest in art, he certainly acted uncivilized.

Leo grimaced, his gaze flickering to Simon for a moment. "We are going to try convince Rubric Mayvel to give up his shares and his contacts. My goal is that he leaves town."

"Not going to cut it, Leo." Natalie spoke up, tapping her polished nails on the marble counter. "He's moving something big, and it isn't ours. I've already lost two guys trying to get inside information. There's no way he gives everything up without a fight. Besides, we've already given him an ultimatum and some convincing. He's had his second chance."

"We are going to try," Leo shot back, his voice strained and his eyes glaring brilliant blue.

The woman's eyes went wide before she replied, her words lost as Clas cut in. Within moments, the discussion morphed into a playground fight full of indecipherable bickering and competition.

Simon's eyes went wide. They might be murderers, but at heart they were nothing but a bunch of toddlers…with guns. Leo looked unimpressed as Clas raised his voice.

"Enough." Leo's voice cut them off, his icy gaze murderous. "We'll make him an offer, and if he refuses, I'll blow his fucking brains out myself."

Simon felt the color drain from his face. He slapped his hands down on the countertop, the sting ringing against his palms. "You promised." He spoke in Russian, so everyone would be able to understand his protest.

"I said I would fucking *try*," Leo snapped back, rounding on Simon. "Stay silent unless you have something to contribute."

"Then why am I even here?" Simon stood, his patience finally snapping after weeks of frustration and anger. None of that had been directed at Leo before, but here he was, talking about killing a man that he promised he wouldn't.

"Sit down." Leo's voice was so deep that it was a growl, and Simon knew immediately that he had crossed a line. His Leo loved to joke around and loved when Simon was a bit of a brat, but this wasn't his Leo. He was dealing with a mob leader and a killer right now.

Simon bit his lip, dropping his gaze to the tabletop. He shook his head, forcing himself to look back up and face Leo's stare head on. He was a grown man, and he was sick of hiding and letting other people tell him what to do. He was sick of being manipulated and mistreated because he wasn't the fastest thinker. He wasn't going to let Leo go back on his word, no matter what Simon had to do.

"No." Simon kept his voice calm. If he let the situation escalate any further, a knife to his throat would be the least of his worries.

Leo faltered, his mouth dropping open as if it were the last thing that he'd expected Simon to say. Hell, even Simon was surprised that he had just discovered his own backbone. But, man, it felt good.

"Mikeal, kill the little shit." Natalie broke in, switching to fluent French. She was probably hoping that Simon couldn't understand her, but after a brief brain delay, he caught every word. He switched to French just a quickly, the vowels flowing over his tongue.

"You know you don't have to kill everyone, right? Just because I piss you off doesn't mean you can't just ask me to leave." Simon crossed his arms, his anger simmering. Surprise lit up her face, her sculpted brows lifting.

"Leave," she shot back, her voice a hiss.

Oh, that was Spanish, which Simon had to admit, he was pretty rusty with. He nodded his head regardless, understanding what she was trying to get across. He chose his words carefully, trying to remember how to get the accent right as he switched his brain into Spanish mode.

"Thank you very much for your time, everyone. I'll see myself out." Simon nodded once, hoping he didn't mix up his pronouns. He turned away, his face blazing at the kitchen full of shocked faces.

Leo's hand on his shoulder stopped him.

"Simon, wait. No one disrespects what's mine, and you *are* mine." He turned a glare to Natalie, who visibly wilted. "I think I have an idea on how to make Rubric pay. He'll never see it coming."

# Chapter Twenty-Two

"I'm sorry," said Leo, kissing Simon's clothed shoulder before sucking at the skin on the back of his neck. There must've been a hickey there that Simon wasn't aware of because it ached more than it should have. Leo had an obsession with marking him, which Simon was more than happy to oblige.

Simon shrugged. A few people were lingering and Mikeal was right beside them, his form completely rigid with his dark eyes staring at them. Leo didn't seem to be dissuaded by the audience. If anything, it spurred him on.

The others filed out until only Mikeal remained. His stare was unyielding, and Simon wanted nothing more than to look away, but he couldn't. Leo's hands were on him, his skin flushing and his cock twitching. Did he not see his brother standing right there?

Mikeal cleared his throat, crossing his arms and leaning back against the kitchen island. His biceps bulged — slimmer than Chris', but thicker than Leo's.

"Enjoying the show?" asked Leo, pulling Simon back to his chest. His hard cock nudged between Simon's ass cheeks, glancing over the plug that was still buried deep.

"Trying to understand," said Mikeal. His thick voice was calm, his face completely flat.

Simon had never been much of an exhibitionist, but he found his gaze dropping, looking for a tent in Mikeal pants. The bulge beneath the fabric looked soft, but still hefty enough to make his mouth water. Simon's cock filled, and he clenched on the plug. *What the hell is wrong with me?*

"Get out," said Leo, seemingly taking Simon's tension for something else entirely. His hands stilled over Simon's pecs, his fingers gently plucking at his nipples. Simon cut back a moan, rocking back into Leo's hardness.

*There!* A rosy blush spread over Mikeal's cheeks, his hands clenching and making his arms look that much more delicious. The man shifted and the fabric of his pants pulled over his soft cock, giving Simon a better shot of it. *Hell, there's a lot of it.*

"I would speak with you, brother." Mikeal shifted again, his discomfort palpable.

"Then speak."

*Oh God*, Leo was not stopping. He nibbled at Simon's earlobe, catching him as his knees went weak. *Why am I not telling him to stop?*

Leo's breath tickled over the back of his neck, and he shivered, going tight. He was sure that his bulge was already apparent, but he'd rather not embarrass himself further. And, as much as he felt like Leo's toy, he actually wasn't.

Mikeal let out a sigh, pinching the bridge of his nose. "It is about Mother. She's been asking questions about the promises you made."

Leo's hands left him all at once, and Simon nearly stumbled as he suddenly had to support his own weight. Simon looked back over his shoulder, and the rage carved into Leo's face made him balk.

"I'm gonna go," said Simon, trying to slip away. Mikeal stopped him, bracketing him in with his meaty body. The scent of his cologne, so much like Leo's, made him shudder with fear and something else. He touched the scar on the center of his palm. The line was nearly invisible now.

"You stay. If my brother wants his toys involved, then you will stay." Mikeal's gaze pinned him, and his heart stuttered.

"I'm not a toy," said Simon, trying to keep his anger from his voice. The plug shifted, glancing over his prostate and he smothered a gasp.

"Says the toy," replied Mikeal, leaning close. "You see why I cannot trust you. A doll doesn't know it is a doll until someone else points it out to them. I can see you are...pretty...for a man, at least, but I don't understand why my brother has allowed himself to be corrupted."

"Is this a gay thing?" asked Simon, incredulous. He hadn't expected this. Leo had never seemed hesitant about his sexuality, and his underlings hadn't seemed surprised. He'd expected it from Chris, maybe, but not Leo.

Mikeal's attractive qualities started to dim.

"Yes," said Leo, pulling Simon's attention back to him. His arms were crossed, his lips tight and the wrinkles at the corners of his eyes in full force.

"I'm pretty sure you're bisexual," said Simon, glaring at Mikeal. "A straight man doesn't blush when he's watching two men together, especially if one is his brother."

Mikeal's gaze turned downright deadly and every muscle in his body seemed to flex, making him look so much bigger and stronger than Simon had realized. He took a step back, his heart pounding.

"You don't know what you speak of." Mikeal's accent thickened, until Simon had to squint as he attempted to decipher the words. He nodded, recognizing suppression when he saw it, and it made his heart break.

"Okay. If you need someone to talk to, please let me know. I know how hard it can be if there's no one to listen to you," said Simon, his voice soft. His plate was already brimming between Leo and Chris, but he could still admit that the man was yummy...unless he happened to have a knife on him. Then he was just terrifying.

The tension that had engulfed the room seemed to dissolve in an instant. Mikeal nodded, his dark eyes wide, before he spun, heading for the elevator like his ass was at risk of being exploited.

Simon let a smile spread over his lips. As hectic as the day had been, at least he was still able to help someone. He turned back to Leo, who was looking at him with unsuppressed awe.

"How did you do that?" He looked to the closing elevator doors. "Whenever I speak with him, we usually try to kill each other."

Simon chewed his lip, a flush spreading on his face. "I just told him the truth. I want to help him, if I can. He's angry at himself—and a lot of other people, by the sounds of it. I think he just needs someone to understand him."

"Fuck, you are unbelievable." A smile spread over Leo's lips, as he grabbed Simon, pulling him close. "You need to work for me. I'll pay you well, and I have a full benefit package." He waggled his eyebrows, pulling Simon in for a kiss before he could retort.

Simon groaned into the kiss, but his mind was elsewhere. He couldn't work for Leo. The man was a criminal of the worst kind, and he couldn't get lost in that spiral, because he'd never be able to dig himself out.

But something pulled at him, keeping the idea in the front of his thoughts as Leo led him to the bedroom. Maybe he could do something to help.

# Chapter Twenty-Three

The bed shifted, rousing Simon from sleep just enough that he had a moment of panic. The bed was too soft, the walls too far apart for him to be in his apartment. He blinked in the darkness, recognizing the glow of the city through the open window.

He was at Leo's penthouse. Of course he was.

They'd spent almost every night there over the last few weeks. Leo didn't seem to mind, despite the fact that there were nights that he wouldn't be back until late. Chris was often back late as well, extending his hours at the strip club since he seemed to enjoy it so much.

Once, and only once, Simon had waited up for Leo until nearly midnight. Chris had gone to bed, but Simon had paced the floor, his heart pounding for no particular reason. He knew something had to have been wrong, and with Leo's plan for Rubric in place, the thought was terrifying.

When Leo had returned, reeking of blood and other filth, he had paused when he'd spotted Simon at the couch. A scowl had marred his tired face, his blue eyes blazing in the low light. He'd brushed by Simon before pushing his way into the shower.

*"I can help,"* Simon had said, following Leo like a lost puppy. It had broken his heart to see Leo so exhausted and so filthy, just for him.

*"Until you are a part of my business, you'll stay the fuck out of it."* Leo had slammed the bathroom door, cutting Simon off before he could protest.

Simon had felt sufficiently spurned, and despite his desire to wait for Leo some nights, he always went to bed with Chris, stretching out on the massive bed that easily fit all three of them with room to spare for elbows and knees.

Sleeping in his own bed felt like a thing of the past. He could hardly remember the coolness of sleeping alone or the scratch of his threadbare sheets against his skin. Leo had refused to sleep in Simon's bed or Chris' larger one, and they'd camped out at the penthouse ever since.

Tonight, Leo had come home early, still smelling fresh with his suit neatly arranged. They'd gone to bed, Leo holding him close until he drifted off. Leo's chest was under his ear, the even thud of his heart pulling him back into sleep even as the bed shifted again.

Simon perked up as Chris grunted and dropped onto the bed. The covers rustled as Chris shuffled closer until his broad chest pressed against Simon's back. The scratch of his beard tickled the back of his neck as Chris spoke, pulling him from the last tendrils of sleep.

"You awake?" Chris whispered into Simon's ear, his breath making him shiver. There was whiskey and mint mixed with Chris' usual scent, intoxicating in its sweetness.

Simon blinked the sleep from his eyes and nodded, letting out a soft affirmative groan. Without the routine from a regular job, his nights and days had become listless. Utter boredom stretched from nine to five as he searched endlessly for a job outside of Rubric's reach. The man was a billionaire, and his shadow seemed to encompass the entire city.

Leo reminded him every day to be patient while he pulled his illegal strings to make Rubric suffer. Simon could be patient, but this was beyond. He could only take rejection so many times before it became personal.

Tomorrow he was going out to look for somewhere to volunteer. They couldn't turn away free labor, and at least he would be doing something with his time.

Chris swept his frigid hands down his sides, pausing at his hips.

"Could you? I mean..." Chris paused, setting his cold hand over Simon's waist. Simon turned, blinking in the darkness. He could only see the outline of Chris against the pillow, big and presumably as beautiful as usual.

Chris grasped his hand, their fingers entwining. He squeezed once, before he pushed Simon's hand over his naked skin. He smoothed over the softness of his treasure trail, dipping lower to where his hair thickened and turned coarse.

Simon gasped when the back of his hand grazed Chris' groin. The man was rock hard and felt even bigger in the darkness with only his imagination and memory to go by. His own cock flexed against his pajama bottoms, perking up in moments.

Somehow, he'd become a depraved sex-fiend since starting their relationship, and he had absolutely no regrets about that.

Simon wrapped his hand around the girth of Chris' cock, letting his fingers dance over the solid veins. He could feel Chris' pulse, beating hard beneath his hand. His favorite part was at the head, where he gently pinched the foreskin and slid it back, before circling over the exposed glans.

"Shit, yeah." Chris went rigid, rocking his hips into Simon's grasp. "Could you?" He paused again, running his hand through Simon's hair before tugging once.

A grin flickered over Simon's lips. After all they had done together, Chris was still so painfully shy and afraid to ask him for what he wanted.

"I can suck your cock, if you tell me what has you so hot and bothered." Simon twisted his wrist in a way that he knew Chris loved. "Quietly, though. I don't want to wake up Leo."

Chris shuddered as Simon tossed the blankets back and made his way down to his prize. The chilly air sank into his sleep-warm skin, but he was sure that the chill wouldn't last for long. He was hoping to get hot really soon.

"The bar," Chris whispered, groaning quietly as Simon closed his lips over the head of his cock as a reward. "I thought that maybe chicks wouldn't turn me on anymore, now that I'm with you and Leo. But there's this new chick, and she's everything that makes a woman beautiful—and she can move. Shit." He tugged Simon's hair sharply as he sank down, taking Chris' cock to the back of his throat before bobbing his head. "I was thinking about you dancing for me on that pole, your perfect cock bobbing in time with the beat. I'd be watching you, just like I watch them, to make sure nobody touches you. No one gets to touch you." He took another shuddering breath. "Fuck, Simon, that feels so fucking good."

Simon hummed, his cock dripping at Chris' words. Maybe Chris didn't realize that he was bi and not gay, but it didn't really matter. Simon couldn't dance either way, but he could suck cock like a champ.

He mouthed over the head of Chris' cock, tracing his foreskin with his tongue before he took a deep breath and plunged down. He nearly gagged as he went beyond the back of his throat, not pausing until his lips touched the thick curls of Chris' groin.

"Oh shit, baby. That fucking mouth."

Simon choked on a chuckle. Chris had been spending too much time with Leo if he was calling him 'baby'.

He grasped Chris' sac, rolling each ball in his hand and smoothing his thumb down the seam. His other hand trailed down to a place he had never touched. He circled the twitching furl, pulling up for a breath as he played with it. It spasmed, but he took his time, stroking it into submission.

"That feels weird," said Chris, twitching his hips to try to get deeper into Simon's mouth, his furl relaxing under Simon's touch.

"You ain't seen nothing yet." Simon chuckled, covertly slicking up one of his fingers and slipping the tip inside of Chris at same time he plunged his mouth back down. Chris clamped down, his entrance going so tight that Simon swore he was going to lose circulation.

He hummed, forcing himself to take Chris deeper into his throat. The man couldn't stay tight, his body relaxing and allowing Simon to slip his finger all the way inside.

It was tight, soft and so fucking warm that Simon groaned again, his eyes falling shut. He was touching a place where no one had touched before, and he could tell by the way Chris clamped down on him that he hadn't even touched himself there.

"Uh, I dunno," said Chris. His grip tightened in Simon's hair. "Is it supposed to feel good?"

It was a fair question, but it smashed Simon's confidence to smithereens.

He pulled out and off, his lips coming away with a *pop*. Crawling across the bed, he reached for the side drawer, feeling his way in the dark. He skimmed over the cold metal plug and something else he didn't recognize, before the cool lube bottle touched his fingertips.

"This should be better." He settled back in the same place, slicking his finger with lube and slipping it back inside as he sucked on the head of Chris' cock. The man's breath hitched. "Better?"

"Yeah. Still weird, though." He let out a huff, his body still tense. Simon tangled his free hand in Chris' rough curls that covered his groin, pulling in a way that he knew Chris loved.

"Do you want me to stop?" He stilled his finger that was inside of Chris. Chris had mentioned that he was interested in trying this kind of play, but maybe he had changed his mind. He started to withdraw when Chris shook his head, the movement barely visible in the dark.

"I want to know what you like about it." His voice was trembling. "So far, I don't get it." He let out a quiet laugh that sounded too strained for Simon's liking.

"It's different for everyone," said Simon, keeping his voice low. He glanced at the outline of Leo's form, but it looked like he hadn't budged. "I like the feeling of the stretch, especially when it's too much too fast. I like it when you push me to my limits."

"That sounds great in theory, but, yeah…no." Chris took another shuddering breath, his body fluttering around Simon.

"Others like this part better." Simon curled his finger along Chris' silken walls, searching for the little nub that was sure to blow his mind. He circled a few times, before he pushed as deep as he could, finally finding the small bump with his fingertip. He stroked it, keeping his touch light.

Chris grunted, his breath rushing out all at once. "Wha—?"

Simon pushed harder, massaging the nub and pressing his finger as deep as he could go. Chris' cock twitched against his face as the man let out a deep gasp.

Simon wished that the lamp were on so he could see the emotions flitting over his features. He could imagine surprise and maybe a bit of wonder. When he'd discovered his own prostate, he hadn't left it alone for *days*.

"Oh, shit, that feels so good."

Simon sucked the pre-cum from the tip of Chris' cock, pulling his hand back to slam two fingers in deep, assaulting that spot with every ounce of effort. He was rewarded with a yelp and a flood of saltiness over his tongue.

"I like it rough," said Simon, grinding his fingers deep. "Do you want it gentle or rough, baby?" He threw the endearment back at Chris, wondering if the ex-cop would even notice when he sounded so blissed out.

Simon gentled his fingers, slowly pulling them out and spreading them wider at the same time. He eased back in, stroking Chris' spot lovingly before repeating the action over and over.

"Fuck, just like that. It feels so good," said Chris. He'd started to lift his hips off the bed each time Simon pulled out, as if chasing the feeling and begging for more.

Simon grinned, teasing Chris' slit and letting the taste sit on his tongue. That was more like it. He loved it hard, because once his body had a taste of pain, everything felt ten times better.

When he pushed three fingers in, he bit back a groan at the sheer pressure inside Chris. He was so tight, his walls silken and smooth...and so responsive for such a big man.

"Simon, please, more," said Chris, gripping the back of Simon's head and gently coaxing him down.

"That's already three fingers." Simon resisted, mouthing at the head. "You're going to have to be more specific. You want it harder?" He slammed in deep, hitting Chris' spot head on. "Or do you want my lips on your cock?" He dropped his mouth, taking Chris to the base.

"Yes — no — I want you inside me." Chris groaned, his hips bucking and making Simon swallow through a gag. Chris had never writhed like that before — like an animal that was fighting at the end of its leash.

"I am inside you," said Simon, gasping to catch his breath and wiping away the tears that had gathered when his gag reflex was assaulted.

"All of you. I want your cock," said Chris, throwing back his head and letting out a low groan. His knees edged wider, opening himself up completely.

Simon's chest constricted. He should have seen it coming the moment he'd grabbed the lube, but it still managed to side swipe him. His cock twitched, all for it, but the chill in his gut stopped him.

"I don't know," said Simon, pulling back as unease started to make him soften. He withdrew his fingers as he sat back on his heels. "I don't know if I can."

In theory he definitely could, and he had imagined it on more than one occasion, but in the moment, his mind was assaulted by nothing but memories.

Memories of Rubric beneath him, writhing and blissed out while Simon pounded him, emptiness radiating in his soul and his ass. Even in those moments, when Simon had longed to beg to be taken, he had kept his mouth shut. Rubric's control over him had been so complete that he hadn't even noticed that it had been nothing but another manipulation.

*Chris isn't Rubric. He isn't.*

"Simon?" Chris sat up, feeling for him in the dark. His hand found Simon's lube-covered one, clasping it despite the slick. "It's okay. Only if you want to."

"I want to," said Simon, sighing as Chris, pulled him closer. "I just don't know if I can." His cock hardened as Chris touched him, throbbing with need. He leaned against Chris, tucking his face against his neck and breathing deep. He smelled fresh from the shower with Leo's bodywash clinging to his skin.

"Then we won't." His breath fluttered over Simon's skin. "Do you need to talk about it? Should I wake Leo up?"

"So he can fuck you?" Simon grumbled, immediately tensing as Chris went stiff. He couldn't blame Chris for wanting that. Bottoming was as wonderful as it was terrifying for the first time. He was so fucking tired of having Rubric hang over him like a looming thunderstorm. Now the billionaire was fucking with his love life too.

"No. That's not what I meant, and you know it." Chris tugged at his hair, but Simon refused to move.

"I know. I'm sorry," said Simon, his voice dropping even lower. "I just feel used. The last time I topped... I don't want it to be like that again." He tangled his fingers in the hair on Chris' chest. It was damp, and he was sure that it would glisten if the lights were on.

"Come here," said Chris, tugging him as he fell back to the bed before gathering Simon in his arms. He fit perfectly, like a ball in a glove or a plug in a socket. "I wish I could take it away, but I can't. Just know that we're here for you, both of us, even if Leo is a bit of an asshole."

"I heard that." Leo's sleepy voice snuck into the cocoon they'd created, the warmth in his voice soothing the ache in Simon's chest. Leo rolled over and suddenly color flooded the room.

"Ah fuck, a little warning, boy," said Chris, covering his eyes as Simon smooshed his face harder into his neck, the sliver of light from the lamp blinding him.

"Call it karma," said Leo, shuffling back over to them. He threw his arm over Simon's hip, pulling him closer until Simon was between them, with his back to Leo and his face still smooshed into Chris' neck.

"You okay, baby?" Leo kissed the back of his neck, running his hand down Simon's side.

Simon shook his head. He was definitely not okay. He probably hadn't been okay in a while, but he'd been hiding it underneath layers and layers of denial. There was a lot of shit buried deep, and Rubric was only the tip of the iceberg.

"You want to tell us about it, or do you want to be held?" Leo asked.

Damn, the man was fast. He was hoping for a yes or no question, but of course, Leo pulled him out of his silence as soon as he tip-toed his way into the situation. The man was starting to know him too well.

"I don't want to talk about it because you'll just start killing people, and Chris will have to do a citizen's arrest." His worlds were muffled, but he hoped they could still hear him. There was no way that he was moving anytime soon.

"Leo's a slippery motherfucker. I never could catch him," Chris mumbled, scratching along Simon's scalp.

"Or you're just slow," Leo replied, pulling a snort from Simon. Fuck, these two made him feel good.

"I want to fuck you," said Simon, moving so he could stare down into Chris' eyes. His cock had gone soft, but it wouldn't take much. It never did.

"Okay," said Chris, swallowing under the intensity of Simon's stare. "Are you sure?"

"Yes." Simon nodded, moving so he was between Chris' legs, before pushing them wide. He knelt on the bed, Leo's eyes burning into him and bringing a flush to the surface of his skin. The light was too bright, casting a soft yellow glow in the room when it should have been dark.

He jerked himself a few times, but his cock stayed limp as his heart pounded. He could do this. He could keep Rubric and every other prick from his past out of his mind for a few minutes...hopefully longer.

"Simon," said Leo, getting up on his knees. "Baby, just tell us what's going on."

Simon shook his head, stroking himself furiously. He cringed as the friction became too much. He needed lube.

He scrambled for the bottle, squirting it onto his hand. It dripped from his fingers, dropping all over the sheets. He added laundry to his 'to do' list for tomorrow after finding a volunteer position. Honestly, he should start to consider just sleeping on plastic at this point. He couldn't count the number of times that he'd changed the sheets, even when the other two didn't seem to care if they slept in a pile of cum.

He slathered his cock, getting himself nice and wet. Even *he* wouldn't be able to resist the slickness of his fist.

Making a tight tunnel with his hand, he jerked and squeezed, pulling so fast that his arm started to ache. He started to harden, his cock flexing in his hand.

He looked down to Chris, spread wide beneath him with his beautiful hole glistening. Concern was etched in his face, but he hadn't moved to stop him. He looked so good, and Simon wanted nothing more than to crawl on top of him and guide his cock between his cheeks, sinking into that perfect heat. Chris would be so tight and so warm, squeezing him just right. It would be perfect. It would be…

His chest went tight as the air evaporated in his lungs. He stroked himself harder, but he was already going soft again, and it was starting to hurt. His balls ached, confused and full as tears prickled at the corner of his eyes.

He stumbled off the bed, reaching for his pants that were tossed on the dresser. He tugged them on, wiping his hands on the front as his fingers slipped over the button.

"Simon?" Leo asked, leaning forward, his eyes wide with alarm. Chris was frozen, his legs still wide with his body on display and so beautiful that Simon wanted to sink back on the bed and give the man what he deserved.

But he couldn't.

"I gotta go," said Simon, reaching for his shirt that was nothing more than a crumpled heap. The tag scratched at the front of his neck as he pulled it on, but he didn't pause to fix it.

"Simon, stop." Leo threw his covers back, marching across the room in all his naked glory. His cock was still semi-hard, the tip peeking from the foreskin like the best kind of promise.

Simon turned away, fleeing the room before Leo could reach him. Fuck, he was a coward. He ignored Leo's yell, cringing at the anger in his tone. He was ruining everything, but he couldn't stay.

He wiped his palms on his jeans, smearing the already slick surface as he scrambled for the elevator, and glancing back over his shoulder when he heard Leo's footfalls. The man was still stark naked, his cock bobbing and swaying with every hurried step.

"Don't leave, Simon. Just talk to us." The anger bled from his voice as he pleaded. The look didn't suit him, and it spread a chill further into Simon's limbs.

The elevator gave a soft ding, and Simon slipped into it, slamming the button to close the door. Leo rushed toward him, his expression falling as he realized that he wasn't going to make it. His face twisted with rage as the doors closed, his top lip curling back.

"You okay, Simon?"

Simon jumped at the voice before spinning toward the concierge. The man looked wide-awake, despite the late hour. Did he ever sleep? Or did he just stand there all day and night, guarding the elevator?

A resounding bang sounded through the closed elevator doors, dimming as they started to descend. The confined box lurched gently, his ears popping as the display counted down the floor numbers.

"I'm okay," said Simon, resisting the urge to run his hand through his hair. His fingers were still sticky with lube, the smell of it thick in the small space. "Thanks, though, Frank."

"I'm not one to judge," said Frank, his face as stoic as a blank chalkboard. "I just want to make sure that you're okay. Would you like me to call you a cab?" His voice was soft and even. Simon hadn't spoken much with him, other than to exchange pleasantries, but he seemed like a decent man.

"Please," said Simon, clearing his throat as the word stuck in his throat. "I would appreciate that." Once he got home, everything would be all right. He needed his own bed, with the blankets that smelled like him and not like his partners, for one night.

He hadn't realized that he'd been relying so completely on them. They were the ones he waited for every day, so grateful that his lonely monotony had finally ended. He needed their embraces to get him through the night and their kind words to ease the humiliation of his past and present.

It had been weeks since he'd slept in his tiny single bed, and longer than that since he'd functioned as an adult on his own. Things were just easier as a group, as he could rely on them to fill his gaps, but it wasn't helping him. He had to be able to stand on his own if he wanted to get through this in one emotional piece.

"You sure you're okay?" the concierge asked again. The wrinkles around his eyes crinkled as he squinted his watery eyes. "Do I need to have words with that boy?"

Simon snorted, covering his mouth then grimacing when lube smeared against his lips. *Gross.* Lube was fantastic in the bedroom, but the second it got on your clothes, it was just a downhill disaster.

"I'm good. I'm actually feeling a lot better." The breathing room alone was enough to clear his head. He had overreacted, as simple as that. And his desire to take Chris' virginity had tipped him into a mild panic attack. It probably didn't help that he was exhausted from his insomnia-inducing focus on Leo's plan. A good night's rest and he would be back to himself.

An animal shelter would probably be the best place to volunteer. Rubric would have never thought to blacklist him there. The guy *hated* dogs.

# Chapter Twenty-Four

His bed was so tiny and hard that he only managed a few short hours of sleep by the time the sun started to peek through the curtains, warming the apartment to unbearable levels. He hadn't realized how scratchy his sheets were before, with tiny runs and balls of lint that scraped over his skin every time he moved. Fabric softener was definitely going at the top of the grocery list.

He let out a long sigh. He was officially used to the finer things in life.

He threw back the covers, stalking to the window shaker air conditioner and spinning the dial as high as it would go. His stomach rumbled, but he hadn't stocked the fridge or cupboards in ages. Someone had even eaten the can of black olives.

He shuddered. Green olives were a go, but black? That was just nasty.

The clunky couch and thin carpet had lost its appeal, along with the stain in the corner that looked like a cat. It was so empty without Chris, and the lack of Leo's presence left a hole at the farthest end of the couch, even if the man detested sitting on the thing.

The only things in the entire apartment that really meant something to him were Chris' pictures on the wall, but they lacked the same life without the ex-cop beside him.

He had overreacted. *Huge.*

It wasn't like he'd been forced. Most of his partners had been decent guys, and they had definitely all been of age and consenting. He just hated topping, and Rubric had transformed that dislike into a phobia. There was too much pressure and too many things to keep track of. He never knew when to go faster, or slower, or deeper. He couldn't tell when his partner needed a break, or even if they would be hard when he remembered the good ol' reach-around.

*Are they faking it?* was always what would run through his mind. At least, as a bottom, he could ask for exactly what he needed, and his partner couldn't fake a hard cock. It was easy enough to tell if they were into it or not.

And honestly, he liked the feeling of someone's mouth on his cock better than a hole. No ass had suction like that — or a tongue. Sure, a mouth wasn't as tight, but it was a whole lot wetter, and most guys were okay without a condom.

"Shit," he said, running a hand through his hair. Chris had probably thought that something very different had happened. Who turned down a sweet ass like that? Apparently, Simon was the only one.

He wanted to call them both to apologize, but his phone was still at Leo's, and they were probably both still sleeping. He did not want to wake either of them up early, especially when they both knew how to use a gun. 'Morning person' was not in either of their vocabularies.

He jumped into the shower instead, scrubbing every inch of himself and finally getting the remnants of lube off his skin. Steam was still clinging to him when he stalked back to his room, grabbing his suitcase from the closet.

There was no reason to stay there anymore — not with Chris and Leo in another bed without him. All his clothes would fit in the case, and he could leave the bed and furnishings for the next person. The cups and pots were replaceable, and they were the only things left in the cupboard. It was shocking how little he actually had in his life.

He folded his dress shirts carefully, humming a tune as he worked. His slacks went next, then his socks. He hid his stash of lube and his solo sex toy in one of the socks. It had been with him too long to leave it behind now. He glanced at his stash of condoms before he chuckled and shut the drawer. It would be a nice surprise for the next person who rented the place.

The suitcase zippered shut easily, only snagging on a pair of pajama pants that he hastily tucked inside. He pulled the case off the bed, grunting as he took the full weight. It would have been the perfect time for Chris to appear with his muscles so he could carry the case for him. The bus ride was going to be awful.

A knock sounded at the front door, as if summoned by his internal musings. He cocked his head in confusion. He had locked it the night before, but Chris had a key, so there was no way that he would knock. That would only leave one person on the other side.

He dragged his case down the hall, snagging his shoes as he went. The knock came again, so much more insistent.

"I'm coming," he said, taking a deep breath. His stomach fluttered and he swallowed against the sudden nervousness. Hopefully Leo wasn't upset when he saw him with his bag packed. Simon hadn't exactly talked about moving in, but Leo had mentioned it a few times.

He slid the lock back, his hand trembling and his face flushing. The chipped paint scraped under his nails as he turned the knob, his fingers trailing over the wooden door. There was a permanent stain there, from hundreds of touches from too many hands to count. He wished he'd had a chance to meet all of them.

He swung the door wide, balking as soon as he saw who was standing in the threshold. Why hadn't he looked through the peephole? Perhaps it was because he missed Leo, and his nervousness and excitement made him skip the most important step when living in an apartment.

*This* was not part of Leo's plan.

"Hi, Simon," said Rubric, standing in the doorway with a small smile on his lips. The man looked like sex dipped in chocolate and served on a platter made of wishes and dreams. His hair had grown in the month since Simon had seen him, but he was still clean shaven, giving him a sophisticated look mixed with a hint of something shameless. His suit was perfect, and the new gold watch on his wrist shimmered.

The watch alone was probably worth more than Simon's apartment, but that was no one's fault but Rubric's.

Simon had known that he was bound to see Rubric again and had played the moment over and over in his head. Faced with Rubric's soft eyes and his sheepish grin, everything he'd prepared to say jumbled at the back of his throat.

He could only stare in absolute horror as Rubric's gaze swept over him, taking in every tiny messy detail. His eyes narrowed at Simon's track pants, as if Simon didn't have the right to wear anything comfortable.

Leo happened to like this pair of track pants in particular, especially when he got to rip them off and fuck Simon over the back of the couch.

*What about Leo's plan?*

"You don't look happy to see me," said Rubric, straightening and pulling his hands from his pockets before crossing his arms. His blue eyes narrowed, his lips turning down. "I tried calling you, but I kept getting your voicemail."

A month ago, Simon would have melted under that expression, scrambling to right his imagined wrong. Coffee? Homemade cookies? A fuck? Anything so that he could make it right and have Rubric smile at him again.

But knowing what the man had done to him and how thoroughly he'd been screwed over, the look just pissed him off.

"I blocked your number," said Simon, his voice strained. He looked down the hall to see if any of his neighbors had been roused by the knocking. It was just after nine o'clock, and most of the rooms were silent behind the doors. He could smell a distant hint of bacon seeping beneath one.

Rubric's frown deepened. "Why did you do that?" He stared down at Simon, looking every inch his impressive height. He was shorter than both Chris and Leo, but he was still an intimidating billionaire. Senators had fallen at his feet, according to Leo.

"I asked you not to call me." Simon took a deep breath, meeting Rubric's gaze. He could still go along with Leo's plan, with some modifications. "Why are you here?"

"Are you moving out?" asked Rubric, taking a step closer and looking down at Simon's suitcase. Simon took a step back, then cursed himself for his automatic reaction.

He nodded, retreating again as Rubric took another step. Cold slithered into his gut, his chest going tight as Rubric loomed over him.

"I was always surprised you could afford this place anyway," said Rubric, looking past Simon and into the apartment. "I hear the prices are crazy on this side of town."

Simon gripped his fists tighter, his fingers aching from the strain. He would not rise to the bait. Rubric was the one who had recommended the place, obviously knowing that it was beyond the reach of Simon's pay. Not punching the guy was becoming harder by the second.

He still didn't understand *why*.

"I have a roommate. You know that." He'd told Rubric that fact on many occasions, although the man seemed to forget it—or he'd chosen to ignore it.

"Hmm, that's right. I always forget about Chris. He never made much of an impression, to be honest. Just another cop sticking his nose where it doesn't belong." A smirk settled over Rubric's lips, and Simon bit back a growl.

Had Rubric always been such an asshole and Simon had just been too clueless to notice? He knew he'd been blinded by the man's charisma and good looks, but this was something else altogether.

"He does good work for the city," said Simon, his voice strained. "But you didn't answer my question, Rubric. I asked you to leave me alone, but you're here, at my apartment. Why?"

Rubric tapped a finger to his chin, humming again as he took another step into the apartment. Simon held his ground, even as Rubric got uncomfortably close. The smell of his cologne was sweet and fresh, and it brought back every memory from the last five years. Surprisingly, most of the memories were good. It had only gone downhill when he'd gone off the rails and kissed his boss.

"I didn't think you were serious. You couldn't be," said Rubric, pausing his advance. His gaze snapped to a bit of curled paint on the door frame and his frown deepened. "I gave you enough time to get over your selfish demands and a little extra so you could take some holidays. But it's time for you to get back to the office. I expect you to be back at your desk tomorrow."

*Un-fucking-real.* Simon struggled to remember what he had seen in Rubric. He had thought that the man was kind and smart. But he had been wrong about a lot of things.

"What? No," said Simon, taking a step back. He had to put space between them. He could hardly breathe through the beating of his heart. "I told you I quit, and that was final. It's not a good idea for me to be working for someone I've had sex with. I can't work for you anymore, Rubric."

Rubric didn't seem fazed. If anything, he looked about two seconds away from smiling. "So, you have another job then? Because word on the street is that no one will hire you. Something about a rumor involving sexual harassment in the workplace? I'm sure it's just a rumor, though. No one would believe that about you."

A stone settled into Simon's stomach. Was that why no one was returning his calls? Because Rubric had spread a rumor about him being some kind of sex offender? He was going to be sick.

"But, hey, if you're moving out, you must've found something great!" A smile appeared on Rubric's face that looked so genuine that Simon was almost fooled. "I'm so happy for you, Simon. You were the best assistant I've ever had, and I really wish that you'd reconsider coming back. I get it, though. I can put in a good word for you at your new place. I'd hate for them to have second thoughts while you're still on probation."

When had Rubric become so downright *evil*? And how had he missed it? According to Leo, the guy had as many illegal accounts as legal ones, but Simon hadn't believed it until now. A month ago, he would have fallen for the act. Hell, a month ago, he'd be back at his desk, with a Tupperware container of cookies in his hands.

"I should be okay, but I really appreciate your offer," said Simon, trying to keep his words genuine. "They have me all set up with a new place, one that's closer so I don't have to take the bus anymore. I was just heading out now to start moving my stuff in. I'm sure the cab is waiting."

Alarms blared in his head as Rubric pushed his way farther into the apartment. He had to get him out of here *now*. If Leo ever found out about this…all his hard work would be for nothing. He didn't want Rubric dead. No one deserved that.

"Did you miss me, even a little?" Rubric's gaze fell at the same time he reached back to close the door behind him. Panic settled in Simon's chest as Rubric plucked at his heart strings. He'd never wanted to hurt the man. Maybe he was blowing this whole thing out of proportion again.

"Yes," said Simon, looking away. It wasn't a lie. There were a few things that he missed, but he missed his job more than he missed his boss. He missed having a purpose every day and the human interactions outside of home. He missed making at least one person smile.

"Then come back to me. I need you, Simon. I can't do it without you. I'm trying, but I've been losing so many clients, and done deals have been slipping through my fingers. I need your help. *Please*." Rubric's voice dropped as he begged, thrusting his hands into his pockets and curling in on himself.

*The plan. Stick to the plan. You can still salvage it.*

"I don't know what I'll be able to do to help, Rubric." Simon turned away, heading for the kitchen. Rubric followed him, as expected, and Simon pulled two mugs from the cupboard. His trembling hand brushed Chris' giant mugs, which took up every bit of space on the cluttered shelf. He grabbed them, walking over to his suitcase and tucking them inside.

He could feel Rubric's eyes burning into him and watching his every move. He was probably waiting for him to continue talking to fill the silence.

"Clients come and go all the time and a deal isn't done until the contract is signed. Even then, there are still loopholes. Maybe you need to look at it from a different perspective and lower your expectations." He filled the two mugs with tap water, handing one to Rubric, who took it with a simmering glare.

"I've lost two hundred million dollars in one week. How is that for lowering my expectations? Every time I call them or try to schedule a meeting, my clients ask for you." His voice had an edge to it that Simon didn't expect. He was obviously desperate.

Leo must've been the most efficient man on the planet. Two hundred million. Simon had never had an ounce of cruelty in his body, but he had to admit that a small part of him loved the sound of that number.

"That's a lot," said Simon, hiding his smile in the coffee mug. He choked on the water as he accidentally sucked it down the wrong hole. "Did any of them give you a reason?"

"Things have gone...missing," said Rubric. He leaned back, a frown tugging at his lips.

"Call the police," said Simon, nodding. "If you suspect some kind of fraud, or sabotage, then get them involved. I can even let Chris know. Maybe he knows someone who has experience with that kind of thing."

Hopefully Rubric had no idea that Chris had lost his job. The man hardly remembered Chris' name, so he wasn't too worried.

"I can't call the cops, Simon. I need you...end of story. What is it going to take to get you back?" Rubric slammed the mug down on the counter, a crack appearing on its base. Water leaked from it in slow drips, tumbling down the counter to the floor. Simon watched them fall.

Rage was *exactly* what Leo had said would happen. Only Leo was supposed to be present for the event so he could tell Rubric that he wasn't welcome in the country anymore.

Simon didn't have a cool catch line planned or enough of a spine to stand up to Rubric...or a gun. All he had was a cup of lukewarm water that tasted like old plumbing with a pinch of lead.

"I need you to leave," said Simon, carefully setting his mug down. He grabbed a hand towel and lowered himself to clean the spill that Rubric ignored, like he didn't even see the mess.

"I'm not going back to the office until you agree to come with me." The edge in his voice was back. There would be threats next.

Simon had heard it all before, grumbled into the phone when a client had tried to back out last-minute, but it had never been directed at him.

"No, you don't understand." Simon shook his head, hanging the towel back up on the hook. He turned to Rubric before meeting his gaze. "You need to leave the country. Close your doors or declare bankruptcy for all I care. Either way, you're done. It's only downhill from here — and I think you know that."

Rubric paled, his face twisting as he growled through clenched teeth. "Leo did this. That fucker. They were supposed to take him out, but all I got were excuses instead. Why are you with him, Simon? He doesn't have what you need."

Was that what Rubric thought? That he had what Simon needed? It couldn't have been further from the truth. The confirmation that he had put the hit out on Leo thudded into his gut.

Simon didn't have time to respond. Rubric's eyes went dark before he lunged across the kitchen, grabbing Simon and slamming him into the stove.

Simon's head snapped back, bumping off the upper cupboards as his vision wavered.

"You're still his little slut." Rubric's hand went to his throat and started to squeeze. "I told you to stay away from him. He's not safe."

Simon scratched at Rubric's hand, gasping as the grip loosened. His temples throbbed, his blood rushing through his ears and pounding in his throat. Rubric had always been an intimidating man, but Simon had never been afraid of him before.

"*You* aren't safe," said Simon, cringing as a cough strangled his lungs.

"Tell me everything he's planning," said Rubric, licking his lips and leaning in so close that Simon could feel his breath on his skin. His cologne was overwhelming, and the mint turned his stomach. Rubric's hand went tight again, and blood roared in through his head.

Fuck, it hurt. Rubric's fingers were digging into the sides of his neck and probably leaving bruises near the tiny line of scarring that Mikeal had left behind. Black spots speckled his vision as his lungs started to burn. Struggling was out of the question, but he couldn't stop himself from writhing against Rubric, doing his best to escape a man who was five times his strength. His head pounded as he went slack, his arms moving back to his sides.

He gasped as Rubric lifted his hand away again, blood rushing into his head so fast that a migraine shuddered over him instantly. He went to his knees, coughs racking his body. His lungs were screaming, but he couldn't stop coughing.

He could just make out Rubric's shoe at the edge of his vision. The toe was scuffed and the hem of his pants was dirty and worn. Two hundred million dollars had seemingly taken its toll.

"He didn't tell you," said Rubric. He crouched down and threaded his hand through Simon's hair, jerking his face upright with a surprisingly gentle touch. Their faces were level, his blue eyes carving into Simon's watering ones.

"Did he tell you how many people he's killed?" Rubric moved his hand down to Simon's face, cupping his chin and tilting his head back. The touch was vile, worsening as Rubric licked his lips. "What I know is only the tip of the iceberg. That man's soul is so black that no one will ever be able to save him — not even you, sweetheart." He ran his finger over Simon's lip, dipping the tip just inside. Simon struggled not to bite him and just breathe. "It breaks my heart to see you with him. You deserve so much better." Rubric leaned in, cradling the back of Simon's head.

Simon turned away in time for Rubric to press his lips to his cheek instead of his mouth. Another set of coughing tore apart his lungs until his sides and stomach ached. He never wanted to kiss or touch Rubric again — romantically or otherwise.

"I deserve someone like you," said Simon. He meant it to sound sarcastic, but his voice was nearly lost.

"Yes," said Rubric, obviously undeterred as he moved closer. "We make such a good team, Simon. I know you agree with me. If only you would have taken my first offer to come and live with me, then we could have taken on the world together. Me and you on top. Us against the world."

"And I was supposed to be…what? Your whore? You certainly had me clinging to your every word — and everything else." Simon pushed Rubric away, getting to his feet and rubbing at his throat. The skin was tender, as if there were already bruises forming. Leo was going to be pissed.

"You mean so much to me," said Rubric. "You're my best friend in the world." Rubric followed his every move, bracketing him against the countertop. There had never been a more powerless moment for Simon.

"Then I would hate to see how you treat your enemies," said Simon. He pushed against Rubric's arm and was thankfully able to slip past him and into the narrow living room. He cursed himself for not going straight for the door in his panic.

He had to keep moving and keep distance between them. He would never be able to get away if Rubric got his hand around his throat again. His best bet was to get outside and yell for help.

"Wait. I do know. You hire someone to kill them. That must be great for business." Simon circled around the couch, putting it between them as he readied himself to run for the door. He could probably keep from keeling over if he tried to run now.

Rubric paused, crossing his arms and raising one brow.

"I never mistreated you, Simon." His tone was so honest, so genuine, that Simon almost wanted to believe him. His throat throbbed in protest, and he clenched his fists.

"You never paid me what I was worth." Simon poked the sore spot of his ego. The money didn't matter, but the principal sure as hell did.

"So that's what this is about? You want more money? I never took you as the type, and you never complained." Rubric's scowl deepened. He settled himself in the doorway, blocking the exit and hammering another nail in Simon's coffin. "You'll get your raise then. A dollar an hour. Any more and you're just being greedy."

"Okay then," said Simon, clutching his anger close to his chest. His heart pounded and his throat throbbed, but Rubric seemed much calmer. He could still do this. "Thank you for the offer, and the opportunity, but I will have to decline." He plastered a fake smile on his face, even as Rubric scowled. "Please leave my apartment. These walls are thin, and I imagine that my neighbors already called the police when they heard the commotion. I don't want you to get into trouble."

He shouldn't have underestimated Rubric's desperation. There wasn't much that a desperate man wouldn't do, especially when he'd always had his way in life. Before Simon could blink, Rubric lunged.

# Chapter Twenty-Five

Rubric made it exactly one step before his obvious plan came crashing down. Over his shoulder, on the edge of Simon's vision, two shadows appeared. Simon sluggishly looked up, peering into the faces of his two avenging angels, bent on destruction. They moved so quickly, and so much faster than Rubric, that Simon didn't even have time to flinch.

Despite Leo's leaner frame and quick reflexes, Chris' police training had obviously kicked in first. Chris threw himself onto Rubric's back, knocking him to the ground and pushing a groan from his lungs. Rubric tried to fight back, but Chris grabbed his arm, wrenching it behind his back before he could attempt to break free.

All Chris needed was a pair of cuffs, and Simon would have witnessed his very first arrest. He distantly wondered if Chris was going to read him his rights like they did on television.

The joy fluttering in his chest sobered when his second angel stepped forward, a gun nestled into the palm of his hand. Simon had touched the gun once, and he knew how cold the steel was and how unusually heavy it would be.

"Rubric, what a lovely surprise," said Leo, kneeling down and tapping his gun against Rubric's forehead. "I was just thinking about you and wondering how you were doing after this week's...events."

"You fucker," Rubric growled, fighting against Chris' grip. Chris smashed his elbow along the top of his spine, and Rubric went still, biting out a second curse.

"Hmmm, an accurate assessment," said Leo, slipping his gun back into the holster at his side. He stood, walking to Simon, and wrapping him up in his arms. His heat was overwhelming, and his body solid against Simon's trembling form.

"Are you okay?" Leo whispered into his ear, his voice soft.

Simon nodded as the words caught in his throat. Leo touched his chin, tilting his head up. His eyes went wide as he spied the bruises on Simon's throat, rage carving across his face.

"Why did you hurt him, Rubric?" Leo turned back to Rubric, his heat disappearing with a shuffle of cloth. He was still wearing a suit, even though it was shortly after nine on a Saturday morning. "He's the only reason you're alive. If I had my way, you'd have been dead ages ago."

Rubric struggled, groaning as Chris wrenched his arm hard. Any farther and it looked like his arm might twist clean off.

"Leo," said Simon, his voice no louder than a whisper. Leo continued as if he'd hadn't heard him at all.

"Give me three good reasons why I shouldn't take care of this now." Leo crossed his arms, his gaze narrowing. Chris wrenched on the struggling man, his gaze fixed on Simon's neck. Rage unlike anything Simon had ever seen stretched across his bearded face.

He hadn't looked that pissed when Kayla had had a run-in with a drunk guy when they had been out for drinks. Chris had laid that guy out on the floor in a twitching pile of his own piss and vomit. He looked like he wanted to do so much worse to Rubric.

Chris was too good. Simon couldn't let him get involved in this. With Leo it was different, but Chris was his delicate bear who held him and whispered sweet nothings into his ear when he thought Simon was asleep.

"Leo," said Simon, taking a step forward. All eyes turned to him, Rubric's struggles growing fiercer until Chris was almost bucked off. Chris grabbed Rubric's other arm, wrenching it back in the same way until Rubric cried out.

"Leo, he's a good man," said Simon, his eyes on the gun as it glinted in the morning light. The shadows of day shifted through the window blinds, painting delicate stripes over them as the air conditioner shuddered to life again. Simon jumped at the sound.

This couldn't happen. He couldn't let Rubric's blood paint the thin carpet, only to be scrubbed away by one of Leo's crew. He couldn't let their relationship and their love be tainted by a man who was simply not worth their time.

Leo snorted, his icy eyes narrowing. "You would call the devil a good man, Simon."

"No." Okay, *maybe*. Everyone had redeeming qualities, after all. Some were just harder to find than others. "He gave me a great job that I enjoyed and employed me for five years. He would always hold the door open for me and eat my homemade cookies, even if they were burned. He never made me work overtime and always offered advice. That's why he is a good man."

"Simon," said Chris, pausing as Rubric started to struggle again. Simon turned away. He couldn't fight all three of them.

"He is an excellent businessman, and his clients would be the ones to feel the backlash if he disappeared before transferring their accounts to other managers."

"His business practices have fallen short of late," said Leo, snickering as Rubric groaned. "Seems like more than one person can start a rumor to fuck somebody over. Apparently, this guy has a problem with foreigners, which is strange, seeing as ninety-five percent of his clients are from other countries. It's really too bad that an inside source gave them the scoop. Luckily, that same source was able to help them out of a tricky situation — for a fee, of course."

"You threatened his businesses partners, planted rumors and redirected his shipments," said Simon. Leo hadn't told him the details of Rubric's ruin, but he had a pretty good idea. "He's not a billionaire just because he's an asshole. I've seen him make money for his clients when everything was in the red. I've seen him take ten thousand dollars and turn it into a million."

"He took advantage of you, Simon," snarled Leo. "He could probably afford to top up those accounts because he was taking a cut off your pay."

*Good point,* Simon conceded internally. "It was good business for him, even if it wasn't for me." He gripped his fists tight, his mind whirling to think of more reasons. He could not have pieces of Rubric all over his carpet. And he couldn't have Leo kill for him.

"Up until today, he never hurt me," said Simon. "He always looked out for me, even when it wasn't exactly in my best interests. He tried to keep me away from you because he thought you would hurt me. He tried to keep me safe."

"He just tried to strangle you," said Leo, throwing up his hands. "Simon, you can't be serious. I can see the bruises from his hands around your throat. He would have to choke you hard enough to almost kill you to leave marks like that. I'm going to fucking kill him."

"No, you aren't," said Simon, stalking forward. "Chris, let him go." The ex-cop scrambled off Rubric, wiping his palms on his pant legs. He didn't look nearly as angry as Leo did, with his eyes blazing and set on revenge.

"I gave you more than three reasons, Leo, and even if you don't like them, you aren't going to kill him." Simon stepped over to Chris, pulling him into a tight hug. He whispered a 'thank you' across his skin before he moved back.

Rubric lay motionless, his hands still behind his back and his chest rising and falling rapidly. His eyes had fluttered closed at some point, his lashes brushing over his cheeks. Simon knelt down, taking his face in his hands and waiting until Rubric's eyes finally opened.

"Will you leave? I need you to be honest with yourself. You can flee the country now and never come back, but you'll have your life. If you stay, I can't promise you anything." Simon smoothed his hand over Rubric's cheek, short stubble scratching along his palm. He was a powerful man, but he was only a man.

"Yes." Rubric flinched away from him, scrambling to his hands and knees. He cast his gaze to Chris, then back to Leo, who still had a hand on his gun. "How do I know you won't come after me?" Rubric took a step back, moving closer to the door. Leo opened his mouth the speak, but Simon cut him off.

"The same way that I know that you won't come back. Because you're a good man, and I trust you to keep your word." Simon stood, brushing his pants off and tugging them up from where they'd slid down his hips in the ruckus.

"Stay away from us, and I won't go looking for you," said Leo, relaxing his grip and shrugging. All eyes turned to Chris, who simply nodded.

"I have clients. I need to talk to them before I close their accounts," said Rubric, paling as he finally seemed to realize the situation that he was in. Leo was the least of his problems. He'd made his illegal investors a lot of money, and they would not take their losses kindly, especially if he disappeared.

"Simon can help me close out your accounts," said Leo. "I'll return any missing items to their appropriate owners, minus an administration fee, of course. As for your existing clients, I've already spoken to most of them and convinced them to pull their assets out of your company. By tomorrow, you'll only be worth a tenth of what you were a week ago."

"My investors," said Rubric, shaking his head. He was probably calculating how much money had gone up in smoke. Simon felt almost sorry for him. But none of it would've happened if he hadn't hired a hitman to take Leo out. Broke was better than dead.

"They will be understandably upset," said Leo, a small smirk playing at his lips. "It would be in your best interest to never set foot on this continent again. Hell, Antarctica will probably be a safe bet."

Rubric looked between them, real fear creeping in. Finally his gaze settled on Simon and he nodded once. "I'm sorry." He looked to Leo and the glint of metal at his waist. "I guess I was wrong… You can redeem the devil."

# Chapter Twenty-Six

*Three months later*

Simon took a deep breath, sliding down as far as he could, despite the ache racking his body. Chris was splitting him so wide that he wasn't sure if he would be able to take him entirely. Every time seemed like the first with him, and Leo was hardly any better. Their positions made him feel that much bigger.

Chris was spread-eagled on the bed, his hips propped up on two pillows with Simon slowly sinking down onto him. The silk sheets twisted in Chris' fists, his forehead furrowing. When Simon looked back over his shoulder, he saw why.

Leo was lining himself up to Chris' entrance, slowly teasing him with the head of his cock. Chris flinched as Leo started to sink inside, his movement slamming his cock directly into Simon's prostate.

Riding a bull was one thing but riding a bear who was getting nailed by a mobster took him beyond the stratosphere. The only thing that would make it better was if Simon had had the guts to be the one penetrating Chris. To be honest, he preferred his current position, with Chris ramming his spot accidentally as Leo worked his way inside.

"Easy, baby, just relax and take my cock," said Leo, his words whispering over the back of Simon's neck. He gripped Simon's hips, using him to force Chris down onto his cock.

"Don't call me baby, you jackass," said Chris, his body taut. "And how am I supposed to relax when you're so fucking big?" A flash of real pain edged over his features, and Simon sensed that it would only be a few moments before it was all over. Their usual fighting was already starting to impede what was supposed to be a beautiful and wonderful moment for the three of them.

"Chris," said Simon, leaning forward and pressing his lips to the ex-cop's. He groaned into his mouth, their tongues dancing as Leo shifted behind them, the sheets rustling as he moved.

"It'll feel so good, Chris. I promise," said Simon, rocking his hips just enough to give Chris some sort of stimulation. "I can take your cock, right? Leo is smaller than you."

"Hey!" called Leo, a moment before his hand came down on Simon's ass, leaving a red blush behind. "I am *not* small."

Chris snorted, rolling his eyes, before hissing as Leo sank deeper, his abdomen settling against Simon's lower back. "You aren't small, but the boy is right. You haven't had cock, until you've had *my* cock."

"So humble." Simon sighed, leaning back until he hit Leo's chest. He turned his head, their tongues entwining.

"You like my cock, baby?" Leo asked when the kiss finished, his icy stare locked with Simon's. "Who fills you up the best and gives you everything you need? Who is always hard for you? Not that fucker." He turned his glare at Chris before he pulled out, slamming back inside.

"Ah, fuck, you asshole, I wasn't ready yet," Chris stammered, reaching for Simon's thighs, his grip going tight.

"I've been waiting all fucking month for you to be ready for me. I'm done waiting," said Leo, easing out and back in with one long motion. "Besides, let Simon answer. I want to know who's the best fucker in this penthouse."

Simon wanted to face palm, laugh and shrivel away to nothing. These two were the loves of his life and the banes of his existence at the same time. He had no idea how they all managed to live together without *some* attempted murder, at the very least.

The first month had been hard, especially when his job search had finally come to an end, and the three of them had started working very different schedules. He'd learned to cherish every moment between them, but he'd worried about what would happen if the mobster and ex-cop were left alone for too long.

Until he'd come home from a long shift to find the two of them curled up on the couch together. Their faces had been flushed from kissing, and Leo had had beard burn on his neck from Chris. They'd stammered when Simon had arrived, ready to push each other away, but Simon had only smiled and headed off for the shower, shouting for them to continue as he'd strode past.

Watching the two of them together was better than any porn, but when the three of them found time for each other, it was like living on the moon. He'd never felt higher or happier in his life.

"You going to move anytime soon?" Chris snarled at Leo, pulling Simon from his musings. Leo had paused, presumably to give Chris a break.

Leo scowled, snapping his hips up to start a punishing rhythm. Each thrust sent Chris up into Simon, his cock pushing so deep that he was sure that he would be officially ruined for any other man who wasn't these two.

"Hey, guys?" Simon called out, breathless as he started riding Chris in earnest. "Do you think sometime we can see if both of you fit in me at once? You could pump me so full that I'd be dripping for days. I'd have to get a bigger plug because you'd stretch me so wide and fill me up perfectly."

"Ah, fuck," Leo cried out, burying himself deep inside of Chris. At the same time, Chris cursed, his cock flexing inside of Simon and coating him with liquid heat.

"Baby, you can't talk like that when we're balls deep," said Leo, mouthing at Simon's shoulder as he came down. "You always make us come way too fucking fast."

"I'm still hard," said Simon, lifting his hips and trying to grind back onto Chris, but the man's cock slipped out, completely spent.

"Don't worry, baby. We'll take care of you."

Their gazes were predatory as they wandered over Simon's body with their hands and tongues, showing him more pleasure than he'd ever experienced.

One boyfriend was amazing, but two? Two were more than he could have ever imagined.

## It's a Kink Thing: Kinked Up
### M.C. Roth

**Coming August 2022**

### *Excerpt*

Nav's apartment key tumbled from his hand as his phone vibrated, rattling his change and his plastic swipe card from work. He fumbled in his pocket, pulling his phone out and groaning at the name on the display.

"This is *not* a good time," he said as he accepted the call, sighing at the laughter that burst against his eardrum. He glanced down, searching for his key that had somehow made it halfway under his apartment door, only the jagged edge visible beneath the crack.

He really needed to get a keychain so the thing didn't disappear on him again. He'd already gone through three keys in the last month, and the hardware store was starting to get suspicious as to why he needed so many spares. There just didn't seem to be much point to getting a sparkly keychain if he wasn't going to keep it for all that long.

"How did it go, Nav?" asked Sasha through the speaker.

No matter how many times Nav lost his things or moved, Sasha always seemed to track him down. He was Nav's self-appointed best friend and number one annoyance.

Nav let out a sigh, leaning his back against the door as he looked down the hall. There were a dozen doors that were identical to his, with grungy numbers barely clinging onto their hastily painted surfaces. At one point, the doors must've been a dreadful forest green, but someone had decided to paint over them with a thin layer of white primer. The results were pale lime rectangles with dark corners where the primer had been rubbed raw. The red apartment numbers completed the nightmarish Christmas look with tacky gusto.

"It went great. Better than great, actually. Everette never wants to see me again, and he got his brother to throw me out of the house." Nav rubbed at his shoulder where he was sure there was a bruise. They'd taken the throwing part a touch too literally, and Nav had found out first-hand how hard concrete sidewalks were.

"Ouch. Not unexpected, though," said Sasha, his laughter booming through the tiny speaker. "Maybe you shouldn't have hit on their dad?"

Nav ran a hand through his hair before he leaned back and let his head rest against the thin door. It sounded hollow to the touch, and it nearly bowed under his weight. "Maybe their dad shouldn't have been so hot. I mean, who the hell walks around in just their boxers then gets offended when they get hit on? I didn't know guys his age could even *have* abs like that. His body was just rocking."

"Gross... I don't need the details," said Sasha, the phone rustling. "How many is that now, though?"

"This year or this month?" asked Nav, sliding down the door until his ass met the thin and filthy carpet. A light flickered overhead, and somewhere a baby screamed. His neighbor down the hall was making their weekly batch of boiled cabbage, if the smell was anything to go by. And who the hell had crushed packets of ketchup at the end of the hall?

"You're such an asshole," said Sasha. "I've never met someone who has as many ex-boyfriends as you have. You must run into one at every bar."

Nav laughed, letting the grief of the situation roll off his shoulders and down the ratty hallway to find a sewer out on the street somewhere. There was hardly any grief there at all, if he were honest with himself. He'd only dated Everette for three weeks, which was two weeks longer than his usual attention span. The guy had been cute, but nothing compared to his dad.

"Most bars are out. Restaurants, too. I ran into Josh the other day, and I swear to God he spit on my salad," said Nav. He'd still eaten the salad, of course. A little spit never turned him off a good meal.

"So, you won't come out for drinks with us tonight?" asked Sasha. "Katie already did her hair up real nice, and I can't wait to fuck it up."

"Your straightness disgusts me," said Nav, letting his eyes drift shut. It had been a long week of too many hours at work and even more wasted on another guy he knew would never work out. His shower was calling to him, and he could definitely hear the cries of his lonely pillow.

"I dunno. I'm really tired, Sash." He leaned his head to the side to cradle his phone against his ear. A noise at the end of the hall made him startle, but he kept his eyes closed. It was probably just one of his asshole neighbors getting home after their day job. They would be able to step by him just fine.

"All the more reason to come out with us. You're in a rut, Nav. You need to relax and stop trying to fuck your way through every gay bedroom in the city. Come out with us tonight for drinks, keep your dick to yourself and I guarantee you'll feel better."

"Drinks do sound good," said Nav, pulling his feet closer when the squeak of shuffling footsteps approached him on the carpet. "Okay, I'll be there tonight. Don't let me fuck up again, okay?"

"Deal." Sasha chuckled. Nav could almost see his best friend's smirk through the phone. "I'll keep you surrounded by women so your dick shrivels up and dies. Then I'll get you so wasted that you forget about Tray."

"Tray was last month, before Scott and Paul, remember? Everette was the guy whose dad I just fucked," said Nav, lowering his voice as the footsteps came closer. He already got enough flack in his life for being gay and he didn't need any more shit from anyone.

"You are fucked up, man. I'll see you tonight. Nine sharp at Pinty's. Bring your long underwear and a chastity belt." Sasha ended the call with a click and Nav sighed, letting his phone slide to the ground with a hollow thump. He could sleep against the door, even with the floor jamming into the bruises on his ass.

Who *actually* threw someone? Concrete was not a fun place for his skinny ass to land. At least they had tossed him his pants.

"You okay?"

Nav's opened his eyes and cursed to himself, scrambling to get up to his feet.

Of course, the person to see him crumpled outside of his door had to be his smoking-hot and totally unreachable neighbor. He was gorgeous, with short blond hair that models would die for, and the softest blue eyes Nav had ever seen. Top that with thick shoulders, strong arms and thighs that could kill and he was everything Nav dreamed of.

The guy was also completely and totally unavailable. His boyfriend was the most average person in the world but had something that Nav couldn't even fathom — commitment. Every time Nav saw his him, the boyfriend was usually close by.

"Sorry... I just lost my key," said Nav as he pushed back against his door, his knees wobbling as his neighbor got closer. His mouth went dry, his throat constricting like nobody's business. His palms went damp as he suddenly began to sweat, his face flushing. Hunger evaporated in his gut like he'd just gotten a whiff of fresh ass, and his priorities had spun one-hundred-and-eighty degrees.

He was also the only one who did *that* to Nav. The beautiful blond specimen transformed him from a bonified slut who was proud of it into a blushing virgin.

Nav had fucked and been fucked by more guys than he could remember, but something about that tall, built frame and those crystal-blue eyes sent him back to his high school days when he'd seen his first cock and decided he was gay for life.

"Oh crap, that sucks," he said, running a hand through his blond locks that were probably softer than actual silk. "Did you call the superintendent?" He shifted a brown paper grocery bag in his hands, reaching into his pocket for something.

Of course he was environmentally aware, too, which made Nav want to drool. There was nothing worse than a hot guy who used plastic bags and drove a car that guzzled more fuel than a loaded transport truck. *Can you be any more perfect?*

Nav shook his head. "N-not yet. I think I probably just dropped it somewhere." Nav wanted to crumple into a ball. His voice was so soft and weak that he probably *sounded* like a virgin, too.

Virgins were the literal enemy. Clingy, flustered and nervous, Nav always steered well clear. He'd been there, done that and returned the T-shirt.

Knowing how thin the walls were in the building, Nav guessed the guy had probably heard his sex adventures from across the hall, which was probably why he was looking at Nav with confusion and concern etched onto his perfectly sculpted face. Statues were probably made of this guy—hopefully the ones with the big dicks and not the little ones.

Nav slid his foot sideways to where he remembered dropping the key, hopefully concealing it. He was such a fucking idiot, but he couldn't even think straight with his neighbor staring at him, his gaze piercing straight through his defenses.

"Did you need a hand? Just let me put my groceries in the fridge and I'll help you look for it." A soft smile settled on his lips as he pulled his own key out before opening his door with one hand.

"No, it's okay," said Nav, his face burning. He slapped his hands to his cheeks as the guy looked away, hoping to draw the heat out with his frigid fingertips. The sight of his wide, strong back had Nav flushing all over again. He looked away and into the apartment instead, his jaw dropping as something caught his eye.

There, on the wall, and hidden in the most unlikely of places, was a painting that he'd never thought he would see again.

"Oh my God, you have one of Brian Maeckery's paintings?" He stumbled across the hall, his key and his bag forgotten as the art drew him through the open door.

Seeing it again was the same as seeing it for the first time. The piece was one that had caught Nav's eye when it had been in the studio. His breath stuck in his throat as his cock swelled against his will, his groin pulling tight.

He couldn't help it. The brushstrokes were perfection, each one laid with such sensual purpose that Nav could almost feel them against his skin. The lovers on the canvas were wrapped around each other in an intimate embrace that made Nav's blood boil. They looked at each other in the peak of their pleasure, love and commitment frozen on their features. It was as unreal as a dream.

But what was his favorite painting of all time doing in a run-down apartment building? Sure, his neighbor had spruced up his place from what Nav could tell, but the painting didn't belong.

"Yeah." He set his grocery bag on the counter, before turning to Nav. "He's actually a friend of mine. He owed me a favor, so he gave this to me as payment. It's a beautiful piece." He shifted, flickering his gaze over Nav once before he turned and started unloading his groceries.

Butterflies erupted in Nav's belly. Brian Maeckery was nearly famous—like a shiny, untouchable doll on television. Nav would have worshiped the ground that he walked on, if only he had been able to find his house.

"I'm so jealous. I'm such a huge fan of his." He let out a sigh, reaching for the muddled color where the lovers' legs met. He hovered a few inches away, his hand trembling. The last price tag he'd seen on it was over one-hundred-thousand dollars. "It must've been one hell of a favor."

It still smelled fresh, the flavors of the paint rolling over his tongue as he inhaled sharply. The wooden frame was pristine, without a hint of dust or fingerprints, but how long would that last? It was something that should have been hanging in a temperature-controlled gallery for the rest of its life behind a pane of thick glass, not in a shitty apartment building soaking up the faint smell of cigarettes and cat piss.

His neighbor paused, a tray of chicken breasts clutched in his fingers. He furrowed his forehead before he let out a small laugh, his eyes lighting up. "Not really, no. My fiancé and I modeled for the painting, so Brian thought it was best if we were the ones to get it."

"Wait...what?" Nav took a step back, his gaze flashing between him and the painting. The faces on the canvas were in shadow, with only their lips visible and a hint of their partially closed eyes. But it *did* look like them, and the hair color was spot-on. And their bodies...*oh God*. Was that really hiding beneath the guy's T-shirt and jeans?

"Shit, I've jerked off to this painting," said Nav, flushing as he smacked his hand to his forehead. "I-I mean, shit. You're Theo?"

His boss had relayed the entire story as they'd hung the painting in the gallery together—how Brian had claimed that Theo was his muse and how he had called to him with each brush stroke. Nav had agreed from the bottom of his balls. That had been the first time the painting made him hard — but not the last.

Nav dropped his gaze, flushing so fiercely that he wasn't sure his cheeks would ever cool again. He couldn't look at him. In fact, it was probably best if he turned around and crawled back to his apartment before begging for forgiveness through the door.

Nav started as his neighbor chuckled. His gaze was dragged back to the gorgeous blond, his heart thudding as he stared at the man with his head tilted back and his lips curled and open as the beautiful sound emerged.

"Theo's my fiancé," he said, wiping the gathering tears from his eyes as he continued to chuckle. "I'm Maverick, but everyone calls me Trick. Thanks for the compliment." He let out another laugh, his body shaking as his chest heaved.

"I'm so sorry. I'm just really tired, and I always say things I'm not supposed to when I'm tired." He bit his tongue as Trick laughed even harder. Trick was stunning when he was silent, but when he laughed, he transformed into an actual Adonis.

Nav looked at the painting again, something new surging from the base of his gut.

As much as he had longed to be the one in the painting in the past, it had always remained an unattainable figment of Brian's imagination. It had been fitting that the only thing that he would ever love was an imaginary scene with a fictional man.

But they were *real*...and the man he'd been fantasizing about was Trick. His heart rate picked up, his chest rising and falling like he'd just run a marathon.

Trick was obviously in love with Theo. He'd smiled, the corners of his eyes crinkling when he'd said Theo's name. And the painting…? Nav hadn't known what true love looked like until he had seen the canvas.

An ugly green monster twisted in his gut, leaving a foul taste in his mouth. It seemed that everyone could fall in love except him, even the not-so-fictional characters in a painting. He was going to be cursed to chase brief hookups for the rest of his life, ditching them before they lost their new boyfriend smell and shine.

"Sorry. I didn't mean to upset you by laughing at you. I was just surprised," said Trick, his humor falling away. "You sure you don't want me to help you find your key? Or I can get you a drink if you want to call the super and wait here."

"No, it's okay. I don't want to intrude," said Nav. He looked back to the painting, but the magic that had enthralled him for months was gone. His stomach lurched as he took a step back.

*I'm just overtired. Alcohol required STAT.*

"Well, it was nice meeting you…" Trick paused as if he were waiting for something.

"Nav." He shrugged, filling the uncomfortable silence.

"Nav. Just knock if you need something or if you change your mind." He smiled, parting his full lips to reveal white teeth that were perfectly straight. His smile was dazzling, pulling a wave of fresh heat from Nav's core.

"Thanks. Bye." Nav rushed into the hall, shutting the door before Trick could say anything further. His heart was still pounding, and for some strange reason, he felt the first prickling of tears at the corner of his eyes.

He took a deep breath and pinched the base of his nose. He must've been more exhausted than he'd thought if he was already starting to get teary-eyed. He usually didn't hit that level until he'd worked sixty hours in one week. He'd only done fifty-five hours in the last five days, so he should have still been in the glaringly frustrated and angry phase.

He reached for his key, easing it out from where it had squirmed through the crack under the thin door. He grabbed his bag, hauling it over his shoulder and turning the key in the lock before pushing inside.

Unlike Trick, he hadn't spiffed up his floors or counters in his apartment. There really was no point if his stay was going to be brief.

The paint was the original faded ivory with a few cracks around the corners and a smudge of purple along one baseboard. The floors were roll-on linoleum with a few holes in the kitchen where someone had repeatedly dropped a sharp knife. It could have been anyone's apartment.

Except for the art that he'd hung on the walls. The art was all his. Most of the paintings were little pieces he'd picked up in estate and garage sales in the city, with a few originals from up-and-coming artists. His work in the studio gallery put him in reach of a few artists who hadn't hit it big yet and had prices that were within his reach.

He stepped up to one of his favorites. The artist was known simply as *Rachel*, and they had a way with traditional techniques that wasn't too common anymore. A frog on a lily pad would have made most artists scoff, but Rachel had elevated the simple idea and done something beyond anything Nav could have imagined himself. The frog was made of stars, and the lily pad was the cosmos, according to the gods. It always managed to take his breath away.

All the works he had managed to collect were beautiful and unique, but nothing like the scandalous and sensual canvas of Brian's work. It was so far beyond his price range that he didn't *deserve* to be close enough to touch it.

His throat clogged as he thought of the painting in its dismal setting across the hall.

"Christ, I need a drink." He pulled his clothes from his body, letting them trail on the ground on his way to the shower. As the water cascaded over him, he tried to push the painting and Trick from his thoughts.

# About the Author

M.C. Roth lives in Canada and loves every season, even the dreaded Canadian winter. She graduated with honours from the Associate Diploma Program in Veterinary Technology at the University of Guelph before choosing a different career path.

Between caring for her young son, spending time with her husband, and feeding treats to her menagerie of animals, she still spends every spare second devoted to her passion for writing.

She loves growing peppers that are hot enough to make grown men cry, but she doesn't like spicy food herself. Her favourite thing, other than writing of course, is to find a quiet place in the wilderness and listen to the birds while dreaming about the gorgeous men in her head.

M.C. Roth loves to hear from readers. You can find her contact information, website details and author profile page at https://www.pride-publishing.com

P U B L I S H I N G

Sign up for our newsletter and find out about all our romance book releases, eBook sales and promotions, sneak peeks and FREE romance books!